"I got the Kentucky Summers series for Christmas. I am now on the fourth book and can't stop reading. I absolutely love your books and please don't stop writing them."

—Sammy

"I just finished reading the Kentucky Summers Series, and there are no words to describe how much I enjoyed the books. I had to actually quit reading because I was laughing so hard that my stomach hurt. Then I would try again and still couldn't stop laughing. They were great!"

—Dottie Button

"I am writing to inform you these are the best, most entertaining, joyful books that have been written in many years! Sir, again, I thank you for these wonderful books and the great talent God has given you. I am anxiously looking forward to the next one."

—Mardell Mullins

"How happy I am to be able to recommend books to my grandchildren that I am completely comfortable with them reading. Thanks for what you do."

—Santa Cliff Snider

Kentucky Summers

Kentucky Snow & the Crow

Kentucky Summers

KenTucky Snow & the Crow

Tim Callahan

Published in the United States of America
ISBN: 978-1545190883
1. Fiction; Juvenile, Adult
2. Fiction; Coming of Age
12.09.06

Dedication

This book is dedicated to my aunts, uncles, relatives and Morgan County residents who have graciously let me use them as characters in my books.

In Memory of:

Aunt Ruth Johnson
6-24-1924   7-18-2012

Acknowledgments

I would like to thank everyone who has worked on my books at Tate Publishing. They have been a pleasure to work with and have helped make my dreams come true.

I would again like to thank my faithful readers who e-mail and stop by at festivals, asking for my next book. It is such an encouragement and lift to keep me going. This is the sixth book in the Kentucky Summers Series, and I imagine there being two more. Beyond that I'm not sure.

I would especially like to thank Kelli Jo Ross, a fifth grade student who e-mailed me wanting to play the role of Susie when the dream of a movie is realized. (You would be a great, Susie.) She has been such a pleasure and joy to communicate with.

I thank my wife who works so hard as a nurse so that I can concentrate on my dream. Thank you. I love you.

I thank my daughter Lauren for her love and smile. You're going to be a terrific doctor.

Thank you, God, for leading me in my writing and giving me all that is good in my life. Thank you for sending the tests and trials in making me a more appreciative person for your blessings and love.

TABLE OF CONTENTS

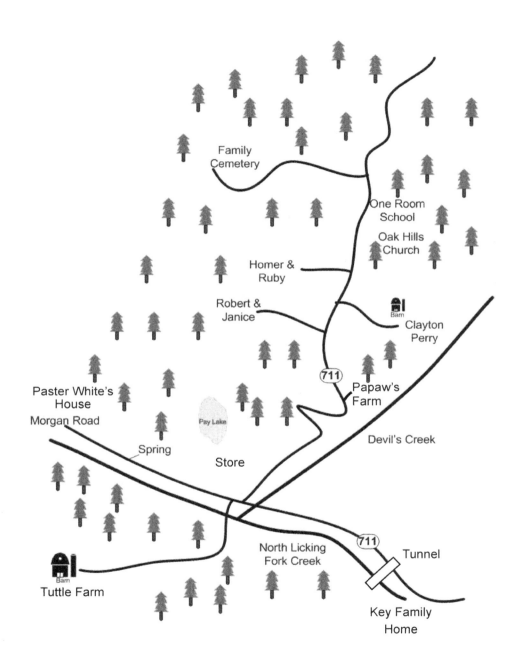

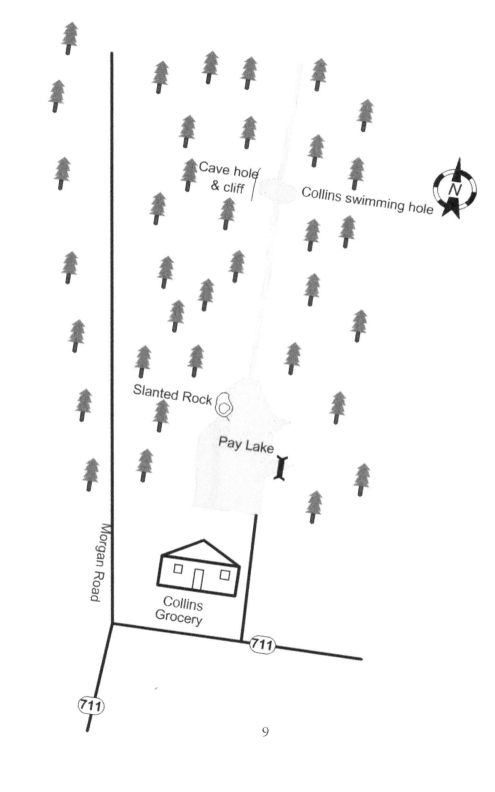

9

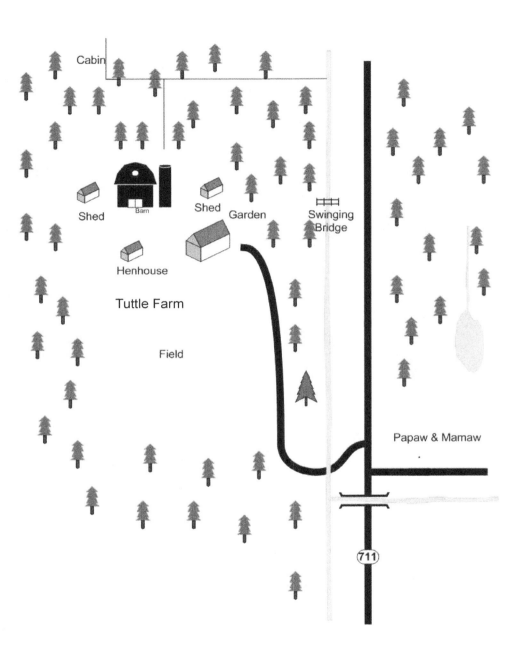

THANKSGIVING

Mamaw & Papaw's Farmhouse

THURSDAY, NOVEMBER 23, 1961 - THANKSGIVING DAY

I stood on the porch at noon as I looked across the lower pasture at the gray November sky. The day was chilly, in the forties, and Mamaw and Papaw's house was filled with their four daughters, their husbands and children, my cousins. I could hear laughter flowing through the house and out onto the porch where I stood by myself.

Generally I would see deer in the lower pasture, but the hunting season had driven them deep into the woods until men stopped shooting at them. Mom's three sisters, Ola, Helen, and Ruth, had come from Ohio to spend the holiday with their mom and dad. When we lived in Ohio I would see my aunts often, but for the past two years I had only seen them mainly on holidays.

Janie was having so much fun with Ruth's daughter, Judy. Janie and Judy were the same age and had always been very close. They had missed each other terribly. The two hadn't left each other's side since Judy arrived. The three husbands, Corbett, Bill, and, Joe were relaxing in the living room with Papaw. Mom had invited Sheriff Cane to eat with our family, and he was supposed to arrive by two o'clock. I knew that Mom was anxious about introducing him to her sisters.

I looked out at the leafless trees that surrounded the farm and thought about the past year and wondered how I survived the many escapades and adventures that had come my way. Today reminded me of my many blessings. Uncle Morton had told me that I was blessed and was being tested for something great in the future. I was hoping the testing was over. I didn't even think I cared if I failed or passed the tests. I wanted them to be over.

But I was thankful that I had survived the summer, and so far autumn had been uneventful and quiet. I had helped many farmers harvest their crops. I helped in the tobacco fields and the cornfields. I helped throw baled hay into the barns. I had picked pawpaws for Susie to eat and for Mamaw to make

Pawpaw jam. Susie and I had found persimmon trees and picked up the ripe ones from the ground. She loved them. I didn't. I had gone to school every day and tried to get good grades. I missed having James Ernest in the schoolhouse. I had to listen to Purty every day be "the man."

James Ernest had decided to eat dinner with Homer and Ruby and Uncle Morton. He figured we had enough mouths to feed, and Aunt Ruby wanted James Ernest to join them. Ruby had also invited the Washington family to her feast.

James Ernest had told me he was doing well in high school and that he liked it but missed the old Oak Hills one-room school. I sure missed him being there. He spent most nights with us and ate most meals with us. At times, though, he would be gone for a few days, spending time alone or with others. Mom had learned to accept it and never questioned him when he disappeared.

With all the harvesting and farm chores that we had to do, the Wolf Pack had not had a chance to build the tree house we had wanted to build. We had stored the wood and knew we would get around to it one day. It was only noon and still two hours before we would eat. I figured I had time to go for a hike. I went into the house and found Tommy, Joe Jr., and King.

"Let's go for a hike," I told them.

They followed me through the kitchen.

"We'll be back by two," I told Mom as I walked through the door.

"Be careful," Mamaw said as my mom looked my way. But she kept talking to her sisters as she watched me walk away.

"Where are we going?" Tommy asked. Tommy was the youngest child of Ola and Corbett, who had ended up with an ice cream cone stuck to the end of his nose in the summer of 1959.

"We're not going looking for coyotes again, are we?" King asked. King was Bill and Helen's son. Two summers before, King and I had walked around the lake after dark one night and came across two coyotes with blood-covered snouts. He hadn't been very fond of my hikes ever since then. At that moment Coty ran up to us. King jumped two feet in the air when Coty surprised him. We headed down the pasture hill toward the woods with Coty leading the way.

Jenny, Vernita, and Janet, my cousins, were standing behind the garage, watching us walk across the field.

"Probably the last we'll ever see of them," Jenny said to the other girls, loud enough for us to hear. I guess my reputation had spread through the family.

"What did they mean by that?" Tommy asked.

Joe Jr. snickered. King looked nervous as we walked into the woods.

Coty quickly chased a squirrel up an acorn tree. The forest floor was covered with multi-colored leaves that were turning brown. I had them follow me along a small path toward Devil's Creek. I turned right, and we followed a rabbit trail that I had found late one evening. It was small but led to a spot I knew the guys would like.

"You sure this is a trail?" Tommy questioned.

"Doesn't look like a trail to me," King piped in.

"It's not much of one," I agreed.

Coty's nose was going crazy as he led the way on the hare-scented dirt path. Suddenly he began to yelp when he caught a glimpse of a small, white tail bobbing up and down in front of him. He took off through the woods after it.

I wondered how many times I had seen the same scene play out, Coty scaring up a rabbit and running after it. He had never caught one that I knew of. I did see him catch a squirrel one day—a stupid squirrel. Coty was right on its tail when the squirrel lit up a tree, and while Coty peered up through the limbs, looking bewildered, the squirrel came back down right into Coty's open mouth. Coty shook it once, and the squirrel was dead. I think Coty was more shocked than I was that he had actually caught one. He probably was as surprised as Purty was the day he shot at a squirrel and a raccoon fell out of the tree and nearly onto his head.

"Won't your dog get lost?" Tommy asked.

"No. He'll come along in a little while," I said. What I wanted to say was, "City boy."

But I liked my cousins and didn't want to poke fun at them. I'd probably be the same way if I had lived in Ohio all my life.

We pushed through branches and bent over to get under limbs as we made our way on the small trail. The trail followed the ridge above the north side of the creek. We finally came to a break in the rock wall and climbed down through the rock opening to a small ledge that had a view of Devil's Fork Creek forty feet below. I turned to the left and led the others another hundred feet along the ledge to a large overhang. I found a large rock and took a seat.

"This is so neat," Tommy said.

I had found the overhang about a month earlier while exploring with Coty one rainy afternoon. I was hoping to take Susie to the spot and build a fire and have a picnic someday.

I knew the guys would like to see it. I hadn't shown it to the Wolf Pack yet. James Ernest might have already known about it. There was a great view of the beautiful creek below. There was a rock wall that had natural drawings on it. They weren't actually drawings but strange-looking carvings that had been made by years of rain and wind on the rock.

Carving or Fossil of Animal Head

When we looked straight up at the overhang we saw trees balancing on the edge, daring each other as to how far they could lean over the edge without falling. Blue was now peeking through the cloud-covered sky. Rays of sunlight shot through the openings of the trees and then down to where we were sitting.

The guys walked all over the area looking at the strange rock formations, the rain carvings, and the different views of the surroundings. They all had smiles spread across their faces. I was happy to think they might be seeing a glimpse into the reasons I loved living here in Morgan County.

I knew we needed to head home if we were going to make it back by two o'clock. I didn't want to miss the Thanksgiving meal. I wanted a turkey leg and knew I would have to battle to get one.

"We'd better get going," I told the guys.

"Is the fishing very good in that creek?" Joe Jr. asked.

"Yeah. Pretty good," I answered.

"Maybe you could take us fishing next time," he said.

"Sure," I said.

Coty found us as we were heading back to the house. By the time we got to the house our families were already filling their plates. The women made us go to the well and wash our hands and faces. The turkey legs were gone. I eyed the large one that Judy had taken. Her sister, Jenny, had taken the other one. What was it with these Johnson girls and turkey legs? My best bet was getting the one from Judy. I knew there was no way she would eat a whole turkey leg. She hadn't even taken a bite from it yet.

"I'll trade you some yams and my turkey for that leg," I told her.

"Nope. I like turkey legs," Judy told me.

"I'll let you play with Coty," I said.

"I've already played with him. That's nothing," she said. I knew she was right.

"What do you want for the turkey leg? What about the wishbone?" I said, knowing that all kids liked to make a wish and pull the wishbone.

"We already did that," she said as she reached across her plate and held up the winning part of the wishbone. "I wished for a turkey leg, and my wish came true."

"How about a dollar?" I said. I knew it was going to come down to money.

"How about ten dollars?" Judy said.

I gave up and took my plate of white breast meat, yams, green beans, and mashed potatoes to the side porch. I knew I was defeated by a four-year-old. I was thankful for the meal, but not as thankful as I could have been.

Later that evening we all gathered at Homer's barn for fellowship and singing. Guitars and banjos and a fiddle were brought to the barn. Pastor White, Miss Rebecca, and Bobby Lee were there. The Washington family was there. Robert and Janice and their daughter Tammy came. Their son, Dana, brought his wife, Pretty Idell. Homer played the banjo and sang some old hill songs. Pretty Idell sang a beautiful bluegrass ballad.

James Ernest was requested to sing I'm so Lonesome I Could Cry. His voice drifted through the rafters and seemed to hang in the loft where Susie and I were watching with a few of the other kids. The folks in the barn hung on every note that he sang.

Mr. Washington and Coal sang two songs that they said were Negro spirituals that touched everyone. The first one was Swing Low Sweet Chariot. Everyone seemed to know it and joined in near the end. The second song was His Eye is On the Sparrow. Raven sang the second verse, and Susie and I thought she was a really good singer.

The ladies had brought desserts for the gathering and everyone dug in during a break in the singing. I filled a large bowl with cherry dumplings.

After eating, Mom and her sisters sang an old song from their childhood. Then Sheriff Cane picked up a guitar and played and sang a song called Handsome Molly. The last verse he sang was "Handsome Betty" instead of Molly, and everyone laughed.

Everyone had such a good time. We were happy and stuffed. Homer told me that my arms would soon grow branches, and cherries would be growing from them. I told him that I would just pick them and have Mamaw fix more cherry dumplings.

Susie and I snuck a kiss up in the hayloft when no one was looking. It was a good day to be thankful for things.

2 A BLACK CROW

School had let out the day before until January the second. We were on a two-week break for Christmas. I enjoyed school but not as much as I did when James Ernest went there with me. The subjects were harder, and Sadie and Bernice made the days so much more unpleasant than they needed to be. They thought they were the rulers of the school and tried to dictate how everyone should do things.

Mrs. Holbrook would smack them with the paddle or a switch every so often to get them to straighten up, but it did little good. It seemed to make them more determined to boss everyone around. They used the paddlings as proof of how tough they were. Daniel Sugarman walked around the schoolyard, following Sadie everywhere she went like a puppy following its master. Susie and Sadie had become mortal enemies since the fight in the creek when Susie almost drowned Sadie. Sadie swore she would get even some day.

If Bernice only carried around a broom and wore a pointy, black hat her persona would be complete. She acted and looked like a witch. She wore mostly black every day, and she had a big nose and white streaks in her long, black hair—one of the many reasons her nickname was "Skunk." None of the boys followed her around. The only way she could ever get one to like her would be if she put a spell on the poor guy—a great curse of some kind.

Even Thelma and Delma were scared of Bernice. They called her "Hattie," which Bernice didn't take very well. They would run when she got too close. Susie's best friends at the school were Raven, Rhonda, Samantha, and Sadie's sister, Francis. Even Francis had nothing to do with Sadie and Bernice at school. Some of the little kids at the school called Sadie and Bernice—"Satan and the switch," which stood for "skunk- witch."

Oak Hills School- One room school house

Daniel Sugarman finally had the cast taken off his arm. He had broken the arm when he attempted to jump from the cliff into the swimming hole. One of the bones had been shattered and was sticking through the skin. Every time I looked at Daniel I thought of that bone. He wondered why I always frowned when I saw him. I told him it wasn't anything personal; I was just thinking about his arm, but I still think it bothered him that I was always frowning at him.

The best thing about school, except for Susie, was Mrs. Holbrook. She was the best teacher. She was nice, always helpful, and always happy to see us each day. At least, she acted that way. She would get upset when kids brought animals into the schoolhouse. I'd seen frogs, snakes, baby birds, insects of all kinds, and even larger animals like Coty. A red fox walked into the front door one day as Mrs. Holbrook was printing something on the blackboard.

The fox slinked over to a lunch sack, which was on the floor. The kids began screaming. The fox grabbed the lunch sack in his mouth then turned and ran out of the building just as Mrs. Holbrook swatted at it with a long broom. It was the last time the kid left his lunch sack sitting on the floor.

On the last day before Christmas break Mrs. Holbrook introduced a new game for us to play. She called it the Preacher's Cat. Mrs. Holbrook explained, "The first player has to describe the cat and give it a name that both start with the letter A. The second person has to use the letter B and so on. An example would be, 'The preacher's cat is an angry cat, and her name is Alice.' I'll call on different students around the room. Everyone can play this game. Purty, would you please go first?"

Purty stood up at his chair and began, "The preacher's cat is an angry cat, and his name is Alice."

All of us kids began laughing. Mrs. Holbrook held her hands up to quiet everyone and then said, "Purty, you used the same thing I said, except you gave a male cat the name of Alice."

"I didn't know I had to make up something different, and this preacher is weird," Purty tried explaining.

"Try it again, using the letter A again," Mrs. Holbrook told Purty.

Purty looked pained but started again, "The preacher's stupid cat is an annoyed cat, and his name is Alex."

Mrs. Holbrook looked to the ceiling, something she did often after Purty spoke. "Thelma, you're next."

Thelma jumped to her feet and said, "The preacher's cat is a bad cat, and her name is Billy Jo."

Raven was picked next and she rose and said, "The preacher's cat is a cute cat, and her name is Calico."

Mrs. Holbrook picked me next, and I stood up, unsure what I would come up with. I knew I needed to come up with D words. I began, "The preacher's cat is a dumb cat, and her name is…Delma."

The class erupted into laughter. Mrs. Holbrook looked toward the wooden ceiling again. I hadn't planned to use Delma's name. It was just the first name that started with a D that popped into my brain.

Delma stood, without being asked to, as the class laughed, and the kids quickly hushed.

"I'll go next," she quickly said before Mrs. Holbrook could say anything. "The preacher's cat is a stupid, ignoramus, ugly cat filled with fleas and ticks and eats nothing but garbage, and his name is Timmy."

Well, this little fun game had gone horribly wrong rapidly. I didn't think that was what Mrs. Holbrook had in mind at all. I felt bad because it was really my fault. I started it.

Mrs. Holbrook called for an early recess. She told everyone to go outside even though it was almost freezing. As soon as we were outdoors everyone began making up sentences about the preacher's cat and using their enemy's name in it. Some were very creative. I was sure Mrs. Holbrook would have been proud of the adjectives kids were coming up with but probably not very happy at the same time.

Mrs. Holbrook left us outside in the cold for a lot longer than our usual recess. Maybe she was trying to freeze us solid to get our undivided attention. It worked. The students were quiet while trying to warm up with the heat the pot-bellied stove provided. She asked Purty to get a bucket of coal from the back of the building. She then stoked up the fire to provide more warmth. The kids next to the stove were soon too hot while the youngest and oldest kids, who were farther away on the ends, were still cold.

We didn't play any more games that day. The day slowly ground to an end. Mrs. Holbrook wished us all a Merry Christmas, and we were done with school for over two weeks. Mrs. Holbrook had a big smile on her face as she waved goodbye to each of her wonderful students.

SATURDAY, DECEMBER 16, 1961

It was Saturday, nine days before Christmas, and I was standing in the store, waiting for customers to walk through the door. We had coal burning in the stove that sat in the middle of the room. There were no fishermen to take care of. The lake would mostly remain empty of fishermen for the next few months. Every once in a while a man would brave the weather for a chance to catch a catfish. Some men even tried ice fishing when the ice was frozen deep enough. Fishermen would come for a chance to get out of the house and away from their wives. At least that's what I gathered from their conversations.

Papaw, Mamaw, and I had spent a week in October watching the World Series on TV. Our Cincinnati Reds, led by my favorite player, Vada Pinson, and Frank Robinson, and the pitching arms of Joey Jay and Jim O'Toole, won the National League pennant and met the New York Yankees for the world championship. We would live and die with each pitch. The Yankees won the first game as Whitey Ford outpitched Jim O'Toole in a close two to zero win.

The Reds came back to win the second game six to two behind Joey Jay's four hitter. The Yankees won the third game three to two by scoring a run in each of the last three innings, one being on a home run by Roger Maris, who had broken Babe Ruth's home run record by hitting sixty-one home runs during the season.

The Reds were crushed in the final two games. But it was a week I'll never forget. I was able to watch the Reds in a World Series with my Mamaw and Papaw. It was great despite the outcome not being what we had wanted.

Kentucky winters could be anything. We could have lots of snow with very cold, long stretches of weather for days at a time, or we could have little snow and mild temperatures the entire winter. Kentucky was considered a southern state to some folks and a northern state to people in the most southern states. I didn't care what winter brought our way. I loved it either way. I liked playing in the snow, building forts and snowmen, and having snowball fights. I also loved having warm temperatures, which gave us hope for an early spring.

During really cold weather or heavy snow Coty was allowed to stay in the house at night. He walked around inside the house during those times unsure of what to do. He would sniff the new surroundings and stand and stare as though he knew he was somewhere he wasn't supposed to be. I would always have to tell him to come and lie down. He would wander over, circle a few times, and then plop on the floor.

The Wolf Pack had nothing planned for the Christmas vacation, except we were going to have a meeting at some point.

Sheriff Cane had been spending more time at the house visiting Mom. They would go for walks at the lake, or down Morgan Road in the evenings, or out to dinner and a movie what seemed like every week. I couldn't believe there were that many good movies to see.

James Ernest spent most of the evenings with us. He couldn't afford to heat the trailer, and he didn't want to freeze. He slept on our couch. Some nights he spent with other families. He had spent nights at Homer and Ruby's house, the Washington's house, with Mamaw and Papaw, and he really enjoyed spending nights with Uncle Morton.

James Ernest had told me that he and Uncle Morton would stay up late into the night, swapping stories about nature and birds, coyotes, and all kinds of things they had learned by studying the outdoors. I wondered if I would be able to contribute anything to the stories. I loved talking to Uncle Morton, and I knew that James Ernest did, also.

The weather was mild for the middle of December. I was walking to the outhouse on that Saturday morning. The sky was a deep blue. The trees that surrounded the lake and store were naked. We hadn't had rain or snow in the last week, and the leaves that lay on the ground were dry and crunched as I walked on them. I stopped and looked at the tree line around me. I could clearly see James Ernest's trailer on the hill. It was usually mostly hidden by the green of the trees in the summer. But the winter brown and gray hid nothing.

I spotted a Red-tailed hawk high up in an oak tree that stood trying to block my view of the trailer. His white chest made him easy to spot in the tree. I knew his eyes were searching the area for prey.

"Caw, caw," came the call of a black crow. I turned toward the lake and searched for where the sound came from.

"Caw, caw," it came again.

I spotted the crow in a tree, perched on a lower limb left of the lake's dam. At the time I thought it strange to see this bird, but I wasn't sure why. I continued to the outhouse. I took my seat and was doing my business when I heard the cry again.

"Caw, caw," echoed around the inside of the small outhouse. It sounded as though the bird had landed on top of the structure. I heard Coty bark. Coty was guarding the path to the outhouse as he always did.

I had always loved the large black birds that swept over the fields and landed around the lake looking for bits to eat. I think my love for the birds began when we read The Raven by Edgar Allan Poe in school one day. I had memorized the beginning of the poem about a raven, which came rapping on a man's door. I remembered that the raven could talk in the poem but only said, "Nevermore."

> Once upon a midnight dreary, while I pondered, weak and weary, Over many a quaint and curious volume of forgotten lore, While I nodded, nearly napping, suddenly there came a tapping, As of someone gently rapping, rapping at my chamber door. "'Tis some visitor," I muttered, "tapping at my chamber door — Only this, and nothing more."

That was how the poem began. It had always been my favorite poem. It was neat. Most poems were about flowers or sunny days or balloons, but this poem was about ravens, forgotten lore, and rapping on a door. I loved it.

Something about the poem woke a desire in me to try my hand at writing poems and also gave me a love for ravens and crows—all black birds. The desire to write poems soon faded after several attempts to write them. I wrote silly things like, "Bing and the Kings can have all the money, I'll just call my sweet love, honey." Or, "Leaping lizards and near-sighted wizards." It definitely wasn't Poe. So my days writing poetry came to an early end, but my love for black birds never had.

"Caw, caw," the crow yelled back and Coty barked again at the bird.

This went on the entire time I was in the outhouse. What did a guy have to do to get a little peaceful time in the outhouse?

I opened the door, expecting to see the bird fly away, but instead he sat on the crown of the roof and stared down at me.

I spoke to him, "Good morning, Mr. Crow."

"Caw, caw," he cried and bobbed his head. It surprised me. The bird acted as though he was talking to me. I wondered what it meant. This couldn't be happening. Coty came up to my side and barked at the bird again. The crow walked the peak of the roof to the front edge and looked down at Coty. Mr. Crow threw his head back and made some kind of gravelly sound in his throat, which reminded me of what a crow might do if he was laughing at a dog. I laughed. Coty seemed frustrated by the crow's antics and my laughing and looked from me to the crow and then howled back up at the black bird.

The bird didn't seem too concerned about Coty at all. Suddenly the crow flew off its perch and down toward Coty. Coty barked with all his might. "Caw, caw, caw," and "woof, woof, woof," bounced around in my brain as I circled, trying to watch the bird and Coty argue. The bird continued to fly around me as Coty circled. Coty every few seconds would jump up trying to snatch the bird out of the air.

I was almost sure that the bird was trying to land on Coty's back. But Coty would have none of that. As I went round and round I caught a glimpse of Mom and Janie on the porch, watching the commotion. After what seemed like an hour, but was actually only a couple of minutes, the most amazing thing happened; the crow landed on my left shoulder. I'm not kidding. It really did!

Coty dropped to his butt and looked up at the bird with a puzzled look on his dog face. The look made me think that Coty was thinking, "What the heck?"

I knew that I was thinking the same thing. I turned and looked at Mom and Janie. The look on their faces was almost the same as Coty's.

"Caw, caw," the black crow screamed into my ear. My sister opened her mouth as if she was going to say something but then slowly closed it, not knowing what to say. I didn't know what to do. I wanted to reach up and pet it. But I was afraid it might bite my hand. I wanted to turn my head and look at it, but I was afraid it might peck my left eye out. I wanted my eye, so I looked straight ahead.

The next thing the bird did I know you won't believe because I didn't believe it, and I was the one he did it to. The black crow lowered his head and nestled the side of his head on my cheek, his soft feathers almost tickling.

What in the world would cause this bird to land on my shoulder and then begin wooing me? I wasn't sure if he was looking for a friend or a mate. All I knew was that I was freaked out beyond anything that had ever freaked me out. And I had been freaked out a lot. Finding Coty in a den had freaked me out. Sliding into a cave filled with Indian drawings had freaked me out. Almost being killed by the Tattoo Man and then the kidnappers had totally freaked me out. Seeing Purty walking around naked, that by far had been my biggest freak out, but this one—it topped all of them.

I just stood there in that place and soaked in every moment of having a beautiful black crow sitting on my shoulder. Coty finally quit barking and howling and sat in front of me kind of like he was soaking it in, also. My mom didn't say anything. I figured she was beside herself, not knowing how she should act. I didn't think there was a parenting guide telling moms what to do if a big black bird lands on your son's shoulder.

I heard Mom tell Janie, "You come back here." Janie had started walking toward me and the bird because she wanted to get a closer look. The crow's claws had dug through my shirt and into my skin. But it didn't really hurt much; if it did I was willing to put up with the slight pain.

I was standing there with a smile on my face that must have stretched across Kentucky, wishing Susie could see what was happening, when the back screen door opened and Susie stepped through to stand next to Janie. Mom put her hand up as if to warn her not to say anything. I saw the look of surprise spread across her face, a look that was half fright and half delight. My wish had come true.

Much to my dismay, the twins were next to open the door and walk out onto the porch. I hadn't wished for them. Their mouths dropped open when they saw the sight that everyone was staring at.

As soon as they stopped, the great bird looked their way, and I could sense the bird tighten its body. His claws drew deeper into my skin.

"Caw, caw, caw," he cried and bobbed his head up and down in anger. Coty stood and howled. The crow flapped his wings, slapping me on the back of my head and in my face, and flew from my shoulder and straight toward the twins. He was screaming, "Caw, caaaw," at them.

The twins dove behind Susie. The crow veered to the left and flew up into the sky and landed in the tall sycamore tree that had been hit by lightning during a storm a couple of years earlier. Susie ran out to where I was still standing, and we looked up into the tree at the crow.

"Caw, Caw," the crow called out.

DEEP IN THE DOGHOUSE

Susie and I went for a walk up to the lake. Coty pranced in front us like he sometimes did. I told Susie all about the crow landing on the outhouse and then sitting on my shoulder. She was amazed. I was telling her about it, still not really believing that it actually happened, when she reached for my hand, which sent a shiver through my body. I loved holding her hand. The crow called out as he circled above the lake. He soon settled on a branch in a tall oak tree.

"Why do you think the crow landed on you?" Susie asked.

"I have no idea," I answered.

"Maybe he's lonely. Have you seen other crows?"

"I always see crows around the lake. They bother the local fishermen all the time," I answered.

"How?"

"They pester them. They try to steal their food and bait and any fish they see flopping on the path. But they do keep the place clean from food garbage."

"I don't see any other crows around," Susie said as she searched the trees and sky. "I thought crows went south for the winter."

"No, they were around here last winter. I remember seeing them around the lake," I said.

Susie turned and looked at me, staring into my face. "Well, I don't see any other crows. Why is your crow all alone?"

"I don't know. And how did it become my crow?"

"I think that he missed out on the plans of the other crows, and now he's lonesome for a friend, and he picked you," Susie explained, having figured it all out.

"I just think he's a stupid bird that made a mistake and landed on me instead of a tree," I said.

"Maybe, but I think it's more than that," Susie said as we walked up the rise toward the slanted rock. "He's watching us."

"Who?"

"Your crow."

"How do you know he's watching us?" I asked her.

"Just a feeling," she said as she looked up into the tree toward the crow.

We made it to the slanted rock. I climbed onto the rock and helped Susie by reaching for her hand. We sat near the top edge of the rock, giving us a good view of the fishing hole and the surrounding area. Coty continued to where the stream flowed into the lake. A slight breeze sent ripples across the lake. The late-fallen leaves bobbed on the surface with the gentle waves. A frog hopped from the bank into the water as Coty passed by him.

Coty was traveling around the bay, searching the trail ahead of him. He was straight across from us when we heard the cawing coming toward us. The crow soared just off the water and then angled toward Coty and landed on the trail a few feet behind him. Coty was oblivious to the crow's being there. The large, black bird began walking the path just behind Coty. Coty peered over the bank toward the water. The crow walked to the edge and peered over the bank toward the water. Coty smelled a small tree and then lifted his right rear leg and peed on the spot and then moved on. The bird walked over to the same spot and put his beak near the spot and then lifted his right leg, mocking Coty.

Susie and I cracked up with laughter.

The crow looked toward us and cried out, "Caw. Caw."

Coty quickly turned his head and saw the crow just behind him.

"Caw."

Coty howled toward the bird. The bird threw his head back and howled with a raspy voice. It was the darnest thing I had ever seen. Coty's eyes popped open, and the fur stood up on his back. Coty began walking toward the crow but in a stalking stance close to the ground. The crow turned, lowered his head to the ground, fluffed out his feathers, and began slinking ahead of Coty, mocking him again.

Coty couldn't take it anymore. He ran at the bird and snapped at it with his opened mouth. The crow flapped his wings and rose just out of the reach of Coty's leap and flew across the bay and landed on the slanted rock below Susie and me.

Coty didn't like that at all. He had watched the crow fly toward us and land on the rock. Coty was barking his head off. He then decided he had had enough of the crow. Coty began running around the bay. The crow was walking up the rock toward us as Coty was making his move. Coty jumped over the stream and headed toward the slanted rock in a full-out run. The crow turned to watch Coty running at him. Coty was at top speed when he made it to the rock. He jumped onto the rock, trying to catch the bird, but the crow flew up into the air. Coty landed on the slick boulder and slid down the rock and into the lake.

The large, black crow drifted back down onto the rock and stared at the dog struggling in the water. Coty finally managed to control himself in the water and swam around the rock to where the stream emptied into the bay and walked out of the lake. He shook the water from his coat, and then with a defeated look about him, walked past the rock and headed for home.

As Coty disappeared over the rise, the crow flew off the rock and down the lake toward Coty. Susie and I then began laughing. We stayed on that rock for another hour, talking about what we had just seen. We had a hard time believing it had happened. But it had happened. We knew no one else would believe what we had seen. You pretty much had to see it to believe it.

We finally got up from the rock and began walking back toward the store. The air seemed to be turning cooler. I wondered if winter was coming. It was a week before Christmas, and we still hadn't seen any snow.

"Have you been Christmas shopping?" Susie asked.

"Not yet. Have you?"

"No. Maybe we could go shopping together."

"That sounds good," I said. "I'm not very good at shopping. You could help me."

"Do I get to help you pick out my gift from you?"

"Sure. Do you know anything about pigs?" I said while keeping a straight face.

"Very funny," Susie said as she hit me in the arm. "Why don't you just buy me a pack of bacon?"

"That would save a lot of time and effort," I teased back.

When we arrived at the store I called out for Coty, "Coty! Coty, come!"

He wasn't anywhere, and he didn't answer my call. He wasn't in the backyard or on the front porch. We walked around the house, searching for him. Susie and I called out for him. I finally went to his doghouse and looked inside. I could see him huddled up deep in his house. I knew instantly that he was hiding from the crow. I looked around the area for the crow, but there were no signs of him.

"Everything is okay, Coty. I don't see that mean crow anywhere. You can come out," I tried coaxing him to come out. He wouldn't budge. I felt sorry for him, but I wasn't going to humiliate him any further by dragging him out of his doghouse. I knew he would come out when he was ready.

"Poor guy," Susie said as we headed for the back door.

"Knowing Coty, he'll get even at some point," I said.

BO GOES TO CHURCH

SUNDAY, DECEMBER 17

Instead of awaking to the crowing of Mr. Tuttle's rooster, it was the cawing of a crow that made me snap awake. I wondered what all the racket was as my sleepy head was slipping out of its deep slumber. The first thing I noticed when I turned my head to the window were the flakes of snow falling outside my window. I liked having my room a little on the cold side and then slipping under warm blankets. I guess it made me feel as if I was sleeping in a tent outside in the wilderness. I had left my window slightly ajar to achieve that feeling.

The next thing I noticed, after the snow, was a small, black head sticking through the small window opening.

"Caw, caw!" the crow yelled.

"What in the world?" I said to myself.

I slid out from under my covers, my bare feet hitting the cold, wooden floor. I hurried to the window. I wanted to close the window, but the crow's head was still poking through. It reminded me of the giant, ugly puppet show that had poked itself in my window months before. I couldn't slam the crow's head with the window, so I opened the window wider to try and get the bird off my window sill.

I opened the window, and the crow hopped inside and jumped onto my bed. From his neck down he was covered with snowflakes. He then shook his body much like Coty would, and the snow fell onto my top blanket. His wings spread across the bed, and he flapped them, knocking the excess snow off. He then nestled himself down into the blanket and laid there as if he was sitting on a nest.

A gentle "Caaaw" came from him after he had settled. I didn't know what to do. It was kind of neat having a large, black crow lying on my bed. I wondered how healthy it was. Didn't birds carry diseases? I wasn't real happy about him depositing the snow on my bed, but I couldn't overlook the fact that it was really cool. The crow had made himself at home really fast.

When I realized how cold I was standing on the wood floor. I quickly closed the window shut, and I slipped under the covers, trying not to disturb the crow. I then realized that maybe I was dreaming. There was no way I could be lying in bed with a crow nestled into the blankets next to me. I had to be dreaming. I closed my eyes, knowing I was still asleep. I wanted to return to the dream and see how it turned out.

About an hour later a tapping came to my bedroom door— a gentle rapping.

"'Tis some visitor?" I asked.

The door opened, and Mom asked, "What did you say? It's time to get ready for chur—"

Before she could finish her sentence, the crow that I thought I had dreamed up flapped his wings and yelled, "Caw! Caw!" His opened wings spread most of the way across the bed.

Mom screamed. The bird screamed. Mom screamed louder. The crow tried to escape by flying back out the window, which I had closed. Thump!

"What in heaven's name!" Mom screamed. The bird staggered across the floor, slipping on the wood planks. He then flapped his long wings and flew at mom's head. She ducked just in time, and the crow flew into the living room. Mom hid behind the door. I ran to my window and flung it open, hoping the bird would try it again for his escape.

I then followed the bird into the living room where I found him perched on the top of our floor lamp. I hurried to the front door and opened it and the screen door, propping it open with a feed sack. I had made another escape route.

I called for the crow, "Come, crow, come." I wasn't really sure how to call a crow to come. I was almost sure that this wasn't the way. I called again, "Caw! Caw!"

Janie walked from the back bedroom. "Is breakfast ready?" Janie was asking when she saw the crow. The crow saw her and screamed a piercing sound nothing like the "caw" from before. Janie stopped in mid-step and stared at the bird who was staring at her.

Janie slowly turned and yelled as she ran, "I'm going back to bed!"

Upon hearing Janie's voice, Mom emerged from behind the door to protect her youngest. The crow jumped from the floor lamp, pooped in mid-air, and flew past Mom's head again and through the store and out the front door, escaping out into the snow once more. I shut the door behind him and hurried to the window in my room and slammed it shut. I flopped onto my bed, hoping that maybe I was still dreaming.

After checking on Janie to make sure she was okay, Mom came into my room and looked at me. She started her sentence a couple of different times. She seemed unable to come up with the right words.

"Why was there a crow on your bed?" she was finally able to ask.

"I thought I was dreaming," I explained.

I went on to explain how the bird got into my room. Mom rubbed her forehead a little harder with each part of the story. She then just turned and walked toward her bedroom to join Janie. Mom and Janie were now both hiding in their bedroom. Coty was deep inside his doghouse, and I was hiding under my covers, hoping again to wake up and realize it was all a dream. How much trouble could one crow cause?

A half hour later Papaw called out from the inside of the store, "Where is everyone?"

We were still deep under the covers, recovering from the morning's visitor. I jumped from the bed and slipped on my slippers and hurried into the store.

"I'm here," I said as I walked in. Papaw was standing behind the counter, straightening a few things before customers began arriving.

"Did you see the snow?" Papaw asked.

"Yeah. My bed was covered with it," I answered.

Papaw was thinking about my statement when Mom walked into the room.

"Good morning, Dad," Mom said.

"Morning, Betty. I thought everyone was still asleep when I walked in."

"We had a very eventful morning with a crow," Mom said before walking back toward the kitchen, leaving me to explain.

I went through the entire story from when I first met the crow. Papaw looked at me like I was out of my mind. "I've seen crows do some funny and weird things in my life, but nothing like what you just made up."

I knew he wouldn't believe it. I just said, "Yep. It's quite a story. I'd better go get ready for church."

I went to my bedroom and put on my church clothes—without the tie. I went into the backyard looking for Coty. I made sure he had food and water by his doghouse. I looked in to see him staring out at me. I checked the trees to see if the crow was anywhere around. I saw no sign of him and didn't hear him.

So I said, "Coty, come on out. I don't see the stupid bird. It's okay. Come on out and see me."

Coty rose and slinked out the opening with his head going side to side and tilting up into the sky. I knew he was searching for the crow. He slowly made his way into my open arms, and I hugged him. I wanted him to know that I loved him and that the crow couldn't ever hurt him or replace him. I was hoping the crow had flown off to find his friends.

Coty then hurried to a tree and peed forever. He must have held it since he hid in his doghouse the evening before.

"If he comes back, you need to let him know who the boss is around here. You're smarter and better than some old crow."

Coty barked and then followed me to the front porch. Papaw was standing against one of the porch supports. He bent down to greet Coty and pet him. It wasn't long before Janie and I got into Mom's car, and we were off to church. I watched out the window for anything black flying in the sky.

I caught a glimpse of what I thought could be a crow but thought I was imagining it.

I was sitting on the pew between Susie and Raven. James Ernest was on the other side of Raven. I told Susie about my morning visit from the crow. She laughed and then noticed that I wasn't.

Oak Hills Church

Pastor White prayed. A woman began singing The Old Rugged Cross. I heard him, "Caw. Caw. Caaaw." The crow was outside the church, trying to sing with the lady. It actually may have added something to the woman's rendition. As soon as the lady finished the song and Pastor White began to preach, the crow landed on the window sill at the end of the row where I sat.

I tried to look away.

Pastor White said, "Please open your Bibles to Second Timothy, chapter one." Then the crow began pecking on the window. I looked away. I knew that everyone would blame me for the church service being interrupted by my crow. I slid down into the pew, trying to hide between Susie and Raven. The pastor continued the sermon. The crow pecked louder at the window pane.

Folks in our section were all looking at the bird who was trying to get my attention. At least, that's what I thought he was doing. The pastor tried to ignore the disturbance. He began preaching about faithful men. The faithful men and women were watching the crow spread his wings and rap on the window with his beak.

Pastor White finally stopped and asked, "What is happening?"

Homer Easterling spoke up, "It seems your preaching has attracted the wildlife, and a crow wants in to hear you speak God's Word."

The congregation erupted in laughter. Men and women all over the church were now standing and trying to get a glance at the creature outside the window.

"Any ideas?" the pastor asked.

James Ernest stood and suggested, "I guess I could sing I'll Fly Away. See if that works."

The church body laughed in unison.

"I've got a rifle in the truck!" a member yelled out.

The women gasped at the proposal. The boys got excited.

"Why don't a couple of you boys run out there and scare it off? Timmy and James Ernest, would you guys take care of the crow?"

44

We slipped out of the pew and started out the front door. I turned back to get my coat, which was hanging on a peg at the back of the church.

We turned the corner to see that the crow was already gone. I heard wings behind me, and the crow landed on my shoulder again. James Ernest stared at me. I shook my head as though saying I wasn't sure what was going on. I began telling James Ernest the story.

We heard Pastor White as he began preaching again. We stood outside in the cold, discussing my new friend. I wondered if I should go inside with the crow sitting on my shoulder but decided against it. I figured Pastor White, my mom, and most everyone, except maybe Purty, would be against the idea.

So I stood along the side of the building in the cold for the rest of the service. After hearing the story about the crow, James Ernest went back inside. The crow seemed perfectly satisfied with being perched on me. I figured if he was going to become a permanent part of me that maybe I should give him a name. So I spent the rest of the church service thinking of names and trying them out.

"What about Blackie?" I asked the crow. His head swayed from side to side. "I didn't really like it, either."

A couple of minutes later I said, "What about Sammy, or Sam? I've always liked that name."

The crow cawed. The message was received, loud and clear, right next to my ear. He didn't like that name, either. I was getting colder by the minute, standing in the two inches of snow that had fallen, and knew that church wouldn't let out for another half hour or so. So I decided to warm up by taking a walk in the woods. The church's gravel lot was surrounded on three sides by woods. The road, Route 711, ran in front of the church.

The woods provided warmth while I walked under the towering trees. The lower branches blocked the cold breeze that I had felt standing next to the building. The crow seemed happy to ride along on my shoulder. I kept thinking of names for him as I walked. I just kept coming up with stupid names such as, garbage eater, cornbread, pecker, and Polly. He wasn't a parrot. I wasn't very good at coming up with names.

As suddenly as a summer storm pops up, I knew what to name him. His name would be Bo - Bo the crow. There was also something formal about crows. They were covered in black; their formal outfit would be complete with a bow-tie attached around their necks. It also was a great southern name. So I told him.

"I'm naming you Bo," I said. I had no idea why I was naming him. He wasn't like a dog that you knew would be there. He could be gone at any moment, and I'd never see him again, at least not that I would know. All crows looked alike. But at least while he did hang around, he would have a name. I wondered if he could learn his name.

"Bo. Your name is Bo. How are you doing, Bo? I reached up and touched him as he sat there on my shoulder. Good Bo," I said. His feathers were soft to my touch. His head nodded up and down as I repeated his name.

I walked on into the trees and came to a small clearing. The silence of the moment was surprising as I stood there. The only sound was the crunching snow under my feet. When I stood still it was as if the whole world stood still with me. I listened to the nothingness—the sound of silence. The crow turned his head, searching the clearing.

"We had better head back to the church, Bo," I said to the crow sitting on my shoulder.

"Bo."

I turned to look behind me. I turned rapidly looking all around me. No one was there. But I had heard someone say Bo—almost as though they had whispered in my ear. It couldn't be. I knew, after looking around and seeing no one, that Bo had said his name. I began to get spooked. Crows aren't supposed to talk. I started walking toward the church. I picked up my pace. I was almost running when I burst into the parking lot.

I stood outside and peered through one of the windows. Pastor White was giving the invitation for sinners to come forward and get cleansed of their sins. One man was kneeling up front. It wasn't long before church let out and folks began filing out the front door. Bo saw the congregation and flew off my shoulder and onto a high limb in the giant oak that stood beside the lot.

Susie and the twins hurried over to where I was standing looking into the tree.

"You and your animals are always disrupting things," Delma said as she neared.

"Where's the crow?" Susie asked.

"Up there. He flew away as soon as he saw the twins' faces," I said, pointing to the limb where Bo sat. "See Bo up there?"

"Bo! You named the stupid crow, Bo?" Thelma criticized.

"Yep," I answered proudly.

"That's a stupid name—for a stupid crow," Delma exclaimed.

"That is really a stupid name. Thought up by a stupid boy," Thelma said just as Clayton called out for the girls to come. They turned to walk away.

"You know something, Thelma. That's fitting that a stupid boy would think of a stupid name for a stupid crow," Delma said as they were walking to the truck.

I heard a loud caw and then saw Bo diving from the tree straight toward the twins. He screeched just as he flew over their heads, and the twins fell to the snow-covered gravel scared senseless. They quickly got up and ran to the truck.

"I like Bo a lot better all the time," I said. Susie and I laughed at the twins as I walked Susie to the truck. Before we parted ways, we made plans for Susie to come to the store later and spend the day with me. I thought it would be a good afternoon.

BAD NEWS

James Ernest rode back to the store with us from church. I told him that I had named the crow Bo. He liked the name. Mom and Janie both liked it, also. I was sure that the twins would soon change Janie's mind.

We were walking up the steps to the porch when Sheriff Cane's cruiser crossed the bridge. We turned to watch him drive into the lot. He slowly got out of the car, turned his back to us and looked toward the bridge he had just crossed. We heard another car coming down the road from Oak Hills. I soon could see that it was Pastor White's car. The sheriff walked to the edge of the road and waved the pastor over. I wondered if the pastor was speeding.

After the sheriff talked to the pastor, he pulled into the lot and Miss Rebecca, Bobby Lee, and the pastor got out of the car and followed us into the store. I saw the sheriff whisper to Mom, and then Mom had Janie take Bobby Lee to the kitchen to play games.

"I had better go to the trailer and change out of these clothes," James Ernest said, making an excuse to get out of the way.

"Please stay. This concerns you," Sheriff Cane told him.

"What's up?" James Ernest said with sadness in his voice almost as though he knew what was coming. "What's happened to Mom?"

I stood still. I knew something important was happening. Mom moved next to James Ernest.

"I'm so sorry, James." Tears welled up in the sheriff's eyes. Miss Rebecca stood with anxiety on her face.

"Their car went off the road and over the side of a mountain in West Virginia. They both died instantly," the sheriff told James Ernest.

Miss Rebecca was helped to a chair by Pastor White. She wept. Mom cried as she held onto James Ernest. I cried for my friend. I knew that he loved his mom so much. I didn't know what to do. I just stood there and wiped at my tears.

"It happened last night, and I just got word about it an hour ago. Apparently, your dad was working in a coal mine in West Virginia. The roads had become slick with the snow, and he slid off the road while trying to make a curve."

The pastor even looked like he was at a loss for words of comfort. We all stood in silence. I felt the same silence that the clearing had given me less than an hour before. James Ernest leaned back against the pop cooler.

The silence lasted a couple of minutes until James Ernest asked, "What about their bodies?"

Sheriff Cane lowered his head and slowly said, "There was a big explosion and fire."

James Ernest and the rest of us knew what that meant. The bodies were gone. There would be no burial. James Ernest also knew that he now would be alone forever. His family was gone—gone for good. He wouldn't wonder any longer if they might come back for him some day.

He lowered his body to the wooden floor, and buried his head into his arms and knees. He cried deep and long. I went over and slid my body down the cooler to be beside him. I put my hand on his shoulder, and I cried with him. It was all I knew to do. Sheriff Hagar Cane went over and held my mom in his arms as she cried. Pastor White and Miss Rebecca held each other.

I heard a long, loud, lonesome caw from the overhang covering the front porch.

A thought raced across my mind, Thing of evil! but I didn't believe it was true—just a thought.

Two hours later families began arriving with platters and bowls of food. Susie's family arrived. Mamaw and Papaw had come before the pastor's family had left. Pastor White decided to stay. James Ernest had gone to the trailer to change out of his clothes. It wasn't long before the store and house was filled with people like the bags of feed on the porch, bulging at the seams.

Susie and I sat on the porch and greeted folks as they arrived. Coty laid by my feet. He helped greet everyone. It was cold outside on the porch but not bad. The inside was warm with body heat. James Ernest still hadn't returned to receive the condolences that the community offered. Papaw came out to the porch and said, "Tim, you ought to go get James Ernest. Tell him he needs to come and see the community. It would be helpful to him."

"Okay," I said.

"I'll go with you," Susie told me. Coty led the way. The snow was already melting off the roads and paths. We followed the trail up the hillside to the trailer.

I knocked on the door and called out, "James Ernest! James Ernest!"

There was no answer. I tried the door handle, and the aluminum door opened. I peered inside and called out his name again. Still, there was no answer. I climbed into the trailer. Susie followed. James Ernest wasn't inside. I checked his bedroom. I looked for his backpack. I couldn't find it.

"Where did he go?" Susie asked me.

I shook my head. I had no idea. Where would James Ernest go? No one knew that answer. He might go anywhere. He could go to the mountains to be alone. He could go to the Washington's to see Raven. He could go to West Virginia to see the scene of the accident.

We slowly walked back to the store. I didn't want to break the news to everyone. I knew they would worry and want to look for him. They didn't realize that it would do no good. I knew that we wouldn't see him again until he wanted us to. That was the plain truth of it.

Bo flew overhead. I watched him circle the lake. He landed in a tall pine and screeched again. It was what I wanted to do for my friend. Bo said it all.

We walked up the steps and across the porch. I opened the door, and Susie and I walked in. All heads turned our way. I saw that the Washington family had arrived. Raven had been crying. I could still see traces of tears on her dark face.

"James Ernest is gone. He won't be coming," I announced. The hush enveloped the folks. I could see their minds racing. Slowly the store and house erupted with everyone speaking at the same time. They were guessing as to where James Ernest was. They were guessing as to why he left.

Someone said above the talk, "We need to go find him."

Others began agreeing and looking toward Sheriff Cane.

Uncle Morton raised his hands to quiet everyone, "It would be a total waste of time. You'd never find that boy. He'll return when he's ready."

"But we can't abandon him in his time of sorrow." Other folks agreed.

"Let's let him do this in his own way. James Ernest is smart. He's going to do what he needs to do. We should pray for him and leave him alone. This is a tough time for him," Uncle Morton offered.

Papaw spoke next and said, "He's been through a lot. The only hope he held onto to see his mom again was taken away last night. Let him go. He'll return. We're not abandoning him. We're honoring him by letting him grieve."

The next two hours were spent talking about James Ernest and his mom. Everyone ate and listened as Mom and Mamaw talked about James Ernest's mom. Hardly anyone knew her very well. Mom probably got to know her better than anyone.

The front door opened, and James Ernest walked in. He had dropped his backpack on the porch. Everyone stared at him, being surprised to see him.

Before any of the women could say anything, he spoke. "I'm sorry I left. I shouldn't have. You all have been so kind and good to me, and I up and walked away from your concern and love. I'm really sorry. I was walking in the woods when I realized how wrong I was. I need your love to help me through this. I can't run away from my sorrow. God put you all in my life for a reason."

Coal rushed over and threw her arms around him. She was followed by most everyone in the house. I knew it had relieved so many people to see James Ernest return.

That evening, after most of the folks had left for home, we were sitting in the living room with Mamaw and Papaw, Pastor White, and the Sheriff.

The pastor suggested, "Why don't we at least have a memorial service for your parents?"

James Ernest looked down at the floor and then up into the pastor's eyes and said, "I think I would like that."

It was decided that the memorial service would take place Wednesday evening at the church. It was the first time I had seen James Ernest smile since he had heard the news about his parents.

THE MEMORIAL SERVICE

It was five days before Christmas, and there was deep snow everywhere. Generally kids would be wild with excitement, and adults would be going crazy with shopping duties and lists that needed to be done as time began running out.

But today the mood was different throughout the community. The country folk's main thoughts were about the memorial service and how James Ernest was doing. He'd been staying with Uncle Morton since news came about his parent's death. I heard Mom tell a customer that there was no better person for him to stay with during this time. I think Mom was right.

Uncle Morton was full of wisdom and always knew exactly the right words to say to a person full of hurt. He had always helped me understand the ways of life. Uncle Morton lived fairly close to the Washington farm, and I knew that James Ernest had also spent time with Raven and her family. If there were people who could relate to heartache and sorrow, I was sure that it was Raven's parents. James Ernest was smart enough to know who to gravitate to after losing his parents.

Snow had fallen daily during the week. Different snow storms would come through and dump three to four inches at a time. There had to be over a foot of snow on the ground that morning. Papaw had put snow chains on his truck. The roads had remained passable because the snow hadn't come all at one time.

I had taken Janie out to build a fort the day before. It was a perfect day for it. The snow packed solid in our hands. Coty bounced around in the snow. I would throw snowballs up into the air, and he would jump to catch them in his open mouth. He liked eating them. The last one I threw a little higher, and as Coty timed his jump, waiting for it to begin its downward fall, Bo, the crow, intercepted it at its highest arc. Bo held the snowball in his claws and flew above Coty's head. Coty barked and howled at Bo. Finally Coty gave up the chase and headed for his doghouse. Bo flew over Coty and dropped the snowball on Coty's head. Coty shook it off and dove into his house.

Bo went to the nearest tree and found a spot to perch.

"Bo is mean to Coty," Janie told me.

"I think Bo is playing with Coty. But Coty has no way to play with Bo since he can't fly."

Janie and I continued building the fort. We made it big enough so the two of us could hide inside and attack others who needed to visit the outhouse. The others mostly were Mom. She wasn't real happy being pelted with snowballs as she tried to make her way down the path. When the fort was finished Bo made a visit and walked along the top of the walls, putting crow prints everywhere. Janie and I made a sign that read "Fort Crow" and stuck it into the snow.

I had gotten a sack full of corn from Papaw's barn, so I could give Bo some food. I stuck an ear of the corn on top of the fort, and Bo enjoyed flying down and eating from it during the day.

The memorial service was to start at six that evening. Papaw went to pick James Ernest up at four so he could come home and get ready for the service. I walked up to the trailer to see him when he arrived. We hadn't talked much since we had learned about the crash.

I knocked on the door and went on in. He was standing in the living room holding a picture of him and his mom.

"Hi, Timmy," he said without even seeing who I was.

"I just wanted to say how sorry I am for what happened to your parents."

"Thanks. I'm okay," James Ernest said. He then added, "It's so hard to believe I won't see her again. Even when she just sat and stared out the window I felt she was here for me. I had a purpose. I was her son. I took care of her. I now regret all those years I went without talking to her, because now I can't." Tears were running down his cheeks as he told me his thoughts.

"You were a great son, and she knew you were. She loved you," I said. I wasn't sure what to say. How is a kid supposed to know what to say at a time like that? Adults don't even know the right thing to say or do.

"Thanks. I needed to hear that."

"Why don't you take that picture to the memorial service? I'm sure others would like to see it."

"That's a great idea. I've got some other pictures I could take, also." James Ernest began rushing through the trailer, gathering pictures and memories of his mom.

"Sheriff Cane is going to pick us at five thirty. I need to go get ready," I told James Ernest.

"I'll be there by then."

Mom made me wear my tie and white shirt. I didn't mind
wearing it this time. I didn't even complain about it. Sheriff
Cane arrived ten minutes early. James Ernest came in the
store shortly after. Mom placed a closed sign on the front
door. It read, "Closed. Gone to Memorial Service."

The drive to the church felt awkward. Kind comments
were made to James Ernest, but mainly it was quiet. I was
thankful that it was only a couple of miles. Mom hugged
James Ernest in the parking lot when we arrived.

He hurried into the church to place the pictures before others began arriving. Pastor White and his family were already
there. When I walked into the church I saw a small table
inside the door with pictures of his family. He had placed
a picture of a field of flowers on the table also. I wasn't sure
what it was for. He had found a picture of the three of them
together when he was very young. Only one of the pictures
was in a frame. The others were placed face up on the table.

Pastor White had James Ernest greet folks near the pulpit
as they arrived. A line soon stretched the length of the church
with well-wishers.

Everyone from the community was there. I didn't see
anyone missing. Even our teacher, Mrs. Holbrook, was there
with her husband. James Ernest had been one of her favorite
students. Mr. Harney, the banker, was there. Mr. Cobb, who
ran the general store, was there. Razor McCall, the barber,
was even there.

As the service started people were standing at the sides
and sitting on the floor, due to the crowd that was there to
support James Ernest.

Pastor White began the service with prayer and then sang the song "On the Wings of a Dove." As the song was winding down I heard a familiar commotion—a pecking at a window. I knew it was Bo. I didn't know what to do. Everyone in the church was looking at Bo in the window as Pastor White finished the song.

I was sitting beside James Ernest. He leaned over and said, "Go get him and bring him in here if you have to."

I stared at him with an expression that said, "Are you kidding?"

"You can't let him interrupt the entire service, and I need you here."

I hurried to my feet and almost ran down the center aisle. All eyes stared at me, especially Mom's.

I opened the door and ran through the snow to the side where the crow was sitting on the window sill. I wasn't even sure the stupid crow would go into the building. I thought about grabbing it and wringing its neck like Mamaw did with the chickens we ate for Sunday dinners. When I neared Bo he rose off the sill and lifted himself into the air. Maybe he sensed my thoughts.

"You're ruining the service," I said angrily.

He yelled back, "Caw, caw!" The same stupid thing he always said.

I waved by arms at him, thinking maybe I could scare him away. But I also worried that even if he did fly away he might return to rap on the window again. I gave up and began walking back to the door. Bo quickly lighted onto my shoulder and hung on as I climbed the steps to the door. I opened the door and walked into the service. Pastor White stopped in the middle of a sentence and looked up at me. Everyone else followed his lead. There were gasps from the people and loud whispering as I stood looking at them with a large black crow on my shoulder, named Bo. I could sense excitement with the kids in the room.

Mom stood up and said, "Timmy, take that bird out of here. Please!"

James Ernest stood and looked at Mom and said, "I asked Timmy to bring the crow inside. My mother would have been fascinated to see a crow so close. She loved to watch the crows in the trees above the trailer. Please let the crow stay. Mom would love it."

I was shocked. I never knew this.

As I took a step toward my seat, Bo rose from my shoulder and flew into the rafters of the church building. The building had an open ceiling with stained crossbeams. Bo found a spot to perch at the back of the church. He fluffed his feathers and settled in for the service. I quickly made my way to my seat.

"Thanks," I said to James Ernest.

"Thank you," James Ernest said back.

I looked at Purty. He was in the row behind me and over a little. He had a shocked look on his face. He didn't know anything about the crow. He then smiled at me.

Pastor White began speaking again, "I feel as though I'm having a Poe experience. If the bird yells out, 'Nevermore!' as I'm speaking, I may have to leave."

Everyone laughed.

The pastor gave a short message about how souls here on earth sometimes go through deep hardships, and it's hard to understand at times. But he said to never forget that God is in control, and we should never doubt it. I turned my head to look at Bo. He was still on his perch. He seemed to be listening to Pastor White speak.

"It is beyond belief how this community comes together to help their neighbor in a time of trouble. I know that this blesses God. If anyone has anything to say about James Ernest's parents, or to James Ernest, now is the time to come. Uncle Morton rose from his seat, and Pastor White helped him up the steps to the podium. He took a piece of paper from his coat pocket and spread it out in front of him. Suddenly everyone began laughing, realizing that Morton was blind.

He looked out at the audience and scanned the mass of bodies, "It's so good to see everyone here," he began as laughter again filled the building, "to support James Ernest in this time of sadness. Anytime we lose someone we loved it's a time of sadness. But James Ernest lost his family. We shouldn't forget this. Yes, James Ernest has been able to fend for himself since he was very young, but he still needs a family. And I believe he's found one in this body of people." Amen's filled the room.

"James Ernest is one of the finest men I've had the opportunity to meet. I'm proud to call him brother and friend. I am so sorry for your sorrow and loss. Even though you were abandoned, you know as well as we all know, that your mom loved you dearly. And always remember that you are in the protective hands of your heavenly Father, the great God. I expect great things from you, for His honor." Uncle Morton folded his papers and made his way to James Ernest, who had left his seat to meet and hug Uncle Morton. There was not a dry eye in the church.

Raven stood next and nervously made her way to the stage. She hesitated before speaking. She looked out at all the white faces staring at her. I wondered how she got the courage to stand and speak. I thought she was going to go back to her pew, but she didn't. She spoke, "I've gotten to be very good friends with James Ernest. We make baskets together. A lot of you have bought them. In the entire time I've known him he's been the kindest boy I know. He never talked about what he wanted to buy himself with the money he made from our baskets. He always talked about what he could buy his mom. I think she needs this or that, he would say. He would strip wood, and weave baskets, until his fingers bled to be able to get her what he thought she needed. I'm so proud to be his friend, and I'm so happy I got to know his mom a little. I know he had to get some of his gentleness from her."

Raven then motioned for her mom to come to the stage, and they sung a Negro spiritual about meeting Jesus on the shores of heaven. James Ernest hugged Raven and Coal.

When they walked off the stage I knew I needed to get up and speak. My times spent on this stage were not the best of memories. I fought with myself over going forward. I didn't even know what I would say. This was a time that I could have used notes like Uncle Morton did. I was allowed to and didn't even think of doing it. I'm so stupid, I thought.

As I began to rise, Mom stood and walked to the stage. She looked pretty up there. I had never heard her speak in front of a group before. I settled back into my seat—a reprieve.

"I had the privilege to get to know Anna Mae, James's mother, a little. She was a sweet lady but was troubled. One thing I know is that she thought the world of James Ernest.

She trusted in him. She knew he would return when the boys were trapped in the cave. She told me as a matter of fact that James would be home soon. 'He's always here for me,' she said. She had become accustomed in knowing that James Ernest loved and cared for her. It had to be hard for James Ernest. He taught me what unconditional love is. He loved Anna Mae despite getting almost nothing in return. I admire James Ernest, and he'll always have a home with my family."

Mom then walked off the stage. Keep going, Mom, I thought. That was good. Why did you stop? Now I have to get up. James Ernest hugged Mom.

I looked around to see if anyone else was going to stand. Everyone was looking at me.

I stood.

I walked to the podium.

I began to say something when I heard the flapping of wings in the rafters. Bo flew over the congregation and circled behind me and then landed on my shoulder. I then had everyone's undivided attention. I knew there was no way I could get Bo to fly back to his perch, so I decided to say something with a black crow attached to my shoulder.

"I'm not sure what I wanted to say. I just know I have to say something. James Ernest has been my best friend for a few years. We were best friends when he didn't talk, and I shouldn't have. It didn't keep us from forming our friendship. He never made fun of the way I talked. He would sneak up on me and scare me to death. But I liked him. He was different. I was different. I always wondered how he could care about his mom so much. I knew I couldn't do what he did.

"He was upset when they told him he couldn't continue going to school since he didn't talk. I thought he had found the perfect way not to have to go to school." Laughter broke out. "So what does my best friend do? He starts talking again so he could go to school. And I always thought he was the smartest guy I knew. I wasn't so sure then." Laughter came again.

"But I was wrong. He was right. He wanted to learn. He wants to be something. But I also know that he is already something. He's the best friend a guy could ever have. I am so sorry for the loss of your mom and dad. I know how hard it is to lose someone in your life. I'll always be your best friend." Tears ran from my eyes, and I knew I was done. I stepped away from the podium, and Bo yelled out, "Caw, Caw!" and bobbed his head up and down as in total agreement with all that I had said. I knew that I had to be dreaming. This was one long dream. Someone wake me, please!

Bo flew back to his perch as I was sitting down. James Ernest waited a little while to see if anyone else wanted to speak before standing and walking to the stage.

It was so quiet you could hear the people breathing in and out as James Ernest walked up onto the stage and stood behind the podium. He looked out at the crowd that filled the church. He knew that most everyone there had never met his mother, and no one had met his father. But he knew they knew him. They had come to support him in his time of sorrow and hurt. He was touched by the expressions of love. It made him feel better, looking out onto the sea of faces—friends that he had made despite his oddities and family.

"Thank you for coming this evening. When it was first suggested that there would be a memorial service, I wondered if more than ten people would come. I'm overwhelmed by your love. I shouldn't be surprised, though. I've seen the care and love that this community has for its people from the first day that Mom and I moved here. We couldn't have come to a better place. I would especially like to thank a couple of folks. Mr. and Mrs. Martin Collins have been so kind to me and Mom. They are grandparents to me. I love you two so much. Thank you, Betty, for being Mom's friend and caring about her. She really liked you."

I looked over at Mom, and she had a tissue out, dabbing the tears from her eyes. Then I noticed that most of the ladies were doing the same.

James Ernest continued, "The Washington family and Raven have been such a blessing to me." He hesitated as he swallowed hard, and then said, "I love the Wolf Pack, Randy, Purty, I mean Todd, and Timmy. I'd never had friends until I moved here. Timmy taught me what it meant to be a friend. He's my brother.

"Mom had a lot of problems, the biggest one probably being me. I'm now so sorry I went years without talking to her. I have a lot of regrets. We both were locked in our own worlds, and we didn't know how to unlock them and get out. When Mom left with Dad I knew it was her way of escaping the chains that bound her. I will never feel abandoned. I feel as though it was her way of saving me. No telling what would have happened if she had forced me to go with them. I loved her, and I'll always love her. I pray that God will comfort her in His arms."

James Ernest wiped tears from his eyes and began to sing.

Amazing Grace had never been sung with more sense of purpose than what I heard that evening in that little church in Morgan County. His deep voice flowed through the rafters and pews of the church and touched each person there. The blanket of snow outside the church carried the words deep into the forest. I was sure that the deer, rabbits, and squirrels heard about the grace of God that night.

James Ernest raised his arms to the sky as he finished singing, and I could feel the crowd praying as he began walking back to his seat. Pastor White took his spot at the pulpit and thanked everyone for coming and said, "I know this means the world to James Ernest. It means the world to me." Then he closed the memorial service in prayer.

I walked out of the church and looked up into the sky at the nearly full moon in the eastern sky. Susie stood beside me and said, "There's Timmy's moon."

I smiled. Because of my love for the full moon, many of my friends and family began calling it Timmy's moon. I wasn't sure why I loved the full moon so much, but I had since I could remember. Maybe it was the mystery of it, maybe because I could see the man in the moon's face in it. Maybe because it wasn't there every night, and it was special when it did arrive. It was kind of like it came to check on me and make sure everything was okay.

I suspected the full moon came that night to check on James Ernest to make sure he was okay. I hoped he was.

Bo flew out of the church and elevated into the sky. We could see him due to the moon's reflection on the snow covered ground. It almost looked like the middle of the afternoon. Susie and I watched Bo fly as he circled the church going higher and higher. Suddenly he passed between us and the full moon, and we could see him silhouetted against the white.

Mamaw and Papaw were having a gathering at their farm for James Ernest. Mom came over to where we stood. James Ernest had walked over to us and looked up into the sky to see what we were looking at.

"Time to go," Mom said.

"I think I need to walk, if you don't mind. I won't be long at all," James Ernest told Mom.

"That's fine. Remember that everyone is coming to see you," Mom said.

"I know. I promise I won't be long."

"Can we walk with him if James Ernest doesn't mind?" I asked Mom.

"That would be great," he answered.

"Sure. You had better ask your parents, Susie," Mom suggested.

After getting permission, the three of us began walking the gravel road along the ridge. Even though it was around thirty degrees outside, it felt much warmer. The church was only a little over a mile or so from the farm. I wondered if Susie's legs were cold. She had on a pretty, flowered dress.

"Are you cold?" I asked her.

"A little, maybe, if you'd hold my hand," she suggested.

I did, but I didn't understand how holding her hand would keep her legs warm. I was happy to hold her hand, though.

"Your song was beautiful," Susie said to James Ernest.

"Thanks. The service was so nice. I really appreciated it. Bo made it very unique."

"Sorry about that," I said.

"No. I'm serious. It was neat. It's not a service that people will easily forget. It was a great way for people to remember my mom," James Ernest explained.

"I think you're right," Susie said.

We were walking around a bend in the road just before the entrance to Homer and Ruby's lane when a large coyote eased into the road ahead of us. We stopped dead in our tracks and watched him in silence. The coyote was standing in the middle of the road, looking toward the opposite side of the road. The coyote turned his head slowly and looked at us and sniffed the air.

"What do we do?" I whispered.

"Shhh." James Ernest hushed me.

The coyote made a step toward us. I knew I was going to pee my pants. My legs were shaking, and I knew Susie could feel the fright in my hand. This was a lot different than the time I saw the two coyotes at the lake. They were lying down and didn't seem too interested in us. But this guy was very interested in us. I could imagine him seeing a T-bone steak when he looked at us, like I would see cherry dumplings.

I thought I had had my fill of surprises for the week. Boy, was I wrong.

James Ernest used his hand to motion for us to stay, and he stepped away from us and walked slowly toward the coyote. James Ernest held his hands straight out in front of his body with his palms up and moved closer. The coyote stepped toward James Ernest. I was ready to run to James Ernest's side and help my best friend wrestle the coyote.

Suddenly the coyote dropped to the ground and then stood again as James Ernest neared. The coyote then walked up to

James Ernest and stood there as he was petted. James Ernest was petting the wild coyote! I had to be dreaming. I had a pet blackbird, James Ernest's parents died in a bad accident, and James Ernest was petting a coyote that was ready to eat us. I knew I was dreaming. How else could I explain this?

"Are we dreaming?" I whispered to Susie.

"I know what you mean, but I don't think so," Susie whispered back.

The coyote heard the whispers and lifted his head toward us. He seemed very weary of Susie and me. "It's okay. She's my friend," James Ernest softly said to the beautiful creature.

James Ernest continued to stroke the top of the coyote's head. "Go now," James Ernest said, and the coyote turned toward the opposite side of the road. The ditch line dropped down a couple of feet, and there was a barbed wire fence beyond the ditch. The coyote began running and leapt off the road over the ditch and fence with ease. A rabbit dashed from the fence line, and the coyote was soon on its tail.

James Ernest turned toward us as we were watching the coyote race across the snow-covered hillside. We turned our heads toward James Ernest and stood there with our mouths open.

"Oh yeah, and walking into a church with a blackbird on your shoulder is normal," James Ernest said, defending himself.

"How were you able to do that?" Susie asked as she dropped my hand and rushed to within a foot of James Ernest, staring him in the face. "That was so cool."

James Ernest hesitated answering.

"Tell me, James Ernest," Susie demanded.

"Okay, okay. I guess over the last few years of roaming the woods at night I've developed friendships with some of the animals. She's one of them," James Ernest explained.

"What? How does a normal person do that?" I asked.

"I don't know. How do you explain Bo?" James Ernest answered. "We had better keep walking. People are expecting us."

"You said some of the animals. What other animals?" Susie asked. I was wondering the same thing.

"A few deer, a bear…" he began.

"A bear!" I shouted.

"…A couple of raccoons, and a bobcat," James Ernest finished, turned, and continued walking toward the farm. "Some others."

Susie and I looked into each other's startled faces and then turned and hurried to catch up to him. His long strides were hard to keep up with since he was in a hurry to not keep folks waiting. We had to almost jog to keep up.

I had so many questions for James Ernest about his friendships with the wild animals. But all of them seemed silly as we walked along the ridge. He was right. Who was I to question what he told us when I had a dog that was part coyote and a black crow that went to church with me? I was beginning to get out of breath trying to keep up with him in the cold weather. Susie was also breathing hard.

"Slow down," I begged.

He slowed to a casual walk.

"Thank you," Susie said.

"I'm sorry. I didn't realize how fast I was walking," James Ernest said.

We were already within eyesight of Papaw's lane that turned left off the road. Cars and pickups were passing us and driving down the lane. A large oak tree stood where the lane turned off the road. I heard a "caw" coming from the top of the tree. Bo was perched on a bare limb at the very tip top of the tree. We walked under the huge tree limbs and followed the lane toward the house. Bo flew from the tree and swooped down and landed on my shoulder. He put his cheek against mine in a loving way. I really didn't think he was being loving; I figured it was some weird thing that the crow did that just happened to seem like he was being affectionate.

We were a weird bunch of kids. How could I ever question James Ernest about his relationship with the wild animals? Susie looked at me and smiled.

"This is the most amazing walk I've ever been on," she said.

I surely did have to agree.

The lights inside the house were glowing as we neared the house. I made Bo fly off my shoulder as we entered the farm yard. He flew up into the large oak trees by the front porch. Many of the vehicles that were at the church were now parked on the side of Papaw's lane. The side door opened and Raven stepped out onto the side porch and waved. She hurried through the yard and hugged James Ernest tightly when she got to him.

They walked hand in hand to the front door. I noticed they let go as they entered the house. James Ernest was warmly greeted by everyone in the house. James Ernest was smothered with hugs and greetings and well wishes. The kitchen table and counters were filled with food and desserts. Pastor White asked grace over the food and the food soon began to disappear. I wasn't very hungry, but I did get a big bowl of cherry dumplings. I didn't have to be hungry to eat cherry dumplings.

I got my big bowl of cherry dumplings and went out to the porch to get out of the crowd. Susie and Raven followed me. Soon Purty, Randy, Francis, and Sadie joined us on the porch. Purty had a plate that seemed to be heaped up halfway to the porch ceiling. I stared at him until he tried to explain the glutton's plate.

"I was hungry. Memorial services and death makes me nervous, and I eat when I'm nervous," he told us.

"Then you're the most nervous person I've ever met," I said and laughed.

"You should be nervous eating that much food," Susie teased.

Purty looked at his plate and defended the size of it by saying, "It's not that big. I've eaten more than this many times."

We all laughed.

I thought about telling everyone about the coyote and James Ernest, but I decided it wasn't the right time. It was hard keeping it a secret. I wondered if Susie had thought about talking about it. There always seemed to be something new I learned about James Ernest, something different to admire about him. He was only a few months older than I was, but he seemed so much older and more mature. He was ahead of me in school by two years, and he didn't appear out of place with the kids in his class.

"I can't believe you brought that stupid bird into the church, Timmy," Sadie said.

"I didn't want to, but I didn't want it disturbing the service," I reasoned.

"Oh yeah, it didn't disturb the service at all. Plus, what kind of person has a pet black crow? Sometimes you are so weird," Sadie laughed as though she was all-knowing.

"It's a lot better than having a skunk as a pet, Sadie," Susie angrily said, referring to Sadie's only real friend, Bernice.

Sadie quickly stood and started toward Susie, but Randy leapt to his feet and blocked her path. "Let's remember where we are. How about you go into the house?" Randy suggested to Sadie.

Sadie took his suggestion, and soon we were laughing and joking with each other again, Purty being at the butt end of many of the jokes and teasing. His plate was almost empty by then, and he told us he was undecided as to what dessert to get. We suggested he try them all. He liked that idea.

THE IGLOO

Snow blanketed everything outside. It was snowing when I went to bed and was still snowing when I awoke. Coty was lying by my bed. His doghouse was lost in the snow. I noticed that the tree's limbs outside my window were heavy with wet snow. There was at least a foot of snow on the ground with what was left from the earlier snows and the snow during the night. The snow was fresh and new, white and pretty. I was anxious to get out in it. I had plans to make the fort bigger. I wanted to make an igloo and then build a fire inside it.

Bo had disappeared the day before, and I wondered where he had gone. It was a great mystery as to why the crow had befriended me, and I liked having him follow me around, except at school and church. I felt more like James Ernest, especially after I learned of his friendship with the coyote and other wild animals. I hoped Bo would return.

I dressed and walked into the store where Mom was adding coal to the stove. The store was warm and cozy. The snow insulated the room, not letting the warmth escape.

"Did you see all the snow?" Mom asked.

"What snow?" I teased back.

"I wonder if we'll have any customers today," Mom said.

"Not many, I reckon," I replied.

"I think you're right. Where did James end up staying last night?" Mom asked.

"I'm not sure. I bet he went up to Uncle Morton's place."

"You think he's doing okay?"

"Yeah. I think so."

"I hope so. He's been through a lot in a short time," Mom said as she walked toward the kitchen. I went into the living room and looked at our Christmas tree. James Ernest and I had gone into the woods and cut the tree the week before. It was a great-looking tree. It had large glass ornaments hanging from the limbs and large colored lights. We had hung silver tinsel from each of the limbs. I even went into the woods and found large pine cones, and we placed them on the limbs to give it more of a woodsy look. As if a tree with silver tinsel could possibly have a woodsy look.

I was actually most interested in the packages beneath the tree. I could tell instantly if there was a new box under the tree. There wasn't, so I moseyed into the kitchen to see if Mom was fixing anything for breakfast. She wasn't. I got a bowl and poured cereal into it with milk and plenty of sugar. I ate my breakfast.

There were no chores to do that morning, so I got dressed and went outside to begin enlarging the fort. It wasn't long before James Ernest appeared next to me. I discovered him after he dumped a bucket full of snow on my head. He laughed as I shook the snow off and dug down the back of my shirt, trying to remove the cold snow.

"Very nice of you, jerk face," I said.

"What're you doing?" he asked.

"Making the fort bigger," I answered.

"Where's Bo?"

"I haven't seen him this morning. Maybe he got tired of me and flew away to join other crows."

"I doubt it. He'll be back," James Ernest assured me.

"Want to help me build a large igloo?" I asked him.

"Sure. That sounds like fun. Where at?"

"I thought maybe at the bottom of the dam. We can slide the snow down the hill to where the igloo will be and save some time and effort."

"Sounds like a good idea. Have you thought about how to build it?" James Ernest asked.

"Well, I was going to make a big, round mound of snow about five or six feet high and pack it real tight and then tunnel into it and then scoop out the inside. We can punch a small hole in the top and build a fire inside to stay warm. What do you think?"

"I think it's a great idea. We could have a Wolf Pack meeting inside it."

"It's not going to be that big," I said as I laughed.

"We could make it that big," James Ernest said.

"You really think so?"

"We have plenty of snow, and what else is there to do?"

"Let's do it. We'll have to make the walls and ceiling thick so it doesn't cave in," I said.

"I can see the headlines now, 'Wolf Pack Dies in Snow Igloo Cave-in.'"

"Bodies Left Inside Till Spring Thaw," I added. We laughed as we walked to the spot where we would build the igloo.

We spent the next few hours stacking snow. We got the snow shovel from the front porch and removed snow from the dam's hill. We would lie on the mound, slap it with our hands, and hit it with the back side of the shovel to pack it down. Coty watched us from the back porch. He looked bewildered as to what we were doing. He would trudge through the snow to look at it and then go back to his spot on the porch. On one trip he decided to decorate the side by adding a little yellow to it. It may have been his way of telling us what he thought of our efforts.

Once it got to around four feet high, we took a break and went inside for some hot chocolate.

"What are you two building out there?" Mom asked.

"An igloo," James Ernest answered.

"Looks like a pile of snow," Mom said.

"That's what it is right now, but it's going to be the best igloo ever built in Kentucky," I promised. We explained to her how we were building it, as the hot chocolate heated on the stove.

"It sounds almost like the way Ulysses Perry built his concrete dome garage," Mom said.

Mr. Ulysses Perry was a man who lived at the end of a lane not far from Papaw's farm. He was an ingenious man who had invented many unusual things. One of the things he had built was a round dome concrete garage. No one could figure out how he did it. It was believed that he had mounded dirt in much the same way we were doing snow and then poured concrete over it and then removed the dirt from the inside.

He had also invented a car that went forward in both directions so he could drive down the lane to get his mail and then drive back without having to turn it around and without having to back up. The car also was able to be driven under water. He was also a big believer in UFOs and followed their course in the sky each night when the heavens were clear.

At that time I did not know Mr. Ulysses Perry very well. I had met him when he came into the store, and I had heard about how brilliant a man he was. It was neat, knowing that someone like him lived in the community.

James Ernest and I had our hot chocolate and a snack and went back out to continue stacking snow. We had to get a step ladder from the shed. We would throw snow on top and then take turns climbing the ladder and jumping off it onto the mound of snow to pack in down. Mom walked out onto the back porch to watch us, and she stood there shaking her head. She looked down at Coty, and I saw her say something to him. Whatever it was, Coty barked in agreement.

The mound continued getting higher and wider. We patted down the sides with our glove-covered hands. By mid-afternoon we had a pile of snow that was as hard as an icy snowball seven feet high with an eight foot diameter. We then got two garden shovels from the shed and began digging the opening for the igloo. We made the opening away from the house so folks couldn't see in from the porch. The opening faced the dam, which also kept the wind from blowing in.

We made the opening just big enough to where we could fit into. Then I had a thought. "If we're going to have a Wolf Pack meeting here we need to make the opening a little larger so Purty can fit in."

"You're right," James Ernest said and chuckled.

He began making the opening bigger. We then were able to begin digging out the inside of the igloo. Once we got so far in, we began filling a bucket and then carrying it out and dumping it. We took turns doing each job, either filling the bucket or carrying it out. As the inside got bigger, we got more excited. It was really beginning to take shape, and we could tell that it was going to be fantastic. We even had to remove some clothing because we were beginning to sweat inside the igloo, which was something I didn't expect. The day's hours flew by, and at supper time we were nearing completion. We still needed to remove some more snow and put a hole in the top for the chimney. We figured we had around two hours more of work to do. As we stepped onto the back porch and started removing our coats and gloves, the snow began to fall again.

I looked out toward the igloo in the fading daylight and felt good with the work James Ernest and I had done. We were hungry and looking forward to the fried chicken we smelled drifting through the back door.

After we ate we settled in front of the TV. We watched Rawhide, The Flintstones, and then 77 Sunset Strip. Before the time the last show was over I was asleep on the floor, and James Ernest was dozing on the couch. Coty was asleep next to me.

I had not seen Bo all day. I wondered where he was as I slipped into bed. James Ernest stayed on the sofa.

8 LET IT BURN

I awoke to a frantic tapping on my window pane. I looked toward the window, and Bo was racing back and forth on the window ledge, stopping every now and then to rap madly on the glass. When I slipped out from under the cozy covers his head began bobbing up and down. His loud caw probably woke everyone in the house. Coty lifted his head and then let it drop back to the floor when he saw Bo through the frosty window pane.

As I walked to the window I saw light flashing through the top part of my ice-covered window. I tried to open the window, but it was frozen shut. I looked for a clear spot and saw what looked like fire on top of the hill. It then dawned on me through my sleepy head that there was a fire on the hill. The trailer could be on fire. James Ernest's trailer could be on fire. I quickly slipped my britches and boots on. I pulled a shirt over my head and began yelling, "Fire! Fire!"

Coty bounced up and followed me into the living room. James Ernest was up and slipping his feet into his boots. Mom was hurrying into the room. She asked, "What?"

"I think the trailer may be on fire!" I yelled out.

James Ernest looked up with a panicked look on his face. I ran through the store and out the front door. James Ernest was close behind. We raced up the lane toward the trailer.

We usually went up the hillside, but the snow prevented us from doing that. We could see flames shooting out the front kitchen window as we got closer. I began throwing snowballs toward the flames, not knowing what else to do. Mom was inside calling the fire department. The trailer would be charred by the time they were able to get men to the station and make their way from West Liberty.

While I was trying to put out the fire by throwing snowballs at it, James Ernest opened the door and rushed into the trailer.

"What are you doing? Get out of there!" I yelled over the noise of the fire.

Coty was standing at the door, barking at James Ernest. Even he knew James Ernest shouldn't have gone inside the trailer. My snowballs were doing nothing to put out the fire, so I ran to the door and yelled, "You got to get out of there!" I shouted. "C'mon, James Ernest, I don't want to have to come in there after you!"

I really didn't want to go into a burning trailer, but I didn't want my best friend to die inside the stupid trailer. I yelled at the top of my voice, "Don't make me come in there after you!" I sounded like my mom when she was mad at me.

I jumped up to the top step and looked inside the door. Smoke had filled the inside, making it hard to see anything except the floor. The fire was beginning to spread from the kitchen back through the trailer to the living room. I didn't see James Ernest. I figured he went into the back of the trailer where the bedroom was. I was hoping he hadn't been overcome with the smoke.

I dove into the trailer. I began crawling toward the bed-room. I coughed as I made my way. I tried holding my breath. I glanced back to see the flames engulfing the living room. I heard voices outside, yelling into the trailer. I couldn't under-stand what they were saying. The noise of the fire was deafen-ing. I made it to the bedroom, and James Ernest was nowhere in sight. I crawled into the small bathroom. He wasn't there, either. Where was he?

I knew I needed to get out quickly. The fire was now com-ing into the bedroom. I looked for a way out. The trailer only had one door, and it now wasn't an option. I crawled back into the bedroom and saw light coming from the wall above the bed. There was only one thing I could do. I grabbed the blanket from the top of the bed and pulled it over me. I held my breath, stood, wrapped the blanket around my head and body, and backed up to the opposite wall. I then ran the two steps and jumped onto the bed, bounced, and threw myself toward the window.

I was expecting to hear and feel smashing glass. I expected to be cut and impaled with shards of glass. Instead, I felt nothing as I bounced through the window until I landed on the soft snow outside the trailer below the window. Suddenly I felt hands grab me and begin pulling and dragging me away from the trailer. I took the blanket down from my head and saw James Ernest, Mom, and Mr. Henry Washington stand-ing over me.

I looked at the trailer to see it totally engulfed in flames.

"That was a dramatic exit," James Ernest said as a smile spread across his face.

I stood up and threw my arms around James Ernest. I was so glad to see my friend alive and standing there. I almost felt like kissing him. But that wasn't happening. I was surprised when I realized I was standing there hugging him with his arms pinned to his side. I quickly released him and turned to watch the fire.

We stood there watching the flames jump high into the air. It was as if James Ernest's entire past was drifting away with the wind. His parents were gone. His home, even though he seldom stayed there, was fading away with each moment. I turned and looked at him as he stared at the walls that were caving in. I then noticed a wooden picture frame clutched in his hands.

I asked him, "Did you get that out of the trailer?"

"Yeah. It was the only thing I needed to save. I also snatched my money I had saved up while I was in there. I figured I might need it."

He held up the frame so I could see what was so important that he risked his life. In the picture James Ernest was around three, and he was standing hand in hand with his mom and dad at his sides. A smile was on each of their faces—a happy time in his childhood. It was the same picture he had taken to the memorial service. No way did he know how different things would be ten years later.

"That's a really good picture," I said. Who was I to question why he would risk burning up to save a picture of his family—a family that abandoned him? I may have done the same thing. He may have been questioning why I would risk burning up to save him from the fire. It was simple; he was my best friend, and he was worth saving. He was important to me. He was the closest I would ever come to having a brother.

I felt something rubbing my pant leg. Coty stood at my feet, looking up into my face and wagging his tail. Then Bo flew down from a high tree and landed on my left shoulder. Papaw, Clayton, Robert, and Homer climbed the hill. We all stood there and stared as the red and yellow flames finished the trailer. The women stood and watched from the front porch.

I heard a siren and looked down the road to see a fire truck coming toward us. They parked at the bottom of the lane and hurried up the drive and stood with us watching the fire burn away.

One of the firemen asked James Ernest, "You want us to try and save what we can?"

"Let it burn," James Ernest answered. "It's okay. There's nothing left to save."

The fire didn't last long. Snow then began to fall again. Within a couple of hours the embers were out, and there wasn't a trace of the home to be seen. It was covered with snow. The firemen had said that the fire was suspicious. They thought someone may have started the fire. James Ernest told them that he couldn't think of anyone who would want to harm him or that held any grudges. But I knew he could.

I thought of Billy Taulbee. He still hadn't been found after the kidnapping. No one knew where he was or if he was even still alive. I also thought of the boys from Blaze. They no longer could make money delivering the whiskey that the moonshiners had made. The two moonshiners were both in jail. I was sure the boys of Blaze weren't so happy about it. I figured they might want to get even for losing their source of income. But I didn't say anything.

James Ernest probably had a reason for not mentioning them, and I wasn't going to butt in.

That afternoon Mom and my grandparents began asking James Ernest what he needed as far as clothes and supplies since he had lost most everything in the fire. He told them he had lost all of his clothes in the fire except for what he had on.

"I also need to get school supplies before school starts back up," he told them.

"I'll take you to Morehead this afternoon so you can get some new clothes. We can stop at the college book store to get whatever supplies you need," Papaw told him.

"That would be great. Thank you," James Ernest said.

I thought about going with them but decided to stay and help at the store. I also wanted to work on the igloo if I got a chance.

That afternoon while I was watching the store, a man walked through the door and asked if he could start a line of credit. I went into the kitchen and got Mom. He told her, "My name is Bucky."

She asked, "What's your last name?"

"Key," he answered as he chewed on something in his mouth. "My first name is Buck. Buck Key. I go through the same thing every time I introduce myself. We just moved in down below the tunnel. I got a job at the quarry, but won't get paid for a week or so."

"No problem, Mr. Key. Pick out whatever you need. Got any kids?" Mom asked.

He looked around at the floor of the store and then walked to the door, opened it, and spat tobacco juice onto the porch planks. The man wore a flannel shirt that was all ripped up. He had on bibbed overalls over the worn-out shirt. His hair was long and stringy, and he had a beard that came down almost where his belt buckle would have been if he had had one around his waist. He didn't wear a coat even though it was winter, and there was almost a foot and a half of snow on the ground.

"A family?" Mom questioned him again.

"A woman, Winona, and eight kids."

That perked my interest even though everything about him sparked my interest.

"Where did you live before you moved to Morgan County?" Mom continued her questioning.

"We lived in a holler south of Pikeville," Buck Key said.

"I don't know much about that area," Mom told him. He opened the door again and spit the juice from his cheek again.

"Not much there 'cept coons and hard times," he said as he closed the door.

"You'll find this to be a friendly community. I welcome you to the area. This is my son, Timmy. Perhaps some of your kids will be going to school with him," Mom said.

He nodded his head toward me.

"We have a few that are still young enough to be going to a school house. I reckon they should learn to read and write and cipher some," he said as he began gathering cans of Spam off the shelves. "Some of the young'ns has done quit schooling. I do have a son 'bout your age that still goes to class some days." He had to talk around the wad of tobacco in his mouth.

I was beginning to sense that Mr. Key didn't value an education as much as Mom did. I wondered what would happen to me if I up and decided which days to go to school and which days not to go to school, or maybe just up and quit school. I didn't even know that was an option. My mom would wear me out with a switch if I skipped a day of school or even thought about it. And somehow she would know if I thought about it.

I also knew he probably didn't value a clean porch at his house.

As Mr. Key was leaving Mom said, "Give your wife my greetings, and I wish your family a Merry Christmas."

"Is it almost Christmas?" he asked as he looked back at Mom.

"Two days," Mom answered.

"I guess I ought to get a few candy canes and lollipops for the kids, then," he said. Mom placed the candy inside the box with his other items.

Who doesn't know when Christmas is? I stood there amazed and stunned as he walked out the door with his large box of food. He spat again as he walked through the door, not waiting till he was off the porch.

After he drove away in an old pickup Mom said, "Timmy, go out there and clean up the porch. How disgusting!"

I was already headed to the kitchen to get a rag, knowing Mom was probably grossed out by the tobacco juice being spit upon the porch by Mr. Buck Key. He wasn't the first man to spit tobacco on the porch. Many men would try to spit off the porch from the rocking chairs, but it wouldn't make it.

There were dark stains on the end of the planks from years of coming up short.

As I cleaned up the tobacco spit on the porch I thought about my mom. I wondered what kind of person I would be if she wasn't my mother. Most of my values and kindness I learned from Mom. I learned to treat people well because Mom loved people and treated people as she wanted to be treated. I knew I would never drink alcohol or smoke because Mom didn't and because she reminded me how it had killed my dad. I've only cussed at two people in my life, and that was when I was eight years old.

FALL OF 1957

One autumn day I was playing football in the front yard with two boys from the neighborhood. I can't even remember what happened; they may have cheated, or piled on, or some other bad thing. But I got so mad at them that I began calling them every cuss word I had ever heard come out of between my dad's lips. Some of the words that I used I didn't even know I knew. I had no idea what most of the bad words even meant.

The two boys stood there looking at me in absolute disbelief. I don't think they had ever heard an eight-year-old use those types of words, and they probably didn't know what the words meant, either—only that they were being called bad things. I had tears flowing down my cheeks as I swore the daylight out of those boys. I was sorry for saying the words even as they flowed from my lips. I was especially sorry when I heard Mom say, "Timothy Allen, you get your hide inside this house!"

Mom had been standing at the screen door, watching us play, and had heard the entire string of cuss words that spewed from my head. She wore out a switch on me. She broke a paddle in half spanking my butt. She made an old belt shine again as she whipped the words from my vocabulary and some sense into me.

I knew I deserved it. I felt so bad using the words. I have never cussed another person in my life. I never use bad words at all. I learned the lesson mom taught me that day. But what if mom hadn't been there to hear me? What if I had gotten away with cussing at the two boys? Would I now be a big curser? My mom was there for me and taught me right from wrong.

Aunt Ruth, Mom (Betty), Aunt Helen, Kathleen (Ruby & Homer's daughter), Great Aunt Mildred

The Twins' Version

Later that afternoon I was able to go back outside and work on the igloo. James Ernest still wasn't back from Morehead with Papaw. The snow had fallen all day and was now just flurries. Another two or three inches of snow covered the top of the igloo. Coty had a hard time walking in the deep snow so he stayed on the back porch and watched me. Bo had perched himself on the edge of the wash basin that was against the back wall. Coty would watch me while keeping an eye on Bo.

I took the bucket and a shovel and continued to dig the packed snow out of the inside in order to form the room inside the giant ball. I would crawl out and dump the snow away from the igloo. I did this time and time again until I heard James Ernest's voice call me.

I was inside the igloo when I saw his head poke inside the opening and say, "What're you doing?"

He knew what I was doing so I asked, "How was shopping?"

"Got everything I needed. We even got you a new pair of overalls. Hey, the inside is getting bigger," he said as he looked around at the snow walls. He crawled on in, and we sat facing each other cross-legged like Indians in a tepee.

I broke the silence by saying, "I'm sorry the trailer burned down."

"It's not a big loss. I wasn't staying there much, anyway. Wasn't anything valuable in it. I'm glad you got out alive. I can't believe you went in looking for me."

"That's what a guy does for his best friend. You would have done the same for me. Wouldn't you?" I asked.

James Ernest smiled and said, "I think I hear Betty calling us for supper."

"I didn't hear anything," I said to his rear end as he was crawling out of the igloo. He was laughing.

"I know you would've done the same thing," I said to no one within hearing distance—unless there was an Eskimo inside our igloo.

As we ate supper Janie broke the silence when she said, "James Ernest, I'm sorry your house burned to smithereens." We laughed.

I nibbled at the peas in front of me. I began stirring them into my mashed potatoes. Mom looked at me but didn't say anything. She knew I liked them that way.

"I saw the longest beard today," Mom said, trying to keep the conversation going. I think it had been a long day, and everyone was tired.

"Where?" James Ernest asked.

"A man named Buck…Key came into the store and opened an account. His family just moved here from the Pikeville area. His beard was all the way down to his waist.

"Are they the ones who moved into the farm house down past the tunnel?" James Ernest asked.

Years before, the tunnel was used by the railroad. A train ran between Morehead and Wrigley called the Blue Goose.

"Yes," Mom answered.

Train track for the Blue Goose:
Ran to Wrigley thru tunnel

"He said they had eight children, one being a boy around our age. We thought the man's name was Bucky when he introduced himself, but his last name is Key," I said.

"Like a key that you use to lock the door. It's a funny last name," Janie added.

It was already dark by the time we were done eating. Mamaw and Papaw came to visit, and then Susie's parents and the twins came walking into the store. Janie and the twins headed for the kitchen table to play games. But not before asking me, "How did you start the fire?"

"I didn't start the fire," I defended.

"You were the first one to see it," Delma said as though that meant something.

"No, I wasn't. Bo saw it first and woke me up. I was in bed when it started," I told them.

"So the devil bird started the fire," Thelma stated.

"How would a bird start a fire?" I scoffed.

"You think the dumb bird is so smart. Maybe he was starting a fire to keep warm," Delma said.

"Maybe he was using the same matches he uses to light his cigarettes," Thelma added.

How do you argue with two bratty know-it-alls? I turned and walked into the store where Papaw and Clayton were leaning against the counter and talking. James Ernest followed me while snickering. Susie and Brenda came through the front door.

"Where you been?" I asked.

"We walked up to see if anything was left of the trailer," Susie answered.

"See anything?" James Ernest asked.

"Nothing but snow," Brenda said.

"From what I hear, you two were lucky to get out with your lives," Clayton said.

Susie's head snapped around and looked at me.

"You should never go into a burning trailer. They can burn in a moment," Clayton continued.

"You guys went into the trailer while it was on fire?" Susie questioned.

"James Ernest went inside to save some things, and when I didn't see him come out I went in looking for him," I explained.

I could see from the look on her face that Susie wasn't very happy with that decision. I was sure she thought I was the stupidest boy on earth. Maybe I was.

"You're right. The trailer was gone before I knew it. Went up in flames like kindling," James Ernest said. Susie shook her head.

"Want to see the igloo?" I asked Susie, trying to change the subject.

"An igloo?" Susie said as she followed me into the living room.

"Be right back," I said as I went into my bedroom to get my flashlight.

I led her out the back door and off the porch toward the giant snow house. I turned the flashlight on and shined it on the igloo.

"Did you build this?" Susie asked, forgetting my stupidity in her excitement.

"I thought of it, and then James Ernest helped me make it bigger." I dropped to my knees and crawled inside. Susie followed me. Soon we were sitting on the floor of the igloo. The flashlight lit up the inside. Susie looked so cute sitting across from me. Her green eyes became larger as they looked around the room of snow. "It's not finished yet. We still need to make the inside bigger and put a hole in the roof."

"Why would you put a hole in it?" Susie asked.

"So the smoke will rise when we build a fire."

"You're going to build a fire inside the igloo? Won't the thing melt?" she questioned our idea. I began questioning the plan myself. It would make sense that the heat from the fire would melt the igloo.

"I'm not sure," I said.

"I guess you'll find out," Susie told me.

A picture entered my mind of me sitting in a puddle of water and the twins pointing their fat, little fingers at me and laughing before saying together, "Even a moronic doofus knows that fire melts snow. Ha, ha, ha!"

Maybe I would talk to James Ernest about the idea again.

Susie and I crawled out of the igloo and walked up to the dam of the lake. The snow had stopped, and the full moon was peeking through the clouds, illuminating the snow on the ground. Snow clung to the limbs that overhung the lake as if trying not to fall into the half-ice-covered water. Limbs of the pines were weighted downward, pointing to the fish that lumbered beneath the surface. The path that I had walked so many times to gather scattered trash was hard to see in the deep snow from where we stood.

I could see a hump on the dam where the rowboat rested upside down for the winter. The lake rules sign was unreadable because the snow clung to the painted letters. The lake was as pretty in the silver moonlight of white winter as it was on a starlit summer night with bullfrogs croaking and nightingales calling.

Susie placed her hand inside my arm and squeezed. "It's beautiful," she said.

I looked at her and nodded agreement before saying, "I'm ready for some hot chocolate."

"That sounds good," she agreed.

SUNDAY, DECEMBER 24

Mom closed the store because she was going to Christmas services with me and Mamaw and Papaw. James Ernest was up and ready when I got out of bed. Bo was nowhere I could see and after Coty went out to relieve himself, he cozied himself on top of my bed and fell asleep.

The church parking lot was almost full when we arrived ten minutes early. Susie and Raven had saved seats between them for James Ernest and me. The church was decorated with holly and greenery. Pastor White gave everyone a Christmas greeting and prayed. Everything was perfect until he announced that Delma and Thelma Perry were going to read the Christmas story and sing for everyone's enjoyment. Whose enjoyment? I thought.

They walked proudly to the stage and turned and smiled big, toothy smiles. I wanted to puke. I knew it wasn't right, but I wanted them to trip and fall or forget their stupid lines, or say that Jesus was born in a manger to save poor, lost turds.

They began telling the Christmas story. Delma began, as always, "Mary and Joseph were traveling to Bethlehem to pay their taxes. Mary rode on a donkey because she was going to have a baby."

"Actually, we think it was a large, beautiful, white horse with a golden mane," Thelma interrupted, causing the crowd to burst into laughter.

"God wouldn't have His son ride on a donkey," Delma added before continuing the story. "When they arrived in Bethlehem they went to the inn to get a nice, clean room—like mine."

Monie's laughter was followed by the church body's laughter.

"Some man, as stupid as Timmy, turned them away, telling them he didn't have any rooms left for them," Delma continued.

"He didn't realize he was turning away the Son of God. If he had known, he should have given them his room," said Thelma, adding her commentary.

"Dejectedly, Joseph turned the donkey around and headed to a stable he had passed on the way to the inn. The owner of the stable said they could stay in a manger, which wasn't even as big as a stable or horse stall. Can you imagine?" Delma told us.

"This was where baby Jesus was born. But he didn't complain or cry or anything because he was God even though He was treated awful," Thelma added.

"A big, bright star appeared above the manger, telling everyone where baby Jesus was born, and people began arriving to see him and bring him gifts," Delma told us.

"That's why we get gifts today—to celebrate Jesus's birthday like they did then," Thelma said before adding, "Shepherds came to see the baby Jesus and brought their animals. There were cows and sheep and horses and the donkey and probably other animals. But there definitely wasn't a black crow there because crows are evil, and Jesus is good."

At this point in the story they both looked at me with their wicked, little eyes.

Delma continued, "Three very smart men came to the manger and brought expensive gifts because they considered

Jesus the King. One brought Jesus a lot of gold, another gave Jesus incense, and the other wise man gave Baby Jesus myrrh. We're not sure what incense and myrrh are, but we're sure they were something babies needed because they were very smart men."

"Jesus became a very nice child, very much like us, and grew up to help people," Thelma added.

"That's the Christmas story about Jesus," Delma said.

Then in unison the twins announced, "Now we're going to sing a song for your pleasure."

They then began singing "Away in a Manger." "Away in a manger, no crib for His bed, the little Lord Jesus lay down his sweet head." Their voices squeaked off-key, broke at every high note, and at times didn't even sing the same words. But they plodded along through the entire song—all three verses. I actually never thought kids could sing so dreadfully. Usually when kids sang it was cute even if they were bad. This wasn't cute at all. I actually saw a couple of older men covering their ears. Bo could have sung better.

I wondered what Pastor White was thinking when he decided to ask the twins to do this. Apparently pastors have moments of insanity. Much like the time Pastor Black had me recite John 3:16-17. By the look on his face, he was thinking the same thing.

When the song was finally over the twins bowed and returned to their seats with big smiles on their faces as if they had given an award-winning performance. James Ernest then stood and joined Pastor White to sing a medley of three Christmas songs: "We Three Kings," "What Child is This," and "Joy to the World." They were great!

Pastor White then delivered a message about the birth of Jesus and how Jesus was born in a manger just to die for us thirty-three years later. Pastor White then gave an invitation, and the service was over.

That afternoon James Ernest and I finished the igloo. It looked great, and we thought there was plenty of room inside to hold a meeting of the Wolf Pack. We decided to call Randy after Christmas and call for a meeting. We wanted to have a winter adventure and needed ideas. There was no time better than the week between Christmas and New Year's Day to have the adventure. School would start again on January 2.

Delma & Thelma - Looks like they're scheming something up. , 1959

10 CHRISTMAS AND GUNS

Rap! Tap! Rap, Rap, Rap! Bo pecked on my frosty window pane. My first thought was, What's on fire this time?

I heard the rooster's crow from the Tuttle's farm. Bo was beating the roosters in waking me up. Boy, is it fun having a pet crow. Then I remembered that it was Christmas morning. I threw the blankets off and slipped into my slippers and hurried to open my door. The Christmas tree stood just outside my door. I looked to see what Santa had brought during the night. We didn't have a fireplace or chimney. Mom told Janie that Santa would probably come down the black coal stove pipe. He'd have to be the skinniest Santa ever. But I figured Santa was magical and could do anything he needed to do to get the presents to all the good boys and girls.

I figured the twins wouldn't be getting any presents from Santa. But there were presents under our tree that weren't there the night before. I had memorized every present under the tree and who they were for. I ran to the couch and jumped on James Ernest who was still asleep on it.

"Ugh!" came from his body.

I rolled off James Ernest and hurried to Mom's bedroom door and began knocking on it and yelling, "Santa came!"

I heard Janie scream and then heard Mom say, "We'll be right out. Call your Mamaw and Papaw and tell them we're up and waiting for them."

I ran back to the couch and saw that James Ernest hadn't moved since I had rolled off him. So I jumped on him again. "Time to get up," I said.

"How old are you?" he mumbled from under the blue-and-white-checkered blanket.

"I'm twelve, and I'll still get excited on Christmas morning when I'm sixty-one," I said.

"I hope I'm not still sleeping on your couch then," he said and laughed. "Go call Martin and Corie."

I rolled off of him again and hurried to the telephone and called their number. It rang and rang. I was about to hang up when I heard Papaw say, "I suppose Santa must have stopped at the store."

"Yep, he sure did. You coming or should I open your gifts?" I asked.

"You open my gifts, and it will be the last thing you ever do," he teased. At least I thought he was teasing.

What seemed like two hours—but was actually only fifteen minutes—passed when finally the store door opened and Mamaw and Papaw walked in.

Mamaw & Papaw with Timmy and Janie

"Merry Christmas!" I yelled out.

Janie ran into the store and jumped into Mamaw's arms.

"I'm ready for some breakfast," Papaw said as he walked into the room.

"Not until after we open gifts," I said.

"Aw, who cares about gifts? Man does not survive on gifts alone. It is food we need," Papaw said. I knew he was trying to get a jolt from me. I figured he was pretty excited to open gifts, himself.

I began passing out the colorful boxes of green and red. I didn't even look at the tags because I had memorized which package went to which person. Janie started to tear open a gift when Mom said, "Whoa! Wait a minute, Janie. Those presents are Timmy's, and his are yours."

"What?" I asked.

"I tricked you. I knew you would shake and squeeze each box until you knew what each one was, so I put your tags on her presents," she explained. My jaw must have hit the middle of my chest as I showed my surprise at Mom's trickery.

Everyone laughed at me. James Ernest was rolling on the floor.

"He had told me what was in each of his boxes," he said as he found time for words between the laughs.

Janie and I quickly swapped boxes. Janie opened her first box, which was filled with a large Fred Flintstone doll. It had a hard plastic rubbery head and a cloth body. I thought it was pretty cool. Everyone began opening their gifts at the same time. My best gift from mom was a really neat hatchet. I knew that Papaw had probably picked it out for her.

We all got handmade baskets from James Ernest. Mine was a small basket with a top on it that I could set on my dresser and put stuff in it. Janie got one almost like it. Mom and Mamaw got large trash baskets. They loved them. When we were almost done, Papaw went into the store and carried in two long packages. I figured baseball bats were in them. He handed one to me and the other to James Ernest.

We looked at each other and then tore into the wrapping. We threw the paper into the air, and Coty jumped, trying to catch it. He thought we were playing. I couldn't believe what was inside. A box with a brand new.22 Winchester pump action rifle had been uncovered. James Ernest had the same thing. I didn't know what to say. Never had I gotten anything like it. I was almost in shock. I figured Mom was, also. But when I looked at her she had a big smile on her face. She had gone crazy. Never would my mom want me to have a real rifle that I could shoot things.

"What do you think?" Papaw asked us.

"This is too much," James Ernest said. "Thank you."

I stammered with my words before saying, "Is this really mine?"

"Yes, but you have to let me show you how to shoot it and teach you to be safe with it," Papaw said.

"Sure."

I had been hunting before with Papaw's shotguns but never had I held a new .22 rifle in my hands before. I felt older but unsure if I should be ready for it. Were they sure I was ready for this? But I had a rifle and a hatchet. I was ready to conquer the world.

Everyone seemed to like what I had gotten them for Christmas. I also got a pair of hiking boots that I could wear in the winter. It had been a good morning. I noticed Coty standing at the back door. In my excitement I had forgotten to let him out to pee. I had forgotten to do the same. So Coty and I slipped out the back door and did what we had to do. It was cold, and we both were quick getting back into the warm house.

Mom and Mamaw were in the kitchen, beginning to make breakfast. I was glad Mamaw was helping. It would be a good Christmas breakfast. Coty stopped in the kitchen and sat, looking up at Mom as she fried the sausage. She finally saw him sitting there, waiting patiently for his portion.

"Go. You're not allowed in here." Mom motioned him out. Coty slithered away, knowing he had done something he wasn't supposed to do.

We had eggs and bacon, biscuits and gravy, blackberry jelly and honey, and sausage—a Christmas morning feast. Mom laid a sausage and a couple strips of bacon on a paper towel on the floor for Coty. He licked his lips for the next half hour.

It had become a tradition that all of our friends would gather at Homer and Ruby's barn for a Christmas dinner around four o'clock. The barn was always decorated with greenery and holly and a big Christmas tree. It was festive. I was looking forward to seeing Susie and giving her the gift I had bought her. I asked Mamaw if she needed for me and James Ernest to go out and kill some meat for the dinner. She assured me they had already killed the meat for the meal. I wanted to shoot my new rifle so badly I almost hoped someone would try to rob the store. Not really, but I truly wanted to shoot that gun.

That afternoon Papaw placed red plastic cups in the snow near the bottom of the dam. He taught James Ernest and me how to carefully use the rifle. We were told to always have the safety on until we were ready to shoot and to never point the gun at another person unless we meant to shoot them. Finally we got to shoot at the targets. I looked down the barrel of the rifle and lined up the sights and took aim at the red cup on the left and pulled the trigger. The rifle jerked back hard against my shoulder and nearly knocked me down.

"Did I hit it?" I asked.

Papaw laughed and answered, "No. If you don't close your eyes you'll be able to see where it hits. Hold the rifle tighter to your shoulder. It won't kick as hard. Slowly pull the trigger. If you jerk the trigger, you'll jerk the rifle away from the target."

I followed Papaw's directions on the second shot at the cup, and I saw the cup crumble as the bullet passed through.

"I hit it! I hit it!" I yelled out.

"Caw! Caw!" I heard Bo scream from the top perch of a bare oak tree.

James Ernest then took aim and followed Papaw's directions perfectly and put his first shot into the second cup. He looked like he had been shooting a rifle all his life. We spent an hour shooting cups and firing bullets into the dam. Our fingers began to feel numb in the cold, so we headed to the house for hot chocolate.

As we waited for the hot chocolate, Papaw taught us how to clean the rifles. What great gifts for twelve-year-old boys! The added gift was that I got to spend time with Papaw.

We arrived at the barn for Christmas dinner at a little past four. James Ernest eagerly went to find Raven and give her a Christmas gift he had bought her. Bo had followed us to the party. I saw him perched on top of the barn as I walked from the car. I searched for Susie. She was helping arrange the covered dishes on a table.

"Merry Christmas, Susie," I said as I neared her. James Ernest and I both wore our new bibbed overalls. I wore a red, plaid shirt under it.

She turned when she heard my voice. She grabbed my hand and led me to an open stall. She stopped at the opening and looked up where some greenery was hanging. I looked at it and then looked at her, wondering why we had stopped here.

"It's mistletoe, you big dummy," she said.

I knew we were supposed to kiss under mistletoe, but there were people around. She was waiting for me to kiss her.

She finally put her hands on my shoulders and stood on her tiptoes and kissed me on the lips.

"It looks like Timmy got Susie under the mistletoe," Miss Rebecca said loud enough for all the other women to hear. They all looked our way. Susie smiled and waved. I stood there with a red face—not from the cold weather.

I pulled a small box from my bibbed overall pocket and handed it to Susie.

"Can I open it now?" she asked.

"Sure. That's why I gave it to you." I said.

We sat on a bale of hay, and she carefully unwrapped the package without tearing the paper. She took the lid off the small box and removed the cotton that lay on top. She lifted the charm bracelet to look at it. A horse charm and a heart charm hung from the silver bracelet.

"I love it," she said as she threw her arms around me and hugged me. I awkwardly hung onto the twine that held the hay together.

"Wait here," she said as she ran to the Christmas tree where packages were stacked.

She hurried back and handed me a small box wrapped in red paper with a large, white bow on top of it that was three times bigger than the box. She took her spot on the hay bale and told me to open it. I tried to unwrap it as she did, without messing up the paper, but my clumsy fingers ripped it, and I ended up just tearing it to pieces. I placed the bow on top of Susie's head. I opened the box and found a leather necklace with a round locket attached to it. I pushed the button on the side of the locket, and the front sprung open. Inside was the prettiest picture of Susie I had ever seen. I put the necklace over my head and down onto my neck. I told her what a great gift it was. She smiled.

The evening was a blast. Families exchanged gifts, and men played instruments as everyone sang Christmas carols. No one asked the twins to sing "Away in a Manger" again. Dinner was truly a Christmas feast. We all were blessed. I looked over at James Ernest. At times I would see sadness in his eyes. I knew he was thinking of the year before when he had brought his mom to the gathering and introduced her to everyone. I wished for him we could go back in time and relive that evening.

I rose from my seat and went over and sat next to him. "I know you're thinking of your mom. I'm so sorry you lost your mom and dad."

He put his arm around my shoulders and forced a smile. "It's okay. I have a new family and Mom's in a good place. Thanks for thinking of me, buddy."

Toward the end of the evening the Tuttles arrived. They had been to Morehead visiting relatives during the evening. Purty loaded up a plate of desserts as soon as he entered the barn.

We kids ended the celebration by going outside and having a gigantic snowball fight.

TRAPPED INSIDE

I ignored the rapping at my window and the crow of the roosters and fell back to sleep. I was really tired from the party and everything that happened over the past few days. Coty was curled up at the foot of the bed and didn't seem too anxious to go outside. I covered my head to keep the cold off my face and tried to go back to sleep. Apparently it flustered Bo because he began making the biggest ruckus, pecking, and flapping his wings and cawing at the top of his lungs.

Coty got up and went to the window and began barking and howling at Bo. Bo was then mad because Coty was inside with me, or at least I figured that was why he was so mad. I folded the pillow around my head and covered my ears as tightly as possible. I could barely hear the noise, but it was hard to go back to sleep in that position. I felt like having dog with a side of crow for breakfast.

I took Coty to the back door and let him out. I soon saw Bo dive bombing him. Coty jumped as high as he could as he tried to snatch the bird out of the sky. I knew he wanted crow for breakfast also. I looked at the couch and saw that James Ernest wasn't there. I went back to bed.

I awoke to the sound of folks in the store. I looked at the clock and saw that it was almost ten. I hadn't slept that late in a long time. I got out of bed, stretched, and put on the same clothes from the night before. I opened the door and walked into the store. A couple of truck drivers had stopped for refreshments and Homer and Ruby were there. Papaw was behind the counter.

"Hey, sleepyhead," Papaw teased.

"Where are Mom and Janie?" I asked.

"They went up to the farm. They're doing some quilting," he answered.

"Do you know where James Ernest is?" I asked.

"I can't answer that. I have no idea where that boy might be. My best guess would be that he's up at the Washington's making baskets," Papaw said.

"Probably," I said.

We were going to have a Wolf Pack meeting that evening at seven. We had agreed at the Christmas party that we would have the meeting inside the igloo. I was looking forward to it. I turned and headed to the outhouse.

I spent the rest of the day helping Papaw in the store. A couple of delivery trucks arrived, and I unloaded the boxes and stocked the wooden shelves.

As it was getting dark, Mr. and Mrs. Tuttle arrived at the store to visit. Sheriff Cane had come by to spend the evening with Mom, also. Only Randy and Purty had come with them for the Wolf Pack meeting. The adults were sitting around the kitchen table, drinking coffee as we made our way outside toward the igloo. James Ernest fired up the lantern on the back porch. Coty led the way through the snow.

The inside of the igloo glowed from the light of the lantern. We had decided it might not be a good idea to build a fire. We decided that building a fire might have ended up with us sitting in a puddle of water. Purty and I spread a blanket onto the igloo's floor, and we sat in a circle facing the lantern as though it was a fire pit. Randy began the meeting.

"First thing I want to say is that this igloo is really cool," Randy said. We all echoed his words in agreement. James Ernest gave me a high five. Coty barked, stood, and circled with excitement.

"The second thing is do we have any ideas for a winter adventure? I think we decided not to build the tree house until next spring," Randy added.

Purty farted, long and loud.

"Gross."

"Jerk."

"Someone get the toilet paper."

"Someone get a corncob, and we'll plug it up."

We all began laughing so hard we were rolling on the blanket inside the igloo.

"I'm sorry," Purty finally was able to say. "It was the way I was sitting. Sitting like an Indian makes me fart."

"Chief Fart-a-lot," James Ernest cried out, and laughter filled the igloo again.

"Maybe you should sit a different way," Randy suggested.

He took the suggestion and placed his feet flat on the blanket and brought his knees straight up with his arms wrapped around his legs and his chin on his knees.

Randy began to ask again if anyone had any ideas when Purty farted again. Coty's nose went up in the air, and he took off out of the igloo in a flash. We all looked at Purty, and then the smell arrived. We all were trying to make it to the small igloo opening. We were falling over and pushing each other.

We were gagging as we crawled and fought our way to the opening and the sweet salvation of fresh night air. My eyes were tearing up.

Purty still sat in the igloo. He peeked out at us and said, "C'mon, guys. Chief Fart-a-lot's farts don't smell."

I looked at Randy and James Ernest and said, "Chief Fart-a-lot must not have a nose."

"That was by far the worse smell ever," James Ernest said.

"It's melting the igloo," I said.

"He ate three helpings of Mom's liver and onions," Randy explained.

"Coty! Coty, come here. Coty!" Purty begged Coty to come back inside with him. Coty stood next to me and looked up into my face.

"I would suggest you ignore him," I said. Coty turned and ran toward the back porch.

Coty barked at the back door and Mom opened the door. Coty hurried inside. Mom saw us standing outside the igloo and yelled, "What are you doing?"

James Ernest yelled back, "Waiting for the air to clear!"

Mom looked up toward the sky and yelled again, "What?"

"You don't want to know!" I yelled back.

Mom shook her head and went back inside.

We finally summoned up the nerve to go back inside the igloo. We warned Purty not to let it happen again. Randy told him to take it outside. We made him sit next to the opening so he could make a quick escape. I figured it was for his own good. If he farted again, he would need a fast escape from getting killed.

Purty spoke up once we all were in place. "Let's try to get across the ledge behind the waterfalls that we found on Susie's farm. You know - the one that leads to the tunnel."

One day we had gone for a hike on Susie's farm. We were going to Devil's Creek when we saw the waterfalls on their property. We had climbed up to a tunnel that then led to a ledge that went behind the falls. The ledge was dangerous and wet and slanted toward the falls. A fall off of it was certain death. But we could see that the ledge led to another tunnel on the other side of the falls, and it looked like the only way to it was by way of the ledge. We had decided it was too dangerous, and I still thought the same.

"It's too dangerous," I said.

"We could use the rope ladder from the top to climb down like we did at the other cave," Purty insisted.

Randy killed that idea, "The cold icy water would be falling onto our heads. We'd freeze to death as we climbed down."

"There's one way. Maybe," James Ernest chimed in.

"How?" I asked.

"In the coldest part of the winter the waterfall may freeze over with giant icicles. The icicles might form a wall. If it does, then it will also form a tunnel behind the waterfall. We may be able to walk right over to the opening."

"Yeah!" Purty screamed. "I knew we could do it."

"But that's a lot of 'ifs'," Randy said.

"I know it is. But it is probably the only way," James Ernest agreed.

"Instead, we could always go on a winter hike," I suggested.

"That would be fun also," James Ernest said.

No one else could come up with another idea, so we voted on the plan. We would wait for the weather to stay cold for a long spell and then try the waterfall. If that didn't happen then we would go on a hike. We all voted 'yes' and then put our hands together and did the Wolf Pack chant and began howling at the opening in the top of the igloo. I could hear Coty howl inside the house. We then together yelled, "Forever the Pack!"

"If there's nothing else then, we are adjourned," Randy announced.

Purty farted again, and his body blocked the escape route. We were trapped inside. The roof on the igloo began to drip on my head as I tried to squeeze my way out.

"Let us out of here!" I screamed.

12 KenTucky

The year 1962 arrived without much fanfare. Mom went out with Sheriff Cane on New Year's Eve to celebrate. Janie, James Ernest, and I spent the night with Mamaw and Papaw. At midnight I was fast asleep in the middle of their living room floor.

I returned to school that morning after the Christmas break. The bare trees had a crystal glistening on their limbs, and the air had a bitter-cold breeze whispering through the trees and the cracks of our one-room schoolhouse. Kids were excited about seeing friends at school again, but the cold tempered the excitement as we tried to keep warm. Mrs. Holbrook had already started a fire in the pot-bellied stove, and kids were huddled around it when she told us to take our seats.

Just as we settled into our wooden desks, the front door opened, and in walked a long-haired boy with well-worn bibbed overalls and a ripped-up red coat opened. He acted as though it was seventy degrees in Florida when he walked in. He had sandy, light-brown hair, which was long enough to touch his shoulders in the back. From his ears forward he had a mohawk. It was the strangest haircut I had ever laid eyes on.

His face was friendly with a big smile spread across his face and he kicked off his boots once he removed his tattered coat. He stood there on the cold wooden floor with bare feet.

"Who in the world are you?" Delma yelled out.

He started to answer but was intercepted by Mrs. Holbrook, "Delma, I think that's a question I should ask. Are you a new student, young man?"

"Yep. I guess I am. My family came to live here last month," he answered. He had a southern hillbilly way of talking. "I thought I might try school for a while."

Mrs. Eleanor Holbrook covered her mouth with her right hand almost as though she was blocking words from coming out. She finally took her hand down and asked, "What's your name?"

"I'm Kenny Key, or Ken Key, either one. I don't mind," he answered. "My middle name is Tuck," he added.

"Do you have any brothers or sisters?" Mrs. Holbrook asked next.

"I got three brothers and four sisters," Kenny answered.

I couldn't take my eyes off his hair. I wasn't paying much attention to his answers. I did wonder what his brothers and sisters haircuts looked like. I knew that he was the son of Mr. Buck Key, the man with the long beard who had spit tobacco juice all over the front porch. He had told us he had a son around my age, and here he was standing right there in front of the whole class in bare feet and a funny haircut.

"Will any of your siblings be coming to the school?" Mrs. Holbrook asked. Kenny stood there looking at her as though he was puzzled. She then changed her question, "Will any of your brothers or sisters be coming to school?"

"Ma'am, I couldn't tell you what they might do or not do," Kenny said and smiled.

"What grade are you in?" she asked.

"Don't know. I can read and write some. I can cipher the number of deer standing in a field." The kids began laughing. I could hear Delma and Thelma laughing above the others. I didn't laugh.

"That's enough!" Mrs. Holbrook yelled at the class. "Why don't you put your shoes back on and take a seat there in the back?"

"Yes, ma'am, but I'd rather not wear shoes inside if that's okay," Kenny said.

Mrs. Holbrook started to say something but instead she closed her mouth and turned to face the blackboard.

Sadie then said, "Does that mean your name is Ken Tuck Key, as in Kentucky?"

Mrs. Holbrook turned around to look at Kenny. Even she hadn't spotted the unusual name.

"Yep, it is. Dad is right funny at times," Kenny Key explained.

All I could think of was, What a great name. I wish I had a name like that.

Purty hadn't taken his eyes off Kenny since he opened the door. Rhonda could have been walking around in a bikini, and Purty wouldn't have noticed her. I think he was as fascinated by Kenny's haircut as I was.

By the time for recess, the morning had warmed up and most of the boys went outside for snowball fights and fresh air. Kenny slid on his boots and followed us outside. He had been quiet the entire morning since his arrival. When he walked out the front door I met him and introduced myself to him.

"I'm Timmy. I live down the road from you at the store. I met your dad the other day," I said.

"Dad had told me about you. Sorry, I haven't been up to see ya. Been plumb busy as a bee in the middle of summer," Kenny said.

"So, how do you like the school?" I asked.

"It's okay. Why does that funny kid keep staring at me?" he asked me.

"Which one?" I asked him.

"That boy throwing the snowball like a girl." He pointed toward Purty.

I laughed and said, "That's Todd. We call him Purty. He's okay. He's probably checking out your haircut."

"He's seems a bit strange to me. It seems like they scraped the bottom of the barrel to come up with him," Kenny said.

"Here he comes now," I warned him.

Purty came slipping and sliding across the snow toward us with a big smile on his face. Daniel Sugarman was right behind him.

"Hey, I'm Todd. I like your hair," Purty said.

"I've only heard girls say that," Kenny said with a grin. Purty grinned back, not realizing he was being poked fun at.

Daniel skidded to a stop and greeted, "I'm Daniel. The guys call me Spoon."

"You live close to us. We're like neighbors," Purty told Kenny, interrupting Spoon.

Kenny nodded toward Daniel, ignoring Purty's comment.

"Who gave you that haircut?" Spoon asked. "My parents would never let me get a haircut like that."

"Yeah, me neither," Purty chipped in.

"My brothers cut it. Why would your parents care about your hair?" Kenny asked.

All three of us froze and looked at Kenny like he was from outer space. What he asked us seemed so foreign to us. Our parents cared about everything we did. We had to get permission to do almost everything we did, unless we snuck around and did it without their knowing.

My mom would go berserk if I got a haircut like Kenny's. She would go berserk if I even asked about getting a haircut like Kenny's. She fussed all the time about my hair getting too long. One day when I told her I wanted to let it grow a little longer her reply was, "That's why we have barbers." Of course my first thought was just because there are morticians didn't mean I had to die for them to have something to do. Mom didn't appreciate my bit of wisdom. I was sent to get a haircut.

"Pa doesn't care what I do as long as the chores are done. I don't even have to come to school if I don't want to," Kenny told us. Daniel and Purty's mouths dropped open. They continued to stand there speechless.

From behind me I suddenly heard Delma's voice say, "You have the weirdest haircut in the world."

Thelma added, "And what kind of name is KenTucKy? That's just plumb silly."

"Let me introduce you to Delma and Thelma Perry," I said, motioning to the girls standing beside me.

"You have the nerve to make fun of my name when your names are Pelma and Felma? What rock did you two crawl out from under?" Kenny told them.

"It's Delma and Thelma, you doofus," Delma corrected him.

"That's even worse, you little ogres," Kenny shot back. "You two look like the 'back door trots'."

Delma and Thelma then stood with their mouths agape. They were speechless, something I hadn't seen too often. They turned and ran away. Mrs. Holbrook rang the school bell, and recess was over. We made our way back into the schoolhouse. I knew KenTucKy would be my new friend. He had already earned my respect.

Papaw was there to pick me up after school. The twins jumped in the cab while Susie and I climbed into the bed of the pickup. Sadie, Raven, her sister, Samantha, and her brother, Henry Junior, also climbed into the truck bed. Purty ran up and asked if he could get a ride to the store.

"Jump in," Papaw told him. "Your sister is back there, also."

"C'mon!" Purty yelled to Kenny. "We've got a ride."

Purty had to climb up and over the tailgate while Kenny took three steps and placed one hand on the topside of the bed and leapt over the side and into a sitting position next to Sadie. Sadie scooted as far away from him as she could get before bumping into Raven.

"I don't bite," Kenny said to her.

She faked a smile and said, "You probably don't have teeth."

He smiled really big, showing her his teeth. "You're 'bout as pretty as a beagle pup."

Sadie looked as though she wasn't sure if he was complimenting her or not. She probably had never been compared to a beagle pup before.

"It's a compliment, Sadie," I said over the rattling of the truck on the gravel road as Papaw pulled onto the main road.

"I don't think I like being compared to a dog," Sadie said.

"Well, I hain't nigh doon complimenting you, Sadie," Kenny told her. I knew then that Kenny was eyeing Sadie to be his girl. I also knew that Sadie liked it—despite her protests.

Kenny looked over at me and saw that Susie was holding my hand. He smiled big and asked her, "Are you Timmy's girl?"

I wondered what Susie would say. Kenny had a friendly way about him, except he was very direct, and I could tell he was honest about everything. He was a person I knew I could believe.

Finally Susie told him, "He's my boy." I smiled, and Kenny began laughing.

Kenny then looked at Raven and her brother and sister. "I hain't never been around Negroes," he said loud enough that they could hear.

Raven smiled at him and said, "We don't bite, either."

We all laughed, and then Kenny said, "That's good to know."

Right at that moment Papaw turned sharply onto the Washington's lane. Sadie wasn't holding onto anything, and she slid right into Kenny's lap. Her face ended up right in front of Kenny's face. As quick as a cat Kenny leaned forward and kissed her on the mouth. Sadie was flabbergasted. She didn't know what to say or do. She pulled her dress, which had slid up her leg, down below her knee and excused herself. She scooted back to where she had been and grabbed the side of the pickup.

Kenny smiled at me and said, "I knew she was fond of me." Sadie was speechless. I had never seen anyone make Sadie and the twins speechless in the same day.

The Washington kids got out of the truck and waved good-bye. Sadie made no attempt to move farther away from Kenny even though space had opened up. Papaw's next stop was at Susie's farm. She jumped from the bed, and the twins slid from the cab. The twins made faces at Kenny as we drove away, and Susie waved.

Papaw leaned out of the window and asked me, "You want to go with me to drop off the others?"

"Sure," I answered.

Even though it was cold in the back of the pickup, I didn't want to miss any fireworks between Sadie and Kenny.

"Maybe we could hang out sometime," Purty said to Kenny.

"Okay," Kenny replied.

"You could even join the Wolf Pack." He did it. I wondered how long Purty could go before suggesting that Kenny become a member. I thought it should be something the Pack talked about before someone was told they could join.

Kenny didn't say anything. Papaw was driving down the hill and around the two sharp curves, and we all were paying close attention to the snow-covered gravel road. Papaw dropped off Purty and Sadie next, which left only Kenny and me in the back of the truck.

Papaw leaned out the window and said, "Why don't you two jump into the cab?"

We jumped over the passenger side railing and hopped into the cab.

"Hey, sir, my name is Kenny Key," he said as he offered his hand to Papaw, stretching it across me since I was riding in the middle. "I live right past the tunnel."

"Yes, I know. The twins filled me in on who you were. They aren't very fond of you, either," Papaw told him.

"Do they like anyone?" Kenny asked as Papaw put the truck in gear.

"Each other," Papaw said, and we all laughed.

"You need for me to pick you up for school in the morning?" Papaw asked Kenny.

"No, but thank you," Kenny answered.

After dropping off Kenny, Papaw looked at me and said, "No. I don't think your mom is going to let you get a haircut like Kenny has."

"What about just the mohawk?" I asked.

"I doubt it," Papaw answered and laughed.

13 THE CAT'S MEOW

That evening, around dusk, I went for a walk around the lake. The sky was covered with clouds. I stood on the dam and looked out over the still surface. A light fog rose from the water and drifted up into the bare trees. I heard a caw and looked up to see Bo flying toward me. I tilted my head to the right, and he landed on my left shoulder. I reached up and touched his chest, gently petting him with the tips of my fingers.

I turned to the west and began walking along the trail. I loved the quietness of the lake on evenings when no one else was there. It felt as though it was all mine—a secret that no one else knew about. I thought about all the adventures and things that had happened at the lake. I thought about the many fishermen who had fished there as I walked the path. The memory of Mamaw watching me catch the large bass in the moonlight flooded my mind.

I thought of the hours I'd spent with Uncle Morton and all the advice he had given me. I thought of him rolling down the dam. I thought of his battle with another fisherman's line when he thought he had a giant catfish on his line. I thought of how I had gotten tangled up with Joe Junior's line as I walked around the corner where the excess pipe was. As I walked past the spot where Billy Taulbee and his two friends always fished, I laughed. I remembered the many hours they wasted at the lake trying to catch a fish. I wondered where Billy Taulbee was, and if he was still alive after escaping kidnapping charges.

I walked past the spot that was my favorite to catch catfish. I climbed the first rise and stood at the top and looked out over the lake. I could imagine all the fishermen there poking fun at each other and laughing. Sam Kendrick, Fred Wilson, Louis Lewis, Mud McCobb, and Roy Collins came to mind. I remembered that the last time I ever saw Mrs. Robbins alive was near the spot I was standing. She was fishing with a large bonnet covering her head.

The snow crunched as I continued along the trail until I got to the spot where Susie and I had first seen the Tattoo Man leaning against a tree. At that time I had no idea he would end up trying to kill me. The hair on my arms stood on end. Bo let out a long, "Caaaw." Coty came running toward Bo and me, barking with every stride.

"It's okay, Coty." I tried calming him. He whimpered and walked by my side, continually looking up at Bo.

We were next to the slanted rock. I wondered how many hours I had spent fishing from the rock. I tried to come up with the number of fish I had caught while sitting there. Trying to figure it out made my head hurt. I stopped trying. Bo began bobbing his head up and down as we crossed the small stream that fed water into the lake. Darkness was quickly coming to the lake. The sun had disappeared behind the western hillside long ago.

Wooden Bridge at Papaw's Pay Lake

I hurried around the eastern side of the lake, across the two small wooden bridges, past the small cliffs, and out onto the dam again. I looked at the bench and thought of my happiest memory, the night I finally kissed Susie on the lips. I also remembered the night we took the rowboat out onto the lake and Rhonda grabbed Purty by the ears and kissed him square on the lips.

There were so many memories. It was no wonder I loved the lake so much.

As I neared the house, Bo flew away. When we got to the porch I picked up the old towel and dried off Coty's paws. Mom didn't want paw prints all over the house. Mom told me that supper was ready. We had spaghetti. I buttered three slices of white bread to eat with the meal. I went into the store and got an RC Cola from the cooler. I wasn't sure where

James Ernest was, maybe at Uncle Morton's house, maybe hanging out with his animal friends.

After eating, I did my homework and then watched TV until bedtime. I watched The Bugs Bunny Show, The Rifleman, Alfred Hitchcock Show, and then had to take a bath, which I objected to, which didn't matter. I ended the evening watching The Red Skelton Show before going to bed. As I was getting into bed, Mom came into my room.

"I wanted to tuck you in and give you a kiss," Mom said.

"Am I four again?" I asked.

"No. I just wanted to let you know I love you and I'm very proud of you," Mom said, rubbing the top of my head.

I knew now was the time to ask. "Can I get a mohawk haircut?"

"No way! Are you out of your mind?" Mom answered. "What would give you an idea like that?"

Maybe it wasn't the right time to ask. Boy, was I wrong.

"Kenny Key has half of one. It's pretty neat," I explained.

"Half of one. What is half of a mohawk?" Mom asked.

"He has a mohawk from his forehead back to middle of his head, and then he has long hair in the back," I explained as I ran my hands through my hair, trying to show Mom what it looked like.

"Sounds absolutely awful. Is he Buck Key's son?" Mom asked.

"Yep."

"I think you should stay away from Kenny Key," Mom said.

"He's nice."

"So you want a mohawk because he has one?" Mom asked.

"Yep."

"If he jumped off a bridge, would you jump off a bridge?" Mom asked.

I hesitated before answering. It sounded like a question that was one of those that a mom really didn't want an answer to. Maybe she was trapping me. If I answered 'yes', she would get mad. If I answered no, she would tell me I didn't need a mohawk then.

"It depends," I finally answered.

She huffed and walked out of the bedroom, closing the door a little harder than I thought necessary.

Wednesday, January 3

I looked for Kenny when I arrived at school the next morning. I didn't see him anywhere around. He wasn't at his desk when we took our seats. School was boring that day. The only thing interesting that happened was when Purty got a paddling for continually staring at Rhonda. Mrs. Holbrook had warned Purty to pay attention to our school work. But his head kept tilting toward Rhonda and then his eyes would begin to bug out of his head until he fell into a trance.

Susie sat behind me in the seventh grade row, so the only way I could stare at her was if I completely turned around or had eyes in the back of my head. Since I didn't have four eyes, I would sneak peeks at her and smile when Mrs. Holbrook turned her back to us.

That evening James Ernest was at the house. We talked about Kenny Key. I told him about Purty inviting him to become a Wolf Pack member. James Ernest said we would have to vote on it. He suggested we invite Kenny to go on our next adventure. The weather had turned really cold and James

Ernest thought the waterfall would freeze up in a couple of weeks if it stayed cold.

After dinner Mom asked if we wanted to play cards with her. Mom loved playing cards. The three of us played Five Hundred Rummy. We played most of the evening.

I had to go to the outhouse before going to bed. The worse thing about the outhouse was using it in the winter. It was cold. I mean really cold. There wasn't a heater in it. It was almost like pooping in the woods except the outhouse blocked some of the wind. Still the wind would blow through the cracks between the wooden boards and into your crack. I would have to pull my pants down and sit on icy wood in freezing cold. Some people had pots inside the house to use when it was so cold. But I hated using a pot even more than I did suffering the cold. I figured a real guy didn't use a pot.

Sunday, January 21

I awoke with rapping on my door.

"Get up, sleepyhead. You need to get ready for church," Mom said through the door.

"Okay," I said through a yawn. I tried opening my eyes, but they seemed to be glued shut. I rubbed them with the bed sheet until I could open them. I hated the thought of getting out of bed. It was cold outside the covers. Every morning for the past two weeks was the same struggle for me to get out of bed. But today was going to be a special day. The Wolf Pack had plans to hike to the waterfall on Susie's property and see if we could walk the ledge to the tunnel that could lead to other caves and treasures.

We voted that we could each invite someone to come along. Of course I asked Susie to join us. Purty asked Kenny Key to come along. He was torn between Kenny and Rhonda. Kenny had come back to school every now and then. In the past two weeks he had been there four days. James Ernest invited Raven to come along. Randy invited Brenda, but Brenda told him she didn't think she would enjoy freezing for no good reason.

So that afternoon, after church, we were finally going to have our adventure.

The Sunday before had been so cold inside the church that folks kept their winter coats on and huddled together for warmth. Pastor White preached the shortest sermon I had ever heard. It was pretty much, "Jesus died for you, accept his love, and have a good week and love others."

But the church was warmer this Sunday. The weatherman had predicted the temperature would soar to thirty degrees by mid-afternoon. It felt a lot warmer than that.

That afternoon after church James Ernest and I had been invited to eat with Susie and her family. Raven had also been invited. Monie fixed fried chicken, mashed potatoes, and green beans. The meal was wonderful.

During the meal Delma warned Susie, "You aren't really going on a winter adventure with these stupid boys, are you? You will freeze to death or die some other tragic way."

"I'm just going on a hike," Susie countered.

"Seems like we've heard this story many times before," Thelma added.

She was right. We had done the same thing many times before, and each time our adventures had almost terrible results. But we had always survived. We hadn't told the girls that we planned to walk on the ledge behind the waterfall, perhaps because they either wouldn't go or because they would try to talk us out of it. Still, even trying it would all depend on whether the falls was frozen or not. Something that maybe we should have checked out before going to all this trouble.

Soon Mr. Tuttle arrived with Randy, Purty, and Kenny Key.

Clayton and Monie stared at Kenny's haircut when they were introduced to him. I could see the puzzlement on Monie's face.

"Interesting haircut, Kenny," Clayton finally said while his mouth was open.

"You wouldn't believe how many comments I get," Kenny replied.

"Oh, I think we'd believe it," Clayton said.

"We comment on it every day he's at school," Delma said.

"But he's not there that often," Thelma added.

"He gets his education the same way he gets his haircuts," Delma continued.

"Halfway," the twins said in unison.

"You sure allow girls to do a lot of yelping," Kenny said, looking at Clayton.

"They came out that way," Clayton answered, laughing.

The twins stood there with a look of surprise on their faces. They seemed so shocked that their own dad would poke fun at them.

"We'd better be heading out. It gets dark early," James Ernest said to everyone. He placed his backpack on over his heavy sweatshirt and led us across the yard and into the field.

It was already two in the afternoon, and darkness came around seven. We didn't have a lot of time.

"This is going to be fun," Purty said as we walked toward the woods. "I've wanted to do this for over a year."

"What, go on a winter hike?" Susie questioned.

"No. Finally walk the ledge to the tunnel," Purty blurted out.

Susie stopped in her tracks. "Are you guys crazy? I thought we were going on a peaceful hike. That's too dangerous."

"Girls! That's why I invited a boy," Purty spouted off.

Susie looked at me with disappointment. She wanted an answer.

"We don't know for sure if we're going to try it. James Ernest has an idea that could work if the waterfall is frozen over. If it isn't, then it is going to turn into nothing but a winter hike," I tried explaining.

"You Perry girls sure complain a lot," Kenny said to anyone listening.

Susie was listening. "Shut up, Kenny. You don't know anything about the Perry girls or girls at all—probably."

"Pa says girls are for cooking and cleaning and gardening and having babies," Kenny shot back and then added, "and not listening to."

I tried saving the situation and the hike. "Hey, let's continue the hike. We can discuss your beliefs later. Let's have fun."

Susie was so mad I thought I saw the snow melting under her feet.

We began walking again. As I walked I heard a caw coming from overhead. I looked up to see Bo flying down toward me. He carefully landed on my left shoulder. Susie and I were bringing up the rear and no one else saw him land except Susie. The crunching snow drowned out the quiet flight.

A moment later Raven looked back at Susie and saw the crow attached next to my head.

"Bo is here," Raven said excitedly. Everyone looked back to see him. Kenny had only heard about the bird but had never seen him.

"I thought y'all were pullin' my leg," Kenny said.

"Nope. Bo is real," Randy told him.

"Isn't that the cat's meow," Kenny exclaimed.

"He's real, Kentucky," James Ernest said.

I turned my head and looked at James Ernest and then at Kenny. Kenny had a smile on his face as if he liked the nickname. I knew then that he would be known as Kentucky or Tucky, just like Todd was Purty. I noticed that everyone was smiling.

We entered the woods where the trail came out. We followed it until it turned to the right. We needed to go straight. Ahead of us we could see the tall sixty- to seventy-foot cliffs where the waterfall was. James Ernest was right; the waterfall had frozen, leaving giant icicles clinging from the top edge of the waterfall. The ice hung about halfway to the forest floor. A small amount of water ran down the ice and dripped onto the frozen ice- and snow-covered rocks below.

"That's beautiful," Susie said to us all. Everyone agreed.

"It's really purty," Purty said in response.

I saw Kenny squint his eyes toward Purty like he was trying to figure him out. I figured that would take a lot of doing. No one else had been able to do it. I could see that the ledge we wanted to cross was out of sight, hidden by the hanging ice. I thought maybe James Ernest's idea would work.

14 THE HIDDEN TUNNEL

"Is everyone ready?" Randy asked as we stood there looking up at the adventure ahead of us.

"Are you sure this is safe?" Raven asked.

"That's what we're going to find out. We need to climb to the tunnel and walk over to the ledge to see what it looks like," James Ernest explained.

Randy led the climb up the hillside. We stumbled and slipped and slid as we made our way up toward the tunnel. Bo wasn't very happy being on my shoulder as I climbed, so he flew into a tall tree and cawed as we scrambled upward.

Once we all were safely at the mouth of the tunnel, Kentucky smiled and said, "That was like climbing a tree covered with pig fat."

It was Purty's turn to stare at Kenny. But Purty's stare quickly turned to a smile.

The inside of the tunnel was dry and warmer. Loose, flat rocks, about the size of arrowheads, littered the tunnel floor. I wondered if any of the rocks were. I had never found an arrowhead. Papaw had a small collection that he had found over the years. Uncle Morton had an even bigger collection he had found when he was young before he started going blind. I began thinking about the cave with the Indian drawings. I had never searched the floor for things Indians may have left behind. I knew then I would head for the cave in the spring.

It only took a couple of minutes before we stood looking out at the snow-covered ledge. We all stood staring at it. I knew what was going through each of our heads; it still doesn't look very safe. The icicles that hung next to the ledge were still far enough away that a person could slip and fall between the ledge and the ice—falling to their certain death—and no one wanted to die. I had promised that I would be careful. I knew Mom had worried enough in the past year to cover ten peoples' worry.

"Who's going first?" Purty asked.

Each of our heads turned to look at him.

"Be our guest," Randy said.

"I don't think it's safe," James Ernest interrupted.

"Sure it is. It's just snow. I can walk on snow," Purty assured us.

"It looks like icy snow. One slip and you're gone," James Ernest explained.

Purty stood there next to the ledge, looking out at it. I knew he was thinking about taking the next step and proving to Kenny he was brave. Purty had been dreaming of crossing the ledge since the day we found it. He had talked about the treasures that were sure to be hidden in the tunnel on the other side. It had almost become an obsession he couldn't let go of.

"Don't do it, Pur—" I was saying when he stepped onto the ledge and took four quick steps across the ledge. We all stood there watching him with our mouths stuck open when the snow gave way, and he slid off the ledge. He flew off the edge and slammed into one of the long icicles. He then disappeared below the ledge as he slid down the giant icicle with his arms wrapped around it, holding on for his dear life.

The girls were screaming. Not as loud as Purty, but still pretty loud. The other three guys began running back through the tunnel to see what had happened to Purty's body. I dropped to the ground quickly and crawled to the edge where it met the tunnel wall and looked over the ledge down to the snow-covered boulders below.

To my amazement Purty was sitting at the bottom of the icicle with his arms and legs wrapped around it, hugging it tightly, on top of a huge, snow-covered rock. He was alive—alive and breathing and probably thanking his lucky stars. The twins had told me I was like a cat that had nine lives. I wondered how many Purty had.

As I lay there looking down at lucky Purty, something caught my eye. I looked under the edge and was amazed to see another tunnel opening right below me going back into the mountainside beneath us. I took my flashlight and hung it down and at the hole. I could see that the opening went a ways into the rock. It was around the same size as the tunnel we were in. It would have been impossible to see from where we had looked at the waterfall from the forest floor.

I realized that the girls were still screaming. I heard one of them say, "Is he dead?"

I then realized that they didn't know how lucky Purty was. I slowly stood and turned to face them and said, "He's okay."

"What do you mean, he's okay?" Raven asked.

"He's okay. He slid down the icicle and landed in the snow at the bottom. He's fine," I explained.

We could hear Randy yelling at his brother as they neared him sitting in the snow.

"You are such an idiot! You could have died! Do you want to die?"

We couldn't hear Purty's answers. I would assume he just smiled with his goofy, toothy smile and pulled some food from his pack to eat.

I got back down on my stomach and yelled down to the guys. "Come back up here!" I yelled.

"Why would you want them to come back up here? Aren't we done here?" Susie questioned.

"I need to show them something," I answered.

"Let's go on with our hike. This is too dangerous," Susie begged.

"What do you want to show them?" Raven asked.

"I'll tell everyone at the same time," I told her.

It wasn't long before the guys were back up to where we were. Susie and Raven hugged Purty, which I was sure made his day, and to him made risking his life worth it.

"Now tell us, Timmy," Raven said.

"What?" Purty asked.

"Timmy says he has something to show everyone," Susie said sarcastically.

I then explained to them what I had found. James Ernest and Randy dropped to their knees and crawled to the edge to look at the opening I had found.

"Maybe it goes over to the other side," Purty said excitedly.

"But doesn't it go back underneath us?" Susie asked.

"Girls, girls, caves and tunnels can go and turn anywhere. No tellin' where it goes. It could go to Johnson County," Kentucky told them.

"We need to lower someone down to check it out," Randy said.

"I'll go," Purty volunteered.

"No way! I found it. I should be the one to check it out," I spoke up.

"He's not going without me," Susie told everyone.

"Bossy girl," Kentucky said.

Susie glared at him until he looked up at the tunnel ceiling and said, "I like it."

James Ernest said that they could lower us to the opening with the rope—one at a time. A rope loop was placed under my arm pits, and I went off the ledge backward. The guys lowered me with the rope. It was only around a ten-foot drop to the ledge that stuck out leading into the tunnel. It was only a few seconds before my feet touched down on the slick, snow-covered ledge.

I walked into the tunnel far enough to get off the snow, and I slipped the rope up over my head and yelled up for the guys to pull it up. A couple of minutes later Susie was standing by my side. We walked into the tunnel, and she took my hand in hers. I shined the flashlight all around the entrance to see what was ahead of us. The tunnel looked a lot like the one we had just come from except that it was much darker, which made me believe it went deep into the mountain. We began carefully walking and looking for other pathways. The tunnel turned to the right.

"It looks like it goes for a ways. I'd better go tell the others they can come down," I told Susie.

"Do you have to?" she asked.

I knew what she meant. I liked it being just the two of us also, but I knew we couldn't leave our friends standing in the upper tunnel. We turned and walked back to the opening.

"Come on down. It looks like it goes back into the mountain!" I yelled up toward them.

I could sense their excitement even from where I stood. Finding large caves was what boys in the area dreamed about. And I was sure that men and women and girls often wondered what it would feel like to discover a large cavern.

The next person lowered to the tunnel was Raven. We helped her inside and then sent the rope back up. Purty was lowered down next, followed by Kentucky and James Ernest. Randy pulled the rope up to him and tied the end of the rope around a large rock in the tunnel. We waited for a while before I asked, "What is Randy doing?"

"He's tying a few knots in the rope to make it easier to climb back up," James Ernest explained.

I couldn't help but think of my stupidity when I got trapped in the cave above the swimming hole. I didn't have the strength to climb the rope, but I would have been able to if I had thought of tying knots in the rope. It seemed as though everyone was smarter than I was—except for Purty, maybe.

It wasn't much longer before the end of the rope dropped to the ledge, and Randy's feet came into view. We all were finally in the newly discovered tunnel.

"I claim this tunnel as the Callahan Tunnel. Forever, we will call it by that name," I spoke out.

Purty started to object when James Ernest raised his hand as if making a toast and affirmed, "The Callahan Tunnel, forever it will be called." Everyone lifted their hands, joining the toast.

"This way," I announced as I led the group into the belly of the mountain even though there was only one way to go.

We soon were back to where the tunnel turned slightly to the right. It wasn't long before guys were shedding their coats, tying them around their waists. Compared to the December cold, the tunnel was nice and warm. The tunnel continued to fade to the right as though it was going around the waterfall to the tunnel on the other side. Maybe Purty was right.

The going got tougher. In spots large, flat, rocks covered the stone floor that we had to climb over. The tunnel narrowed at one location. We thought we might have to leave Purty behind. Through great determination and our pushing and pulling he managed to squeeze between the walls.

"No sweat," Purty announced afterward.

Kentucky proclaimed, "Maybe it was no sweat to you, but I'm sweating more than a cotton picker."

Three flashlights flashed onto his face. I looked toward Raven. The arc of the light lit her dark face. She smiled and said, "Cotton pickers do sweat a lot."

Tucky realized what he had said, and his face showed his embarrassment. "I'm sorry, guys. I truly didn't mean no disrespect. Where I came from coloreds and whites picked cotton, and they all sweated like crazy in the heat."

Raven walked up to Kenny and reached her hand out and placed it on his arm and said, "No problem, Kenny. You're right."

We moved forward. I was still leading the way with Susie still beside me. Suddenly the tunnel widened and led into a large, circular room. We walked ten feet into the room, and then we all stood in awe of the size and wonder of what we had found. The ceiling had to be thirty feet above our heads. It was probably seventy feet to the opposite wall. The bottom on the cave was clear of any flat stones and boulders that usually cluttered cave floors. It reminded me of a large ballroom where folks would dance the night away.

It seemed as though no one could say anything. We all were speechless until Purty declared, "I claim this as Purty's Cave."

"I think this is still part of Callahan Tunnel," Randy said.

"This isn't part of a tunnel," Purty argued.

"It's okay. I think the name is appropriate. It is a really purty cave," I said, giving up any claim I had on it. Then a thought came to me, "In fact, it's so pretty it should be named Susie's Cave."

Susie squeezed my hand and smiled at me.

"It is on her family's property," Raven added.

"All in favor of naming it Susie's Cave, raise your hand," James Ernest said as he raised his hand.

We all raised our hands. Purty hesitated before finally agreeing that we were right and lifted his hand to make it unanimous.

"Let's explore the room," James Ernest then said. "I'll go this way," heading to the left.

Randy, Purty, and Tucky went the opposite way, to the right.

Susie, Raven, and I followed James Ernest along the wall. While walking, I shined my light onto the ceiling and noticed that there were bats clinging to it. There weren't nearly as many as had been on the ceiling of the other caves we had been in, but there were quite a few. I lowered my light and followed James Ernest without saying anything about the bats.

A couple of minutes later Randy called out from the opposite side of the room, "We've found the tunnel! It continues over here." His voice echoed around the room. There was no need to talk loudly to be heard. The acoustics were unbelievable.

"Let's keep searching the room. We'll follow the tunnel later," James Ernest almost whispered.

"Okay," Randy whispered back.

The echo of the whispers gave me an eerie feeling, especially with the words bouncing off the walls in the darkness. I knew the bats were overhead, and I had a funny feeling something bad had happened here in this cave or was about to happen. I wanted to leave suddenly.

"Let's go," I whispered, not knowing why. I tugged on Susie's hand toward the tunnel.

"No, Timmy. This is exciting. I've never seen anything like this," Susie said.

"What's wrong?" James Ernest asked, having stopped his search to see why I was being such a weenie—or at least, that was the way I felt.

"Nothing, it's okay. Let's keep searching," I told him. I fought back the thought to run, to get out of there as quickly as possible. Everyone else was fine. I told myself to stop being a big baby.

We slowly moved around the room searching the walls and darkness with our flashlights. James Ernest and Raven were in the lead, and suddenly a scream echoed the insides of the cave, sending goosebumps up my entire body. Susie quickly hugged me tightly. Raven continued to scream. When Susie loosened her death grip on me we moved over next to James Ernest and Raven. I shined my light into an alcove that James Ernest had found, and there sitting, leaning against opposite walls, were two skeletons. Susie screamed, causing Raven to scream again.

Randy, Purty, and Tucky were hurrying across the room to where we stood. They arrived, and the next sound was the maddening cries of Purty's screams. Raven's and Susie's screams had bounced around in my head, but Purty's scream almost burst my eardrums. The shrieking caused the bats to let go of the ceiling they were clinging to, and they began flying around the room, searching for the prey they were sure to be coming after them. How many times had I seen this scene play out? The frantic flapping of the wings made the three girls, one being Purty, to scream all over again.

I held my hands over my ears and dropped to my knees. I tried drowning out the sounds by placing my forearms over my ears and squeezing as tightly as I could. The echo of the screams and flapping wings was enough to drive a boy insane. Within a few seconds we were all huddled on the stone floor either covering our ears or screaming. I finally jumped on Purty's back and placed my hands over his mouth and clasped my fingers together and held on, not letting a sound come out of his mouth.

Within a few minutes the bats quit circling and were reattaching themselves to the ceiling. Purty had fallen to the floor, and I had lost my grip. I wondered if maybe I had suffocated him to death. At that moment I didn't even care. Susie and Raven had calmed due to Purty's silence.

After a minute of quiet James Ernest asked, "Did you kill him?"

"I don't know," I answered.

James Ernest bent over to see if he was breathing. "He's alive. I think he passed out."

"You mean he fainted?" Tucky asked.

"Maybe," James Ernest answered.

15 Two Dead and Petrified

James Ernest took his canteen from his neck and poured a little water onto Purty's face. His eyes slowly opened into the ray of a flashlight. He squinted and asked, "Where are we? Am I in heaven? Is that the light at the end of the tunnel?"

"Yeah, it kind of is," I answered.

"Timmy, you're in heaven with me?" Purty quietly said.

"Not yet. We're in Susie's cave. You passed out," I said.

"Is Rhonda here?" Purty asked.

"You're delusional," Randy said and then laughed.

"Don't scream again," James Ernest told him.

"I haven't heard screaming like that since our cow had a two-headed calf," Tucky said. We all looked at Kenny, being unsure if he was serious or not.

I arose from the floor and made my way back into the alcove where the two skeletons had made their home against the walls. Everyone followed. Randy again told Purty not to scream.

I then noticed a chest that was on the floor to the left of the two bodies. It was exactly what I thought a treasure chest would look like. It was old and was covered in dust and dirt. It had old hinges and a large silver lock on the front. I knew that we all were staring at the chest.

I heard, "Wow," come from Purty's mouth.

I walked closer to the skeleton on the left and discovered that a knife was sticking out of the shirt that still covered the skeleton where his heart would have been. Both skeletons had tattered, rotting clothes covering their bones except for their heads and hands. The off-white color of the bones shimmered in the beams of the flashlight.

"It looks like this poor guy died by taking a Bowie knife to the heart," I said while leaning over him taking a closer look.

"And it looks like this guy took a bullet between the eyes," James Ernest said while sticking his finger into the hole made by the bullet and wriggling it inside the skull.

"It looks like they had a tussle over the chest and killed each other," Tucky reasoned. "It gives me the willies."

"Me too, but where's the gun?" I asked.

The flashlights began searching the cave floor for a gun. The gun wasn't to be found.

"How long have they been dead?" Raven asked.

We all looked at James Ernest as though he was an expert in determining things like that. He looked at the bodies again and said, "Probably around thirty or forty years."

"How did you come up with that?" Purty asked.

"Their clothing. The style of the clothes look like something men wore in the nineteen twenties or thirties," James Ernest said.

"Why isn't there a gun? If this guy stabbed the other, and he in turn shot the other, and they both died then there would have to be a gun lying here," Susie explained.

"You're right," I said.

"Unless there was another person," Randy jumped in.

"Yeah," Purty chimed in.

"Yeah, what?" Tucky asked.

"Yeah, I was just agreeing that there could have been another guy," Purty told Tucky.

"Then why is the chest still here? I would think that's what they were fighting over," I said.

"Hey, yeah, the chest. Let's open it," Purty suggested, his eyes bugging out of his head.

"Don't you think we should report this to Sheriff Cane? We shouldn't mess with the chest," Susie said.

"No," Purty begged. "I've dreamed of finding a treasure chest my entire life. We can't give it up because a couple of guys died thirty years ago. What is Sheriff Cane going to find out? If there was another guy, he's probably dead by now. And why didn't he either come back for the chest or take it with him?"

Purty made good arguments. I agreed that the sheriff would never be able to determine who murdered who or who the chest belonged to.

"I agree with Purty. The chest is now finders' keepers, and we found it. What good would it do to tell the sheriff or our parents about this? It would just get me grounded again for being in another cave," I told everyone.

"If there is gold or silver or money in the chest, then what do we tell everyone? How do we explain where we got it?" James Ernest said.

"Let's open it. If there's nothing in it then it won't matter if we tell the sheriff," Purty suggested.

For once I thought Purty made sense. Why hadn't we already tried to open it? It was a treasure chest!

"He's right. Let's open it," Raven chipped in.

"We need to find a big rock to bust the lock," Randy said.

"Here's a good one," Randy said as he carried a large rock toward the chest. He hit the lock with the rock, and nothing happened. He hit it again and then again. The only thing that busted apart was the rock. We spread out looking for bigger rocks. Each rock we tried led to the same result. The lock remained locked and solid on the chest. Soon we were hitting the top of the chest, trying to bust the wooden chest open. The chest must have been made out of the strongest wood in the world, or the wood was petrified.

"We're going to have to get a bolt cutter or a crowbar or something else to get this thing open," James Ernest finally said as we gave up with the rocks.

"Maybe we should hide the chest," I said.

"Where?" Susie asked.

"Why?" Randy asked and then added, "It's been here for thirty years. I don't think it's going to disappear in the next day or two."

"You're right," James Ernest said.

"We have to promise not to tell anyone else about the chest or the skeletons. Does everyone agree? I mean it. We can't tell anyone. This stays with us seven," Randy looked each of us in the eyes by shining his flashlight in everyone's faces. We all nodded yes.

"We won't be able to come back before next Saturday or Sunday. We have school all week," James Ernest reminded us.

"We could come back tomorrow night," Purty said.

"It will be dark," Susie said.

"So what? It's dark in the cave now," Purty argued.

"I can't go out on a school night," Raven told everybody.

"We should wait until everyone can come. We all found it. We should share in the excitement of seeing what's in it," James Ernest stated as the final argument. Everyone finally agreed that he was right. So we planned to come back the next Saturday to open the chest, and we were keeping everything a secret among the seven of us.

We decided to follow the tunnel out the other side of the cave to see where it led. We entered the tunnel and followed Randy's lead.

"I bet there's gold coins in the chest," Purty said as we walked.

"I think there are diamond-covered jewelry and other gems," Susie guessed.

"Spoken like a girl," Tucky teased.

"What do you think is in the chest?" Raven asked him.

"I think there's books filled with maps showing where other treasures are hidden. Maybe some gold goblets and golden candlesticks," Kentucky said. Then he added, "Or maybe another dead guy."

"You really think so?" Susie asked Tucky.

"Nah, I'm just shucking you," Tucky said and laughed.

Susie punched him in the arm.

"I think there's a bunch of old clothes that's worth nothing," I said in a moment of silence.

"I don't think the two men would have killed each other over some old clothes," Purty said.

"How do you know the skeletons were men? They could have been women," Raven asked.

"No, they weren't," Purty argued.

"How do you know?" Susie asked.

"Because the skeletons didn't have boobs," Purty spouted. We all laughed.

Suddenly we saw light ahead. When we were close enough I could see the frozen waterfall ahead. We had made our way around to the opposite side of the falls. We could see the rope hanging from the mouth of the tunnel where we started.

"All we can do now is turn around and go back the way we came," Randy said. That's what we did. Within forty-five minutes we were back to the dangling rope.

It was a lot harder getting up the rope than it was going down. James Ernest climbed the rope first, using the knots that were tied in the rope to help him. Then we either climbed up, or the rope was slipped over our bodies and we were pulled up, or a combination of the two. We all finally made it into the first tunnel, and soon we were hiking through the frozen field back to Susie's house.

When we walked into the kitchen Monie greeted us and asked, "How about some hot chocolate? I saw you walking through the field and heated some for you."

It sounded great. We were cold and tired and the cocoa hit the spot.

"How was your hike?" Monie asked.

"It was exciting," Purty spoke up.

"What was exciting about it?" she asked.

We all turned to see what Purty would say next. What kind of lie would he come up with? Purty was always getting himself in a pickle, but he was just as good at getting himself out of jams.

"Well, for one thing, Bo went with us," he said. I thought that was good, but Purty couldn't stop with that. He had to make the hike even more exciting by adding, "And we saw a black bear and four cubs."

We all 'bout spit our chocolate out of our mouths and noses.

"You saw a bear and four cubs?" Monie's eyes grew wide while repeating Purty's lie.

"Yeah. It was pretty neat. The cubs were sliding on the ice beneath the waterfall. They were having a blast. We watched them for a long time before the mother saw us," Purty deepened his lie-filled story.

"Then what happened?" Monie asked.

"The mother bear made the cubs go in their den, and then we didn't see them again," Purty finished.

The twins had made their way to within hearing distance, and once Purty was done with his fantasy of lies, Delma said, "Did baby bear find that his porridge had been eaten?"

"Was someone sleeping in their beds?" Thelma added.

We all began laughing. Purty quickly hid his head inside the hot chocolate mug.

Delma continued, "And you probably found a big treasure chest filled with gold coins, and you had to walk over skeletons to get to it."

Delma and Thelma began laughing like they were the funniest comedy team on TV. Monie even snickered at them. We tried Purty's approach; we tried hiding our faces behind the mugs.

Friday, January 26

It was one o'clock, and the day was creeping by. Every minute seemed like an hour. I was sitting at my desk, pretending to be working on my math problems but thinking other things.

The seven of us who had found the chest were going back to the cave Saturday to open it to see what treasures were tucked away inside. I had never been so excited with anticipation. All week long I'd imagined what could be inside the chest. Were we all going to be millionaires? I tried to not expect too much, but it was hard not to think about there being a real treasure inside. It was like seeing a big package under the Christmas tree with my name on it and imagining what great thing was inside it and having to patiently wait until Christmas morning to open it. But this seemed a hundred times worse.

The wind was blowing hard outside, and the cold drifted through every crack it could find to come inside the schoolhouse. I was huddled at my desk with a sweater on and my arms folded tightly around my body. Mrs. Holbrook had Purty continually refill the pot-bellied stove with coal, trying to get the thing to put out all the heat it could. I believe it was doing all it could. It was just miserably cold outside. The weatherman had said on the evening newscast the night before that the temperatures were to reach zero and for folks to stay inside to avoid frostbite.

Mrs. Holbrook had a hard time getting the words to come out of her mouth correctly, and she blew on her clinched hands every minute or so. The smaller kids had their winter coats on even though she had moved them closer to the stove. A light snow began falling during lunch. No one had asked permission to go to the outhouse even though the woods might be warmer than the inside of the school building.

I was looking out the window at the snow that was coming down heavier. The flakes were small, but they quickly covered the window pane, making it hard to see out. I liked being able to look out the window from my desk at any time of the day and see the dark-green limbs of the pine tree that stood at the edge of the woods. Next to it was a holly tree with its prickly leaves and red berries. The heavy snow made it impossible to see the two trees. I could make out a green haze through the icy snow-speckled pane.

"We're going to have a spelling bee," Mrs. Holbrook announced.

I figured she knew all of the kids were looking at the snow fall and shivering at their desks, so she needed to do something to gain their attention and get them up and moving around. She had us move the desks to the sides of the room, and then she separated us into two teams. This time she did it by grades. First, third, fifth, and seventh grade children were on one team and the other grades formed the other team.

We stood in two lines. The student whose turn it was to spell would be closest to the stove, thereby thawing out while spelling their word. After spelling they would go to the end of the line, and everyone moved up a spot. If they misspelled the word they would have to return to their desk, which now was next to the freezing walls of the schoolhouse. We had lots of incentive to spell the words correctly.

First and second graders were first in line. They spelled words such as *cat*, *dog*, *hat*, and *out*. One first grade boy spelled *dog* wrong. He got confused and spelled it g-o-d. I felt sorry for the little kid as he sat at his desk and pulled his coat up over his head. The good thing was that when we lost a member of our team it meant we would get close to the stove sooner. I was wishing for everyone on our team to quickly misspell, leaving only Susie and me so we could huddle around the stove and take turns spelling words.

The first round was going quickly. The twins had spelled correctly. Susie spelled dictionary. Purty spelled vacation. Even Tucky spelled his word right. It was now my turn.

"Timmy, your word is *porcupine*—a gnawing animal with long, sharp spines in its coat," Mrs. Holbrook announced.

I knew what a porcupine was. I had even seen them before. But I couldn't remember ever seeing it spelled before. It sounded easy. I thought for a minute or so, trying to stay next to the stove for as long as possible.

"Please spell the word, Timmy," Mrs. Holbrook announced. I could hear Delma whisper to Thelma, "He has no clue." Thelma chuckled.

"P-O-R-K," I began. The twins' laughter escaped into the room, and Mrs. Holbrook threatened to let them take their seats for being disrespectful. I figured they would never stand again in their lives if that was the case.

"Please start again, Timmy," Mrs. Holbrook begged.

I had finally warmed up. It fact the stove was now hot, and I needed to get away from it. I knew by the twins' laughter that I was spelling the word wrong. But it seemed right. I was a seventh grader, and they were only in the third grade. I figured I knew more than they did, so I spelled the word, "P-O-R-K-Q-U-P-I-N-E."

"I'm sorry, but that's wrong. Please take your seat," Mrs. Holbrook said. I walked quickly to my desk and pulled my coat up over my head.

16 Open It

Saturday morning I stood in the store waiting on customers, not that we had that many. It was still freezing outside, and not many folks were shopping. Some men left the warmth of their homes to journey out for necessities. The seven of us who found the treasure chest were still planning a trip back to the cave that afternoon, hoping it would warm up some. We were supposed to meet at the store at one o'clock, and Mr. Tuttle was going to drive us up to Susie's farm. Five inches of snow had fallen by morning light, and it was beautiful outside.

I was standing next to the black coal stove when Homer and Ruby opened the front door and walked in. Ruby was rubbing her hands together and complaining about the cold.

"It's colder than a witch's heart out there," Ruby said while looking at me.

"You should know," Homer teased.

"Homer Easterling, you've never known a kinder woman than your sweet wife," Mom said as she entered the store from the living room.

Homer looked at her, and before he could say anything Mom and Ruby headed for the kitchen.

"No sense of humor. For being such a funny lot, women sure have no sense of humor, Timmy," Uncle Homer said, turning toward me.

I wasn't sure how to respond, so I just smiled and warmed my hands by holding them close to the stove. Homer came beside me and held his hands out to warm.

"How cold do you think it is out there?" I asked.

"I doubt if it's reached ten yet," Homer answered. "It may not get up to ten degrees all day. I figured you'd be out building another igloo or fort."

"I like it fine right here by the stove. Coty is still bundled up on my bed. He won't even go out to pee."

"He's smarter than I am," Homer laughed.

"What brings you out in the cold?" I asked.

"Ruby needed some Martha White flour and a few other things."

I walked over to the shelf and removed a bag of flour.

"Go ahead and give us two. It might save me another trip in the cold," Homer said.

"What else?"

"Give me two cans of Prince Albert pipe tobacco," Homer directed. "We'll have to wait for Ruby to return for the other items."

I moved around the counter and reached up to the shelf with the Prince Albert cans. I told Homer, "Purty called the other day and asked if I had Prince Albert in a can. I told him 'yes', and then he said, 'You better let him out.'"

Homer laughed and then said, "That's an old one but still funny every time."

Coty finally moseyed into the store and greeted Homer. Homer reached down to pat him on the head. I opened the front door and told Coty to go out and pee. He looked up at me like I had lost my mind.

"Go," I demanded.

He crept through the door and down the steps to the parking lot. Thirty seconds later he was at the door, wanting back in. He came in and curled up by the stove in a ball. A minute later Papaw opened the door and came in.

"It's too cold for these old bones," he said as he made his way to the stove.

"You beat me spitting out those words," Homer said.

"So what does my grandson have planned for today?" Papaw asked me.

"This afternoon I'm going on a hike with some of my friends," I answered.

"In this cold?" Homer questioned.

"Yep. I guess so," I said, not too convincingly.

"Did your brain melt from standing too close to that stove?" Papaw said. "This sounds like another one of the Wolf Pack's stupid ideas."

"Oh, to be young and foolish again," Homer chuckled.

I was ready when Mr. Tuttle pulled into the snow-covered gravel lot in front of the store. I yelled good-bye to Mom and left. Coty had no intentions of following me. I saw Randy, Purty, and Tucky in the car with Mr. Tuttle. I wasn't sure where James Ernest was. He had left before I woke up that morning.

"Hey guys," I said as I opened the back door and got into the car.

"Good day for a hike," Purty said while laughing.

"I can't believe you boys are really doing this. Be very careful that no one gets too cold. A person could freeze in this weather," Mr. Tuttle told us.

"We're always careful," Purty said. I wasn't sure who he was trying to fool. No one in the car was buying it, not even me, and especially not his father. It was almost as if the Wolf Pack made it one of our rules—do not be careful!—and voted unanimously to accept it.

We found James Ernest and Raven inside the Perry house when we arrived. Susie's mother, Monie, had made sugar cookies for us, and we dug in. Mr. Tuttle had told us to call when we were ready to be picked up. We were soon putting on our coats and hats and scarves and gloves and heading out the door for our great fortune that we knew awaited us.

The sun was out and made the snow-covered fields glisten like jewels that we hoped to find in the chest. I had my flashlight in my coat pocket. James Ernest had bolt cutters sticking out of his backpack, and Randy said he had a large hammer and a crowbar in his. I hadn't seen Bo for a couple of days. I figured he was perched in a warm pine somewhere. I looked around to see if he was anywhere about. I didn't see him.

We were leaving footprints in the pristine field as we hiked across it. I figured we would be easy to track if we needed to be rescued. I hoped that wouldn't be necessary.

"I've been dreaming about this every night this week," Purty told us as we hiked.

"In your dreams, what did we find in the treasure chest?" Susie asked.

We all listened.

"The first night we found another skeleton in the chest like Tucky said. I woke up screaming." We laughed, and I figured everyone in the house would have woken up with Purty's screams.

He continued, "In my second dream I found the head of a giant catfish, and it was still alive and tried to eat me."

"What did you eat before you went to bed that night?" Raven asked.

"I had Mom's meatloaf," Purty answered. "The only other dream I remember I was all alone opening the chest. For some reason you guys had fallen off the ledge and died. I continued on to the chest and opened it. I pulled the lid up, and big hairy bats flew out of the chest, and I fell backward onto the skeleton and got my arm caught in his ribcage. We wrestled for a while, and then I woke up screaming again," Purty said.

We all laughed, and Randy said, "We haven't gotten a lot of sleep this week at our house."

"Let's hope we find something other than what you dreamed about," James Ernest said.

"We don't need any more squealing like a pig caught in a barbed wire fence," Tucky said. We all agreed with that.

It was cold. My breath seemed to freeze in the air. It was as though words had a hard time carrying between us, especially the longer we walked. The only one not having trouble speaking was Purty. I reckon he had lots of practice. My bones were freezing. The only thing that kept me going was knowing that I would soon be inside the tunnels and caves and in a warmer climate. I couldn't remember seeing a prettier site than the snow-covered hills and fields and trees, the pines with snow lying on the green sagging limbs. The only thing prettier was the girl I was walking next to, Susie.

We made it to the edge of the woods and entered the path. It wasn't long before we stood looking up at the frozen falls. I thought of Purty sliding down one of the giant icicles and laughed. I received so much laughter from knowing Purty. I couldn't imagine not knowing him. We began making the climb to the tunnel entrance. It was difficult and slippery. Purty slid back down four times before making it to his destination.

The anticipation grew with each step as we entered the tunnel. Could we possibly leave with a fortune? Could we have more money than we knew what to do with it? I had never really cared about money very much. The only time I had ever worried about money was when Dad had been on one of his long drunks, and Mom didn't have money to buy groceries or pay the rent. But even then she made do with what she had, or we found another place to live.

I had everything I wanted now. I was happy living in Morgan County. I couldn't ask for anything that would make me happier. So I wasn't sure why I was so excited about possibly finding great riches. I guessed any kid would be.

We came to the end of the tunnel. We would need to climb down the rope to the tunnel below. James Ernest had left the rope there from when we had used it before. He had coiled it up and left it behind the rock that he had tied it to. He uncoiled it, and we quickly made our way down the rope into the safety of the bottom tunnel.

The upper tunnel had still been cold. A wind was blowing through it. But the bottom tunnel was warmer, and the farther we followed it around the falls, the warmer we got. Soon we were taking coats and hats off and carrying them. Purty couldn't contain his excitement. He was bobbing up and down, constantly talking about what might be in the solid box.

"I think there are gold coins and thousands of dollars in the chest! We are going to be so rich. I'll take anyone's share that doesn't want it," Purty said. He must have been out of his mind thinking that one of us might not want their share. I might not have cared, but I certainly wasn't about to give away my portion of the treasure that Purty was positive would be in the chest.

Susie and I brought up the rear as we paraded toward the enormous cave ballroom. Randy led the way. My breathing was getting heavy, either from the fast pace in which we were walking or the excitement that I felt over opening the chest or probably from the combination of the two. The only person to speak in the lower tunnel was Purty, and we couldn't shut him up. He talked in his nervousness, and he was talking non-stop—so much like his mother.

Purty rambled on about everything, nothing of which I was listening to. I was sure that no one was paying him any mind. Randy suddenly stopped, and we all nearly ran into each other. He was carrying a lantern, and it lit up the cave that opened up before us. It was so much bigger than it seemed before when we only had flashlights. This cave was probably twice as big as any other cave I had ever been in. It was enormous.

We walked to the center of the cave. I looked behind us and could see our shadows casting eerie figures on the wall of the cave. They looked like monsters coming out of the wall crevices. I was spooked all of a sudden. I felt scared, probably because of the anticipation, the enormous cave, and the eeriness of the shadows. I had never had such a feeling come over me for no good reason. I grabbed Susie's arm and held on. I never would tell the guys about the feeling that had overcome me. I was afraid something horrible was going to happen, but I kept it to myself.

"C'mon, let's go open the chest, guys," Purty commanded.

I could sense that everyone felt something was very wrong, except Purty. No one said anything, though, like we were all afraid to mention it. Randy turned the lantern toward the opening, and we slowly made our way to the side room that held the two skeletons and the chest. We made it to the chest. I looked around at the skeletons. I wondered what was so important that two men died because of it.

"Hurry up. Let's open it!" Purty cried out. Everyone stood staring at the chest as though it was haunted. "Give me the bolt cutters. I'll open it if no one else wants to."

James Ernest slipped his backpack off and pulled the cutters from his pack. He handed it to Purty. Purty quickly grabbed the cutters and fell to his knees to where he could lift the old lock and place it inside the jaws of the cutters. He tried cutting the lock by squeezing the handles together with his hands. Nothing moved as he grunted. He then placed one handle into his flabby gut and used both hands on the other handle and pulled with all his might. The bolt cutters slipped off the lock, and the handle and his hands slapped him in the face, and he went sprawling onto the rock floor, his head within inches of the skeleton with the bullet hole between his eyes.

Purty's eyes almost exploded from his head as he looked up into the skeleton's face. He tried to scurry up from his spot but slipped and fell onto the skeleton. The bones rattled and fell apart, and the head snapped off and rolled into Purty's face. He fainted. I was somewhat relieved because I didn't want to hear his screams. It was probably mean of us, but we were laughing so hard that we didn't even care that Purty had passed out on the pile of bones.

Randy picked up the bolt cutters and cut the lock within seconds. James Ernest slipped the lock from its resting place and asked Raven, "Would you like to do the honors?"

Raven stepped over and grabbed the lid and slowly opened it. We all, except Purty, stood around the chest, glaring into it as the top was raised to show the contents. The first thing I spotted was a handgun, which was lying on some books and papers. There were no glistening jewels, no gold coins, or silver goblets. There weren't any bundles of cash or gold watches. Tucky reached in first and lifted out the gun. He spun the receiver.

"It's loaded—except for one bullet," Tucky told us.

"I would guess the missing bullet made its way into his head," James Ernest said, pointing toward the skeleton that Purty still lay on.

Purty was waking up. He rolled off the skeleton and opened his eyes. Randy walked over and unscrewed the cap from his canteen and poured water onto Purty's face. Purty began gagging and rising to a sitting position. His eyes focused on the chest and saw that it was open.

"How did it get open? I must have cut through it before I fell and blanked out," Purty said. He then saw Tucky standing there with a gun. "Are you stealing the chest?"

Everyone laughed.

"We found the gun inside the chest," Susie told him.

"What other treasures are inside the chest?" Purty asked as he crawled to the chest.

"It just has some papers and books in it," I said as I was lifting the contents, looking under them to see if something else might be there. "There's nothing else in here."

"What did you guys do with the treasure? I know there was treasure in the chest," Purty demanded.

"There wasn't," Randy told him.

"You guys are lying to me. You're trying to keep my share. Where is it?" Purty asked before bursting into tears.

"I'm sorry, Purty. There was nothing else. Randy is telling you the truth." Susie tried consoling him.

"There has to be a treasure. It's a treasure chest. I needed there to be a treasure," Purty sobbed.

"I know you had your hopes built up way too high. There was nothing in the chest except what you see," Randy said.

Purty sank back to the stone floor and stared at the chest.

James Ernest was going through the books and papers, checking them to see what they were. His eyes bugged open and he said, "These are journals, not books, and they tell about one of their lives. We need to load these into our backpacks and take them with us. It might tell why they were killed. We need to read them in good light."

I had my backpack with not much in it. We had brought empty packs to carry the treasures we found back home. It was stuffed with journals and papers. Just what I wanted—reading material.

"What should we do with the gun?" Tucky asked.

"Let Randy keep it for the Wolf Pack, if that's okay with everyone. It may end up being evidence," James Ernest said. Everyone agreed.

"What about the skeletons?" Purty asked.

"What? Do you want them for a souvenir of when you passed out?" I asked Purty.

"I didn't pass out!" Purty argued.

"You did, too," I argued back.

"Did not," Purty shot back.

"Did, too!" the two girls blasted toward him.

"Who invited girls, anyway?" Purty finally said.

"At least we didn't invite your boyfriend," I told him.

Everyone laughed. Tucky seemed to have no idea that we were talking about him. The argument reminded me of the fights I had with the twins, Delma and Thelma. Did too, did not, did too, did not. I knew that Purty was actually just mad about the chest not being filled with riches beyond our imaginations. He had been counting the money and planning what he was going to do with it since the moment we found the chest. I guessed we all were a little bummed out about what was inside.

"We'll leave the skeletons here. I think we should tell Sheriff Cane about them and see what he wants to do with them," James Ernest told us.

"He'll probably want to plant them six feet under with a stone and no name," Tucky suggested.

"Maybe the journals will tell us who they were," James Ernest reasoned.

"Are you going to split them up so we all can read some of them?" Purty asked him.

"I don't want to read nothin'," Tucky said.

"I think we should read them while we're together. We can meet at one of our houses," I suggested.

"Good idea. That way we can compare anything we find. You don't have to read anything you don't want to, Tucky," James Ernest said.

"Good, because I get enough reading in the schoolhouse," Tucky said.

I stared at Tucky. I couldn't believe he had said what he had said. The few times he came into the school I had never seen him crack a book. I wasn't even sure if he could even read. No one else questioned him, so I left it alone.

"Let's go," Randy suggested.

We began walking back across the stone floor of the large cave toward the tunnel opening. I wasn't looking forward to the freezing cold again. We walked in silence with Randy and his lantern leading the way.

Finally James Ernest said, "Someday I'd like to come back for the chest. It's a great chest."

We all agreed that James Ernest could have claims on it. He didn't have much else in his life. I would be happy to help him lug it out.

Before we left the tunnel and went into the cold James Ernest said, "I think we should read the journals and papers before we mention the gun and skeletons to the sheriff. He may want us to hand over the papers when we tell him."

I thought that was good thinking, except that I didn't know what James Ernest thought we would find in the journals and papers that we would care the slightest about.

Reading the Journals

Late that afternoon I was at the store waiting on customers. I stayed close to the stove when not behind the counter. The gang was all coming to the house that evening so we could begin reading through our find. I told mom that we had to read some old journals for school. She didn't even question it. I knew that if I told her the truth about finding the journals in a chest and about the skeletons, she would insist on telling Sheriff Cane.

Mud McCobb and Louis Lewis filed into the store and straight to the stove.

"Colder than a…" Louis began to exclaim.

Mud shot him a look and interrupted, "Watch your language."

"What?" Louis asked.

"I don't think you should use colorful language in front of Timmy. His ears might not be use to your foulness," Mud explained.

"All I was going to say is that it's colder than the outhouse seat in the middle of an ice storm," Louis defended himself.

"I thought you were going to use your potty mouth." Mud said.

I could see Uncle Homer's car pull into the parking lot and Uncle Morton get out of the passenger door. The front door opened at the same time Mom entered the store from the kitchen.

As Homer was closing the door Uncle Morton rubbed his hands together and said, "It's colder out there than a snowman's butt."

"I was just telling them how cold it is outside," Louis said.

"And just how cold is that?" Mom asked.

"Purt-near zero, I'd say," Uncle Morton answered.

"As cold as it gets," Louis chipped in.

I heard another truck pull up and Papaw and Mamaw were soon entering the store. Papaw looked at the men huddled around the stove and said, "Men, it's colder than a witch's heart out there."

"I think we've determined that it's cold outside. I've got work to do." Mom said as she and Mamaw headed for the kitchen.

It was near dark when the gang began arriving at the house. James Ernest had spent the rest of the afternoon with Raven at her house. Clayton and Monie brought them and Susie along with the rest of the Perry family, except Brenda, who stayed home alone. Mr. Tuttle dropped off Randy, Purty, and Tucky. Coty was huddled near the stove in the store, staying warm with the other men.

My bedroom was too cold for us to gather in, so we took over the kitchen table. The twins were watching TV with Janie, and the adults were in the store, sitting around the potbellied stove. James Ernest began passing the journals and papers out to everyone.

I began reading one of the journals. The date on the first page was February 5, 1931. From the date I assumed that

James Ernest had been right about the murders taking place in the thirties. The name at the top of the page was Lou Phillip Boone. Of course, it made me think about Daniel Boone and the possibility that the man who wrote the journal was related to him. He talked about the weather on that date and the cold spell that had been in the mountains around Cumberland Gap since that Christmas.

He talked about the loneliness that he felt since his wife and baby boy had died earlier that winter.

The next day he wrote about being hungry and that he was going hunting to find something to eat.

There were five journals in the chest, and five of us were reading them. James Ernest had asked Tucky if he wanted to read one or not, and he said he would. Randy and James Ernest were looking through the papers and letters that had been written by different people. We quickly discovered that all the journals had been written by Mr. Boone. The earliest one had been started in the fall of 1929. I had the last one that he had written. I skimmed over the pages that didn't interest our investigation or me in general.

I was anxious to see what light the end of his journal would shed. Would he tell who was after him or anything about bringing a chest to Morgan County? I was assuming that Mr. Boone was one of the unfortunate skeletons that occupied the cave. The room was quiet while everyone read. I noticed the gunfire on the TV in the living room from Bonanza that the twins were watching. They had a crush on Little Joe, and he was shooting someone again.

"Mr. Boone didn't have much," Susie said. "A wife and two sons seemed to be all he had."

"He tells about his wife and a son dying in 1931 and how crushed he was. He never mentions a second son," I told the others.

"That's strange," Susie commented.

"It's really sad," Raven added.

As the evening wore on we continued to discover little things about the family but not much about the murders. James Ernest had discovered a letter written to Mr. Boone about money that had possibly been buried in Morgan County and that no one had found it yet.

I turned the page and noticed a small picture shoved into the binding, holding the picture in it. I pulled the picture from its location and studied it. It was a picture of his family. The back of the picture had names written on it. From left to right was written, "Myself Lou, wife Lucille, Marcus (2), Franklin (9)."

I looked closer at the image of Franklin. Something was familiar about his face. Suddenly I knew who the picture looked like. I did some quick figuring. If the picture was taken in 1931 and Franklin was nine at that time, then he would have been born around 1922, which would make him around forty or so in 1962 and more importantly, around thirty-seven in 1959 when I first met the Tattoo Man.

The boy in the picture looked like a younger version of the Tattoo Man. The same long, rough-looking, dishonest face was connected to the boy in the picture. It had to be him. I shoved the picture in Susie's face and said, "Look at this. Who does the oldest boy look like to you?"

All of the other kids looked up from their reading to look at Susie who was studying the picture. She turned the picture from side to side and even upside down. She moved the picture so that the overhead light didn't glare on the picture.

She handed the picture back to me as I waited for her confirmation and said, "I have no idea. Doesn't look like anyone that I know."

My shoulders slumped to my sides. I gathered myself from the disappointment and then said, "Are you kidding? That is the Tattoo Man as a boy."

Susie tore the picture from my fingers and looked at it again. The others jumped from their chairs and moved behind her to have a look for themselves. There was no way the others could confirm that the boy in the picture looked like the Tattoo Man because none of them had seen him because they all moved to the area after the Tattoo Man had died. The only other one around then was James Ernest, but he had never seen him very close up. Only Susie and I had ever laid eyes on him in good light—and Susie only once when we saw him at the lake. No wonder she couldn't recognize him.

But when a person picks you up by the collar of your shirt and looks in your face from six inches away, you learn what they look like really well. I knew that the boy in the picture was definitely the Tattoo Man.

Susie laid the picture down on the table, and James Ernest snatched it up. Purty moaned because his hand wasn't quick enough to the photo.

"I'm not sure. I only saw him the one time. It could be him, I guess," Susie said.

As James Ernest looked at the photograph I could see questions beginning to form in his mind. I had been around him long enough to know what he was thinking.

`

"Didn't you say that he roamed the trails around here like he was looking for something?"

"Yep," I answered him.

"And didn't you say that he was always asking himself questions like he was out of his mind?"

"Yep," I answered again.

"What do you think, James Ernest?" Purty asked. Purty looked like he was going to burst with excitement.

"I think that if the boy in the picture is the Tattoo Man, like Timmy thinks he is, then maybe the Tattoo Man came here looking for the chest. He was searching the area for the cave that his father was murdered in and maybe looking for the chest," James Ernest surmised.

"But what is so important in these journals that he would need to find them?" Raven asked.

"Thirty years later?" Randy questioned.

"It's just a theory," James Ernest explained. "We need to keep searching. It may not even be the Tattoo Man."

"Maybe he just wanted the journals because his father had written them," Susie reasoned.

I felt as though we were making headway. They may not know it for sure, but I did. I knew the boy in the picture was the evil Tattoo Man. The more I looked at the picture, the more I could see the Tattoo Man staring back at me. I shivered.

I turned the picture upside down on the table and went back to reading my journal. We read and searched the writings in front of us for the next hour. I watched Tucky as he read. I got the feeling that he wasn't really reading the pages. When one of us would turn a page, he would turn a page right after. His eyes didn't move side to side as he read. He just looked at the page blankly and never told us about anything that was written in his journal.

Finally I asked Tucky, "What is he writing about in your journal? Tucky?"

He looked at me and then lowered his eyes and said, "Not much. It's boring."

Susie said she had found an interesting passage in her journal. Susie told us how Mr. Boone talked about his son, Franklin, that I felt was the Tattoo Man. "Here he writes, 'My oldest son is a strange sort. He roams a lot, and I can't get him interested in work around the farm. I order him to do chores, but his heart is never in it. He seems to have an evil side to him, and I've caught him abusing some of the farm animals. I believe he is a bit touched in the head. When he is of age I figure he'll go off to fight in a war.'" Susie finished and looked up.

"I wonder if he did. What war would he have fought in?" Purty asked.

"World War II started in 1939. He would have been seventeen or eighteen in 1939. He probably joined then, and that's where he got the tattoo," James Ernest reasoned.

"It makes sense," Randy said. We all agreed.

Monie walked into the room and asked Susie, "Are you ready to go?"

"Not yet. We need a little while longer, please," Susie begged.

"We need to get home for bed soon. We have church tomorrow," Monie told her.

"Okay. Just a while longer if that's okay," Susie told her.

Delma and Thelma walked into the room. They stood there looking at the seven of us with our faces concentrating on the journals and papers.

"You boys ought to do that with your school books, and you wouldn't be such morons," Delma said.

"I didn't know they could read. I don't see any pictures," Thelma insulted.

Purty threw his journal at the twins.

"You missed," Delma said and smiled.

"Just like when he shot at a squirrel," Thelma told her.

"Poor raccoon," Delma said as they headed back to the living room, laughing. Randy began laughing, followed by others at the table. We then had to tell Tucky about the poor raccoon.

Susie had finished her journal. Tucky laid his down like he was done. Raven, Purty, and I were still reading. I was always a slow reader. I read well, but I would always stop to think about what I had read. I had always done that.

Near the end of the journal, Mr. Boone had written that he was embarking on a trip to Morgan County. That piqued my interest. I told the others what I had found. On the next date in the journal he wrote about how he was meeting two other men, Steven and William, the next morning and starting on their big adventure, looking for buried riches. I began reading the passages out loud so everyone could hear.

"We have been given the location of a cave that holds a clue that should lead to the money. I'm looking forward to the search. We were told that we had to make our way through a tunnel near a waterfall and then slip below into another tunnel which would lead to a large cave."

"That's the cave where we found the chest and the skeletons," Purty said as if the rest of us were stupid.

"Thanks, Sherlock," Susie teased.

"This is getting good. Go on," Purty said.

I read on while Purty was interrupting. "The next day he wrote about their trip by automobile and things like where they stopped to eat and things they had seen. But then the next day's entry he wrote, 'We have found the cave. I'm sitting here against the wall in a small alcove, dreaming of the riches that are ahead of us. We found the clue written on a scroll in the cave just like we were told. We were disappointed because the letter says the final clue is inside a cave, protected by three boulders less than two miles away.'"

I looked up at Susie, and then we both looked at the others.

"We know where that cave is. It's the cave that the Tattoo Man died in! Ain't it!" Purty almost screamed.

I continued, "It says, 'The clue is inside a small tunnel inside the cave. The scroll also told us that a man held a young black lady as his slave and mistress for years after the Civil War had ended and that she had been burying silver coins that she had stolen from him for the day she would be set free. She died with the coins still hidden. The clue will tell us where the coins are buried. How in the world are we going to find that cave?"

I stopped and looked at all the faces that stared toward me.

"Is that it?" Raven asked.

"That was the last word he wrote. It looks like there's blood spatters on the page," I told them sadly.

James Ernest scooted the book into the middle of the table, and everyone except me stood and bent toward it to get a better look at the dark spots that sprinkled the page.

"He was shot between the eyes as he wrote his final word. Oh God! I fell onto Mr. Boone!" Purty cried out.

"Why would someone bring the chest into the cave? We thought they had brought the chest into the cave," Randy quizzed.

"They apparently thought the treasure would be inside that cave and was going to place the treasure inside it and carry it out. After the murderer killed the other two men he had no way to carry the chest out, so he left it there and took the scroll with him. We don't know if the murderer ever found the cave or not." James Ernest tried putting the pieces together.

"Who killed Mr. Boone?" Raven asked.

"Either William or Steven. There were three of them, and two of them died. It had to be the other one. He stabbed the one and then turned and shot Mr. Boone between the eyes," Randy reasoned.

"But why?" Raven asked.

"Greed, apparently. The killer didn't want to share the fortune with the other two, and he didn't need them any longer. He had the clue," James Ernest answered.

"We don't know if the killer ever found the cave or the buried money. It could still be out there," Purty said excitedly.

"We know where the cave is," I said.

"We do?" Tucky said.

STUPID, MORONIC, IDIOTIC BOY

I was explaining to Tucky about how I had found the cave when we heard Mr. Tuttle enter the store. I looked at the clock on the wall, and it was ten o'clock. Monie came into the room and told Susie it was time to go and that Mr. Tuttle was there to pick up the boys. Everyone looked at me.

"Maybe we can get together tomorrow and finish this," I said.

"Man, I can't believe this," Purty complained.

"C'mon, lard butt, we have to go," Randy told him.

"Well, that's not very nice, Randy," Monie said.

"You don't know him as well as I do," Randy said as he continued walking. Purty was close behind.

The only adults still in the store were Mamaw, Papaw, Mom, and Sheriff Cane who had arrived around eight. James Ernest and I were still looking at the journals.

"You or Randy didn't come across a letter telling them how to find the cave the murders took place in, did you?" I asked.

"No such luck."

"I don't get it. Why would someone leave a scroll lying on the floor of a cave, giving clues about the hidden money?" I asked.

Then a thought hit me, "Maybe we're thinking wrong. Maybe the chest was already in the cave with the letter in it. They didn't carry the chest in. That never made sense to me."

"But Mr. Boone's journals were in the chest."

"Yeah, so was the gun. Mr. Boone probably had his journals in a knapsack and placed them in the chest when they found it. He was going to take the chest. The killer put the gun inside the chest with the journals after he killed them, and locked it up. He took the knapsack. He would have to get help to carry the chest out. He couldn't have carried it out himself," I guessed. "Or maybe he didn't even care about the chest."

"It makes sense," James Ernest agreed. "I think we should tell the sheriff about the murders. We'll keep the treasure and this journal to us seven."

He placed the journal in his pack. I still didn't know why the chest with the clue in it had been left in the cave in the first place, and we probably would never know. It probably didn't matter. Why was a treasure chest ever left somewhere?

We casually walked into the store. Mamaw and Papaw were getting ready to leave.

"You may want to stay for this," I told them. James Ernest and I proceeded to tell them about finding the tunnels and the large cave and the skeletons and the chest. We told Sheriff Cane that we had found the gun in the chest that we thought was used to kill Mr. Boone, and that Randy had it for safe-keeping.

We told them everything except about the journal that had the clues inside and the picture of the Tattoo Man. We didn't tell them anything about the hidden money. We figured it wouldn't help solve the murders, anyway. Then I realized that the journal contained the names of the two men who were traveling with Mr. Boone. One of them was the murderer.

Just as I was going to tell him about the other journal the sheriff said, "You did the right thing by telling me about the skeletons, but I don't think I'm going to spend time investigating murders that happened thirty years ago. I'll have you lead us to the cave so the skeletons can finally be buried. We can notify any next of kin about Mr. Boone."

I decided the sheriff wouldn't need the journal after all if he wasn't going to look into the murders. I was relieved. I really didn't want to hide anything from the sheriff.

Later that night when everyone had left and Mom and Janie were in bed, I was sitting with James Ernest on the couch. He was almost ready to go to sleep. I told him, "I guess we can use the rope ladder to get down into the cave. I searched a lot of that cave when I was trapped in there. I didn't see any clues."

"Did you search the entire cave?"

I thought about it before answering. "No, I guess not. Once I found the opening into the Indian cave I didn't go on around the cave. There could be something down there."

"We'll go down and search it real good," James Ernest said.

"What if the guys see the opening to the Indian cave?" I asked.

"We'll tell them that we can't fit in it and that it would be too dangerous for anyone to try, anyway," James Ernest said.

"I guess. I want to make sure that everyone doesn't find out about the Indian cave."

"I know. I agree," James Ernest assured me.

We sat there in thought for a couple of minutes before James Ernest said, "I think we should vote on asking Tucky to become part of the Wolf Pack."

"Yeah. We should," I agreed.

I liked Kenny Key. He would make a nice addition to the club. But I worried about him. I didn't think he could read.

"Do you think Kenny can read?" I asked.

"I thought I was the only one who noticed it. No, I don't think he can read much. He didn't read much of the journal that I gave him."

"He pretended to. I think he doesn't want us to know he can't read," I said.

"He's probably embarrassed about it. We already know that his parents aren't partial to education. But I thought he could at least read some. I'm going to read the journal that we gave him to see if anything is in it," James Ernest said.

"That's a good idea. I guess I'll go to bed. Good night," I said as James Ernest was looking for the journal.

Coty was already curled up on the end of my bed. He raised his head when I entered the room. I petted his head, and then it dropped like a sack of rocks back to the bed.

It wasn't but a few minutes before I was in a deep sleep.

I dived from the snow-covered rock and into the hole we had cut in the ice. The water was colder than any water I had ever felt. My body tightened as I made my way under the rock ledge. It felt as though I would stop mid-stroke and be frozen in the swimming hole. I struggled until I finally popped my head out of the water inside the Indian drawing cave. I managed to get out of the water and plop onto one of the rock seats. My body quickly froze over, and I sat there like a statue of a stupid boy.

My eyes could still move, and I saw something to my right. The figure moved to the front of me and came into focus. The

Tattoo Man began singing a Gene Pitney medley. He started with "The Man Who Shot Liberty Valence" and ended with "Only Love Can Break a Heart." He started dancing on top of the rocks and singing the songs that went with each dance. He sang "The Twist" by Chubby Checker and twisted his body in gross positions. Next he sang "Monster Mash" by Bobby Pickett. I already knew he was a monster. "The Loco-Motion" was next in the dance monologue followed by "The Wah Watusi." He had all the motions and hand gestures down perfectly.

The Tattoo Man closed his concert by singing and dancing to "Who Put the Bomp in the Bomp, Bomp, Bomp?"

The Tattoo Man then started yelling at me, "I found the clue! I beat you to the clue! I found the clue! Who knows where the red curtains are?" He then picked up a chainsaw and came toward me like he was going to carve me into an ice sculpture.

I screamed in my bed. Coty began barking and howling. I heard a loud pecking at my window, and Bo was there, checking on the commotion. I was sitting straight up in my bed and breathing heavily. Coty began licking my face. He knew something was wrong and it probably scared him. No one ever came to my room to check on me. I stayed awake the rest of the night despite my sleepiness. No way was I going back to sleep.

Sunday, January 28

I was in the kitchen placing coal in the stove when Mom walked into the room with her housecoat on. She had a surprised look on her face.

"Thank you for getting the fire going," Mom said and gave me a hug.

"I've already got the one in the store going also. I've been up for a while," I said.

"Couldn't sleep?"

"Not very well," I said.

"What was the screaming last night?" James Ernest asked as he walked into the kitchen in his pajamas.

"Who was screaming?" Mom asked. They looked at me.

"I think I had a nightmare," I told them. I didn't want to tell Mom that I had a nightmare about the Tattoo Man, Franklin Boone. He now had a name. "I forget what it was about. Something about dancing and singing."

"Doesn't sound like a nightmare," Mom said as she turned on the stove.

"It must have been Delma and Thelma," I told her.

"That would do it," James Ernest said.

Later that morning we drove into the church parking lot. Smoke rose from the stove pipe, heating the building. I knew it would be cold inside. Maybe I could snuggle up close to Susie to stay warm. Susie and Raven were saving seats for us in our usual wooden pew. I scooted as close to Susie as I could without sitting in her lap. Pastor White greeted everyone, and then one of the ladies sang a song about heaven.

The pastor began preaching about the grace of God and the beauty of heaven. I was soon sound asleep. I was awakened when everyone stood for the invitation and closing prayer. Pastor White prayed as he walked to the exit door. He closed the prayer with, "Amen," and then proceeded to shake everyone's hand as they left the building. Susie and I were at the end of the line.

"How did you like the sermon, Timmy?" Pastor White asked me.

"It was good—and short," I said. I knew what the pastor was getting at. He had probably watched me sleep the entire sermon.

"What was your favorite part?" Pastor White asked.

"The…uh…" I stammered for an answer.

Miss Rebecca was standing next to him. She poked him in the ribs and said, "You quit teasing him and let him be."

I looked up at the two faces and said, "I'm sorry. I had a rough night."

"It's okay. But Susie, next time poke him in the ribs, like my wife here does to me. Okay?" Pastor White directed.

"I will. I enjoyed the sermon, Pastor," Susie smiled.

"You two behave yourselves," the pastor waved good-bye.

In the parking lot James Ernest told Mom and me that he was going home with the Washingtons. Raven asked if the gang could come to her house to talk about our plans to search the cave. It was fine with me and Susie, but I wasn't sure about Randy, Todd, and Kenny.

As Mom drove home, snow began to fall heavily again.

When I entered the store I went straight to the phone. I dialed the number to the Tuttle's house. They weren't at church that morning, and I needed to tell them about the plans. Sadie answered the phone.

"Tuttle residence. Hello, this is Sadie."

"Hi, Sadie. This is Tim. Can I talk to either Randy or Todd?" I asked.

"You didn't call to talk to me?" Sadie said.

"What reason would I have for calling you?" I asked, confused.

"I thought maybe you got tired of boring Susie," she answered.

"Can you get Randy or Todd on the phone?" I almost begged. I didn't want to have this conversation with Sadie. Why did everything have to be so hard?

"Hold on," she said as I heard the phone clunk against something hard.

I stood patiently waiting for one of them to come to the phone. I waited five minutes. Finally I heard a voice.

"Hello? Hello?" a lady's voice said. "Is someone there?"

"Hi, this is Timmy. I was waiting for someone to come to the phone," I explained. This happened frequently with party lines.

"Hi, Timmy. This is Rebecca. I was going to call your mom," she said.

"I'll get her. Apparently I'm getting stood up, anyway."

"I'm sorry. You're not having a very good day," Miss Rebecca said.

"Mom! Phone!" I shouted.

"You don't have to shout. I'm only two rooms away," Mom scolded.

I went to my room and flopped onto my bed. Why did it seem like every girl hated me except Susie?

A few minutes later Mom came to my room to tell me that Randy was on the phone, wanting to talk to me. I hurried to the phone and said, "Hello?"

"Hey, what's up?"

"James Ernest wanted everyone to meet at Raven's house to continue our meeting."

"What time?" he asked.

"I guess after dinner. Maybe around three," I said.

"Hold on." Soon he was back and said, "Dad said he would take us up there. We'll pick you up then."

"Okay. Don't forget about Kenny. James Ernest and I were talking about asking if he wanted to be a member of the Wolf Pack. What do you think?"

"I'll talk to Todd and tell you later."

"You know Todd would want him in," I said.

"You're right. It's okay with me," Randy said. We hung up.

Around three-fifteen Mr. Tuttle drove up. The snow was still falling steadily and really mounting up. Two to three inches had already fallen. I saw Kenny in the car. I hurried out and jumped into the back seat with Purty and Kentucky.

"What are you boys up to this afternoon?" Mr. Tuttle asked as he was driving the car up the incline toward Oak Hills.

"We're doing homework together," Purty lied.

"Yeah. You have to come up with a better one than that." Mr. Tuttle laughed. "You don't even have any books with you."

"Oh, yeah," Purty realized. He didn't try to deepen the lie.

"Can you stop and pick up Susie?" I asked Mr. Tuttle.

"Sure. We have room. We can squeeze her in here."

Then Mr. Tuttle asked the awkward question, "Why didn't Sadie come since it seems like everyone is going?"

Kenny kept quiet. I didn't want to tell Mr. Tuttle that his daughter wasn't very well liked by any of us. Purty pretended he had dropped something on the floorboard and dipped below the top of the front seat. Randy looked at me and then said, "She must have been doing something."

I wondered in that moment if they liked their sister. I had never thought about it. I knew they realized what a jerk she could be and how stuck she was on herself, but maybe they knew her differently since they lived with her. They hardly ever talked about her.

I knew that all of us were different. All of us had something—some strangeness. I couldn't talk very well. James Ernest hadn't talked in seven years or so until recently and was very spooky the way he disappeared and appeared. Randy wasn't very outgoing. Purty was just strange. Kentucky definitely had a lot of weirdness going on. There was nothing wrong with Susie and Raven that I knew of. But we all still liked each other despite our differences. I figured it took all kinds of kinds.

Susie ran through the snow and jumped into the front seat with Mr. Tuttle and Randy, who had scooted over to the middle.

"Hi, guys. Thank you for picking me up, Mr. Tuttle," Susie said.

"You're welcome, young lady."

We pulled down the Washington's lane. We began piling out of the car and racing to the house. A snowball fight broke out on the way. I socked Purty right in his old kisser with a big snowball. Paybacks are rough, I thought. I was surprised when I saw Mr. Tuttle walking toward the house. Henry and Coal had come out onto their porch to watch the snowball fight and greet everyone.

I was watching Mr. Tuttle shake hands with Henry and not paying much attention to the snowballs flying all around, when I suddenly got plastered with two snowballs in the face. I gave up, jumped onto the porch, and hid behind Coal. I knew it was the cowardly way out, but that was okay with me.

"We better get into the house before we become a part of this fun," Henry said. "Please come on in and sit a spell, Forest. I don't believe you've been by to visit since we done moved in."

"No. I haven't had the privilege," Forest said. Of course Forest had bought the Washington family the farm because he had burned down their other house, trying to run them out of the county. Mr. Washington had saved Mr. Tuttle's youngest son, Billy, from the fire, and since then Mr. Tuttle had abandoned his thoughts of a 'white-only' county.

The inside of the house was clean, but none of the furniture was very new. The couch and chairs in the living room were threadbare. There wasn't a TV in the room. The kitchen table was old with mismatched chairs. The walls in the living room were wallpapered with what I thought was paper from the forties or so. Some of the rooms had been freshly painted, probably since they had moved in. I felt comfortable in the house, and Coal and Henry made sure to let us know that we were welcomed guests in their home.

Samantha, Henry Jr., and Mark Daniel, the youngest, came downstairs to say hello to everyone. They seemed excited that someone had come to their house to visit. Apparently they didn't get many visitors. I knew that Mom and Miss Rebecca visited Coal often, but probably not many other folks.

They soon ran back upstairs and left the seven of us around the kitchen table to finish our meeting. They all looked at me. I knew that most of them wanted to know about the cave.

I started by saying, "I found the cave opening when I almost fell into it. I thought the ground was giving way. I wanted to see what was inside, so I went back to the store and got a rope and a flashlight and climbed twenty feet down into the cave. I didn't have the strength to climb out. So I started looking for a way to escape."

I slowly realized that I was talking my way into a corner that I wouldn't be able to talk my way out of. How would I explain to them how I got out without telling them about the other cave? Then they would want to see the cave someday, and then they would see the Indian drawings. I had to think of something.

"You didn't see any clues when you were inside?" Purty asked.

"I wasn't looking for clues. I pretty much was only looking for a way out," I explained.

"He didn't search the entire cave, though," James Ernest said. "The clue could still be down there."

"Wait a minute," Purty said as he looked at the ceiling in deep thought.

I thought, Here it comes.

"How did you escape from the cave?" Purty continued.

I could see that Susie and James Ernest were staring at me, wondering how I was going to get out of my situation. The others were staring at me waiting for an answer. I wondered if I should go ahead and tell them about the Indian cave with the drawings. I trusted them. But I didn't know Tucky very well. Purty was likely to do or say anything without thinking. Maybe I couldn't trust him to keep a secret.

I was really surprised that this question hadn't been posed to me before now. I guessed that no one had thought about it in all the excitement with the Tattoo Man dying.

"I got my strength back and climbed back up the rope," I lied.

They all looked at me as though they didn't believe my lie.

"Wait a minute, Timmy. When you were in the cave with the Tattoo Man and you stabbed him in the foot, how did you get out of the cave that time?" Purty asked again.

"I climbed up the rope again while he was screaming and hopping around on one foot. That's how I was at the top when he tried climbing out when I threw the dirt and pebbles in his face and he shot at me," I lied again. I thought I had come up with a good story.

"He shot at you?" Tucky asked excitedly.

Kentucky had never heard the story of the Tattoo Man's death. I went on to tell him about the shot scaring the bats and the bats scaring the Tattoo Man and that he then fell to his death.

"I have a hard time believing you could climb up a twenty-foot rope," Purty said as he looked at me with a puzzled look on his face. I knew he thought I was lying. He was right.

"It's amazing what a person can do when they're scared for their life. I've heard some amazing stories about what a person can do when his adrenaline kicks in." James Ernest tried saving me.

"When are we going down into the cave and look for the clue?" Randy asked.

"Why not just wait until spring?" Raven asked.

"I agree with Raven," Susie said.

"That's why we don't allow girls in the Wolf Pack," Purty said.

I could see steam coming out of their ears. Finally Susie said, "You mean because girls are more sensible and not stupid and moronic like some idiotic boy they know?"

"You shouldn't talk about Timmy like that. You might hurt his feelings. He's sitting right there," Purty said, pointing at me.

Raven looked at the other three members of the Wolf Pack and said, "I can't believe you selected him over us." She was pointing at Purty's face.

"We can't believe it, either," James Ernest said, laughing. Tucky had been quiet the entire time, just taking it all in. He laughed at Purty being slammed.

When the laughter died down Randy said, "Why don't we plan on doing it next Saturday?"

"Okay," most everyone said.

"We still have the rope ladder we built," I said.

All the guys agreed. It seemed like we had a plan. I wasn't real sure about it. But I didn't say anything to discourage it. At least they weren't asking about my escape any longer.

19  The Key Kids

Mamaw stood at the top of the cliff outside of the three boulders that guarded the hole that led to the underground cave. She had tickets in her hand. I then saw a line of folks traveling an escalator up the hillside and lining up in front of Mamaw. Why hadn't I ever seen the escalator?

Mamaw yelled out, "Get your tickets here! Only four bits for the time of your life!"

I could see the excitement on the faces of the crowd of people that couldn't wait to hand over their four bits. Mamaw placed the cash in her money belt and then handed each payee a ticket, and she let them line up between two of the boulders.

I waited to see what the folks were lining up to see when an elevator popped out of the ground and scared me half to death. The elevator came straight out of the hole between the three boulders. A man and wife and their eight-year-old son got into the elevator when the doors slid open. I snuck into the elevator just as the door was closing.

"I can't wait. This is so exciting," the young boy said to his parents inside the elevator.

"Where are we going?" I asked.

They ignored me, not as though they were rude but like they couldn't see me standing next to them—like I was invisible.

The ride only took long enough for me to ask the question. The doors slid open again, and the family walked out into the cave. The stone floor had been polished, and there were chairs sitting all around the sides and pictures hung on the walls. I looked up to see that all of the bats were gone. There was a picture of me hanging on the wall. Beneath it was written,

"Explorer Tim Callahan—Discovered Caves and Indian Drawings in 1959 at the age of nine."

The family walked over to Papaw and handed him their tickets. One by one they jumped into the expanded opening and slid down the slinky tube and into the Indian drawing cave. I started to say something to Papaw, but he waved me on toward the opening and frowned at me.

I easily fit into the opening. Large Larry could have fit in the shiny, new opening. I let go of the installed handle and slid down into the cave. I expected to splash into the water, but instead I fell into a large container of plastic balls. I sank to the bottom and had to fight my way to the top. I looked around the cave at the new decor. A chandelier lit up the small cave. The rock benches had been replaced with movie cushioned seats.

I took a seat next to the young boy. A large, red curtain opened in front of us, and Susie was standing there in front of the Indian drawings. She spent the next ten minutes telling the story about how the cave was discovered and told us what each drawing represented.

I yelled out, "There were square rocks in here that the Indians put here! Right here where I'm sitting!"

They couldn't hear me.

She opened a door marked "Exit."

"Have a nice day and please come back," Susie said.

Susie acted as though she couldn't see me, either. The only person who acted as though he saw me was Papaw, and he didn't seem very happy about it.

Outside the door where the swimming hole used to be was a wooden shed that sold pictures of us sliding down the slinky tube. Souvenirs and postcards were for sale. James Ernest turned around and asked, "May I help you? We have anything you would want. Raccoon hats, key chains, photo albums, posters, and cave magnets for your fridge. How about a polished tobacco stick for your hiking excursions?"

"What are you doing? What happened? Why are you doing this?" I screamed.

"This is a state park now. Everything changed because you told everyone about the cave, and then they made the opening bigger. Everyone wants to see the drawings. We're going to be rich!" James Ernest smiled, and he had gold teeth filling his mouth.

I woke up in a sweat despite the cold.

It was cold! I mean really cold. No way did I want to untangle myself from the inside of my quilts to get up and go to the outhouse. I didn't want to get up to do anything. It had snowed almost every day the past week. Snow was everywhere. School was cancelled every day the whole week. I heard someone up putting coal in the stoves. I figured it was James Ernest. He took care of the fires during the nights that he was here.

I had to pee so badly I couldn't stand it. I saw that Coty was snuggled up in the indents on the top quilt when I poked my head out of my blankets. I got up and went to the window. I unlocked it and pulled up, trying to open it. It was frozen shut. I tried to break it loose by hitting the jams with my shoe. I was planning to pee out the window and then go back to bed. No such luck. I stuck my feet into my boots and hurried to the coat tree in the kitchen and grabbed my coat and threw it on. James Ernest watched with laughter.

I opened the back door and went out onto the porch and peed off the edge into the deep snow. Coty had followed me and made his way into the snow and turned a section yellow as I had done from the porch. He also left a present that I would have to pick up later. I'd wait until it was frozen. It is probably already frozen, I thought.

I rushed back into the house and sat on the couch with James Ernest. We had his blankets covering us. James Ernest had turned on the TV to the Saturday morning cartoons, and we watched Bugs Bunny outwit Elmer Fudd again.

"Are we still going down into the cave tomorrow?" I asked.

"I guess so. That was the plan," he answered.

"It's awfully cold out there," I told him.

"It'll warm up," he said as if it was May and the sun hadn't risen yet.

"Are you kidding? It's only supposed to get up to fourteen degrees tomorrow," I protested.

"Yeah, but it's only eight degrees now," he grinned.

"I'm worried about doing it," I said.

"You're worried about doing what?"

"I'm worried that once we get into the cave everyone is going to begin questioning me about my escape again. Plus, they may see the opening that I really did use to escape into the Indian cave," I explained.

"I promise we won't tell them about the Indian cave. But I think we have to look for the clue with them," James Ernest said.

"Why couldn't just me and you go down and look for it?" I asked.

"Because we're a pack, and we have to do things together so we can keep our trust in each other," he explained.

"I guess you're right," I said.

I was so relieved and glad to have James Ernest in my life. He was like a brother to me. We went back to watching Bugs just as he said, "What's up, Doc?"

Mamaw and Papaw had come to the store Thursday evening and Mamaw, and Mom made snow cream, which is ice cream made out of snow. Mom always told me and Janie that we couldn't make it until the second big snow of the year came. She figured the first snow cleaned all the pollutants out of the air, so the second snow was clean. Clean or not, it was really good.

Timmy and Janie beside the store

Mom came into the living room ten minutes later. "It's cold this morning," she said.

Mom came over and leaned over the back of the couch and kissed the top of my head. She rubbed James Ernest's head in greeting, and I saw him smile.

"You'd better get dressed in case we get early customers. We may get some crazy ice fishermen," Mom said and then laughed.

We would get ice fishermen every once in a while. Mud McCobb and Louis Lewis were the main ones who liked to ice fish. They were known to put up a tent on the lake and cut a hole in the bottom of the tent cloth where the ice hole was to fish and keep the wind off of them.

I got up during a commercial and got dressed quickly before Donald Duck was back in the next cartoon. The house was beginning to warm up as the coal stoves threw out their newly found heat. Mom went into the kitchen after saying she would make French toast for our breakfast. That sounded good. I loved French toast with lots of butter smothered in Log Cabin syrup.

After we ate breakfast James Ernest went to the phone and called Randy and Todd. He told them that the plans were still a 'go'. He also told him that we would walk up to Kenny's house to let him know since we hadn't seen him in a while. I heard him say 'okay' and then hang up.

"What did he say?" I asked.

"They said they were anxious, and Randy called for a Wolf Pack meeting this evening. He asked us to invite Kenny to come. He said something about replacing you in the Wolf Pack with Kenny." James Ernest laughed and punched me in the arm.

"Where are we going to have the meeting?" I asked.

"Their house at seven," James Ernest answered.

Mom came back into the living room and asked if I had seen her silver bracelet. The bracelet had a charm on it, and Mom wore it a lot.

"I haven't seen it lately," I answered.

"I remember laying it down at the sink on the back porch a couple of days ago, but now I can't find it anywhere," Mom said as she turned and walked toward her bedroom. She turned back around and said, "Also, we're missing a couple of spoons. Did you take them for some reason?"

We both said, "No," at the same time.

Janie came running into the room and jumped into my lap and then crawled under the blankets and began watching the cartoons.

Around eleven that morning the store door opened, and there stood Louis Lewis and Mud McCobb.

"We've come to slay fish!" Mud yelled out. "Get your sorry butt in here and take our money."

I got up and walked into the store and laughed at the two of them. I had never seen so many clothes on two people. "I'm guessing that you two want to do some ice fishing."

"It's a great day for it," Louis said.

"The ice is definitely frozen, if that's what you mean," I said.

"We need a dozen night crawlers and a package of chicken livers," Mud ordered.

I hurried to get the order. I added up the cost, and they paid me. "I won't be coming up to the lake to take your orders, by the way," I told them.

"What happened to full service around this establishment?" Mud asked.

"That's only for sane people," I teased. They laughed.

"We're going to put up the tent, if that's okay," Louis said.

"I would hope so. It's colder than a witch's house on the lake. Don't freeze up there. I may be up later to check on you," I said.

"You put up the tent while I get the poles ready," Mud said as he hit Louis in the arm.

"I'm not putting the tent up by myself," Louis argued.

"Okay then, you big baby, I'll help you. Grab the tent," Mud said as he closed the door behind them.

I walked into the kitchen and told Mom that James Ernest and I needed to walk down to Kenny's house.

She said, "Your Papaw is going to be here in a little while to watch the store. Please wait until he gets here."

As the words were leaving her mouth I heard Papaw say hello to Janie and James Ernest. James Ernest, Coty, and I were soon on the road walking toward Wrigley. I figured Coty needed some exercise. We hadn't been to Kenny's house before. Therefore, we hadn't met any of his family. I wondered what they were like.

I had on my winter coat, gloves, a stocking hat, and a large, red scarf around my neck and face. I left an opening so I could see.

"Have you met any of Tucky's family?" I asked.

"No. I've saw some of them on the porch or in the yard when the school bus passes their house. He has a lot of sisters."

As we walked I began to get a little warmer or accustomed to the cold. I was able to let my scarf fall around my neck. Suddenly I heard a, "Caw, caw," and then felt Bo land on my shoulder. I hadn't seen Bo for a while, and I had been worried about him.

"Hi, Bo," I said as he began to bob his head up and down.

Bo began poking his beak at my metal buttons that were on the collar of my coat. They seemed to really interest him. Coty came out of the woods and saw Bo and took off again. Bo saw him and flew off my shoulder and was chasing Coty back into the woods. It wasn't long before we came to the rock tunnel that the road passed through. It was one of Morgan County's landmarks. Licking Creek ran on the west side of the road, and it also went through a tunnel that most folks couldn't see for all the overgrowth on the side of the road. A lot of people called the area "The Twin Tunnels." Kenny's house wasn't far from the tunnels.

The Tunnel

After going through the tunnel I saw Bo flying above the tunnel. He was cawing as he flew. He soon came back and landed on me again. I saw Coty lagging behind us. He didn't seem to want anything to do with us as long as Bo was around. We rounded a bend in the road, and we could see the house standing before us on the right side of the road. There was laundry frozen on the clotheslines in the yard. An old wringer washer stood on the front porch next to wooden milk boxes used as chairs. A ripped up flowered sofa was propped up on rocks against the wall under the front window.

Two cats hissed at us as we walked up the steps of the porch. Bo flew into a tree and perched on a high limb. Coty didn't like the hissing cats, and he took off toward the creek. I saw an old hound dog hunkered down inside a doghouse at the side of the house. He looked at us but didn't move. I knocked on the door and heard a lot of commotion from inside the house. The door opened and a fairly pretty girl about my age stood before me. She had sandy colored long hair and a twinkle in her eyes. She was cute.

I forgot to say anything as she stood there. James Ernest spoke, "Is Kenny here? We're two of his friends."

"You must be James Ernest and Timmy," she said and smiled. "I'm Rock, Kenny's twin sister."

Kenny's twin sister—why hadn't he ever said anything about having a twin sister? And did she say her name was Rock, Rock Key.

"Come on in," she told us.

Kenny was sitting on the floor playing jacks with three younger kids. The room was full of kids. All eight wore old, worn-out, bibbed overalls—even the girls. There wasn't much space left for us to enter the room.

"Hey guys," Kenny greeted us without getting off the floor.

"We needed to talk to you about this afternoon," I said as a tall lady with hair down to her waist walked in from what I supposed was the kitchen area.

"Well, we have company. Kenny, did they say they came to see you?" she said.

"Yes'um," Kenny answered.

"Then why don't you get up and introduce everyone?" his mom told him.

Kenny quickly rose from the floor and began making introductions, "James Ernest, Timmy, this is my oldest brother, Monk. Everyone calls him Big Monkey. He's seventeen and my oldest brother. Chuck is my next oldest brother. He's sixteen."

He pointed to a girl in the corner with bright red hair and freckles and said, "Her name is Sugar Cook. We call her Cookie, or Sugar Cookie. She's fourteen."

Sugar Cook! I thought, What kind of name is Sugar Cook? I couldn't but think what a strange family they were. Of course, who was I to judge? I walked into their yard with a black crow named Bo on my shoulder.

Kenny continued since he had a lot more to go, "You've met Rocky, my twin sister. This is my ten-year-old sister, Chero. You can call her Cherokee. Everyone else does."

He then pointed to the floor and said, "This is my youngest sister, Adore. She's seven, and the little pipsqueak next to her is our youngest brother Luck. We all call him Lucky. He's four."

"We named him Luck because we weren't planning on having any more children after the first seven. So he's lucky to be here, and we're lucky to have him," Kenny's mom told us.

Lucky just smiled at us.

None of the kids had shoes on. They all seemed friendly and happy.

"It's a pleasure to meet you boys. My name is Winona. Kenny has mentioned you often," she said.

"We're very happy to meet all of you guys," James Ernest told them.

Chero asked, "Did you have a big, black bird on your shoulder when you walked into the yard?"

I was surprised. I didn't realize they had seen us coming.

"Yes, his name is Bo," I told them. "He's a crow."

"Is that your dog that was with you?" Cherokee asked.

"Sure is. His name's Coty. I named him that because he's part coyote," I explained. "But he's real friendly."

The kids became more excited when I mentioned Coty being part coyote.

"We had a pet groundhog once," Lucky told us.

Everyone laughed.

"He wasn't really a pet, Lucky. He just lived near us," Winona corrected.

"He did until Buck shot him, and we ate him for supper," Big Monk added.

"He was plumb good eatin'," Chuck added.

"They taste better when you shoot them instead of scraping them off the road," Big Monk told us.

I looked at James Ernest. His face was turning green.

"I've never tried eating groundhog," I said.

"Tastes like chicken," Sugar Cook told us. She then added, "If you fix it right."

I knew that this had to be one of my dreams. I was hoping to wake up soon.

"Possum tastes more like squirrel than chicken," Chuck added so we would know.

"Have you ever ate possum?" little Lucky asked us.

I was beginning to think that Lucky's name wasn't so appropriate.

"No," I answered as my stomach began to churn. James Ernest was turning greener.

"It was nice to meet everyone. But I think we had better be going," I said. James Ernest slowly nodded his head in agreement. Nodding his head too much might bring up something.

I turned toward the door when Kenny asked, "We still on for tomorrow?"

We had forgotten why we came in our haste to leave.

"That's why we came, to remind you. But also to tell you there's a Wolf Pack meeting tonight at seven at the Tuttle house. We would like for you to come," I told him.

"See you there," Kenny said.

"You want us to pick you up?" I asked.

"Thanks, but I'll be there," Tucky said

James Ernest and I hurried out to the yard. Bo flew back onto my shoulder, and Coty ran up to meet us. I looked around to see all eight kids looking out the windows as we walked away. The cold air seemed to help James Ernest's face turn back to its normal color.

"Well, that was interesting," I finally said as we walked under the tunnel.

"They sure have a lot of kids," James Ernest said.

"The girls were pretty," I said.

"You noticed that, huh?" James Ernest teased.

"As if you didn't."

"You should tell Susie how pretty they were," he suggested.

"I think I'll keep it between you and me," I told him.

"They sure have strange names. Sugar Cook Key, Rock Key, Chero Key, and, what was the other one's name?"

"Adore Key," I answered.

"Is that supposed to be like A Door Key?" James Ernest asked.

"I don't know. I guess so. It's by far the strangest name," I said.

"Maybe, but Monk Key is not far behind," James Ernest said, and we both laughed.

"He kind of looked like a big monkey," I said.

We walked on for a few minutes, and then James Ernest asked me, "Would you eat possum if your mom or Mamaw cooked it and put it on the table?"

"I think that's what she said we're having this evening," I grinned.

20 POSSUM SPAGHETTI, COOKIES, AND MOHAWKS

Mom had spaghetti and meat sauce for dinner that evening. Janie was slurping the long strings into her mouth.

"It's really good tonight, Mom," I said.

"Yes, it's really good," James Ernest echoed.

"It's unusually good tonight. Did you do anything different to it?" I asked.

"Instead of hamburger I used possum meat," Mom said with a straight face. "Your papaw killed it this morning."

James Ernest laid his fork down on the table and stared at his plate of spaghetti. He started coughing, and then the coughing turned to gagging.

Mom, Janie, and I burst into laughter. We got him.

James Ernest looked at the three of us. His face had turned red, and he said, "That just ain't right. You shouldn't treat a guy like that."

Papaw and Mamaw came to the store later. Papaw said he would drive us up to the Tuttle house for our meeting.

We piled into the cab of the pickup when it was time to go. Papaw pulled around the Tuttle's circular gravel drive and let us out at the front door.

James Ernest opened the door and started to get out when Papaw said, "Enjoy yourselves. I heard Loraine is baking possum cookies for you."

"Your family is not right. I'll save you some," James Ernest said as Papaw and I laughed.

I was still laughing when Sadie answered the door.

"Hi, Sadie," I politely said.

"Hello, James Ernest," she replied, ignoring me.

Kentucky was already there and sitting next to Francis on the couch. He was barefooted.

Purty came into the living room and said, "Hey, guys. How the heck is everyone? I was in the kitchen helping Mom bake cookies."

I snuck a peek at James Ernest. He ignored me.

"You were in there eating cookie dough is what you were doing," Francis said.

Everyone knew she was right. I hoped he wasn't eating raw possum.

After all the greetings were over, Randy led us upstairs to his and Purty's room. They had a bunk bed against the back wall. A large, wooden desk covered with junk was against another wall. A dresser was cockeyed against another wall. Clothes were hanging out of each drawer. Clothes were on the floor and on the beds. Odds and ends cluttered the rest of the room.

"Mom made us clean our room, or she wasn't going to let you guys come over," Purty told us. I had a hard time believing the room had been cleaned in the last year. It looked like an atomic bomb had gone off in the room.

Randy called our Wolf Pack meeting to order. The four of us gathered in a circle and did our chant, "Wolf Pack, Wolf Pack, Wolf Pack, Wolf Pack, forever the Pack!" Then we howled to the light on the ceiling.

Tucky sat on the floor, watching us and grinning. I wondered what he was thinking.

"We have a lot of business to take care of tonight. The first thing we need to do is welcome Kenny Tuck Key to our meeting of the Wolf Pack, and we would like to ask you if you would like to be the sixth member of the pack," Randy said, opening the meeting, and we all looked toward Tucky.

"I'm not all that good at math, but wouldn't I be number five?" Tucky asked.

"We forgot to tell you that Coty is a member of the Pack," I explained.

"We only allow boys in the club, and Coty was always going on our adventures anyway, so he became a member," James Ernest explained further.

"Well, what do you say?" Purty said excitedly.

"Okay, by me," Tucky answered.

"You have one thing you have to do to become a full-fledged member," Purty said.

Randy continued, "You have to share a secret with us that no one else knows about. It will then become something that the Wolf Pack will carry to our graves, sealing our trust and bond with each other."

The room was quiet as we waited for Tucky to tell us his most intimate secret.

"I kissed a girl at school during recess the last day I was there before all the snow came," Tucky shared.

"Where did you kiss her?" Purty asked.

"On her mouth," he answered with a big smile.

"No, I mean where were you at?" Purty tried again.

"In the outhouse," Tucky answered.

"Yikes!" "Gross!" "Yuck!" and other strange sounds came from each of us as we imagined kissing a girl in the smelly outhouse.

"Who was the girl that you kissed?" I asked. I needed to know what girl would go into the outhouse to kiss a boy.

"Yeah, who did you kiss?" Purty was standing with excitement.

"Bernice," he answered.

We all were stunned. Purty collapsed onto the floor in a heap. I sat there with my mouth agape. Randy was rolling on the floor, shaking his body as if he was trying to shake the image from his head.

The thought of Bernice "the skunk," with her skunk-looking hair, and Tucky, with his wild mohawk and mullet hair, kissing in the outhouse was more than we could stand. I had thought eating possum was bad. Eating possum would be a delicacy compared to kissing Bernice in a one-hole, poop-smelling outhouse. This was a secret that wouldn't be hard to keep at all. I not only never wanted to talk about it again; I never wanted the image to enter my brain again. It would be an easy secret to keep.

After we had enough time to get over the initial shock of his secret James Ernest asked him, "Why? I mean, why in the outhouse?"

"I needed to go. So when I got to the outhouse someone was already in there. The door opened, and she grabbed me

209

by my neck and pulled me inside. She then commanded, 'Kiss me.' So I did."

"I'm going to have to be a lot more careful when I go the outhouse," I told the Wolf Pack.

We talked for another ten minutes about Bernice and the kiss.

"One of the other pacts we made is that we will never use tobacco, smoking, or chewing," Randy told Tucky.

I quickly wondered if this would be a problem. I knew his old man chewed tobacco, and one of his brothers was chewing in the living room the day we visited. I had seen a spittoon in the room.

"No problem. I don't like it. I've tried both. Just leaves a bad taste in my mouth," Tucky said.

"I think that's everything. Everyone who agrees to make Kenny Tuck Key the sixth member of the Wolf Pack, raise your arm," Randy directed.

We all did, and Kentucky became a member of the Wolf Pack. Finally, the main reason for the meeting was brought up.

Randy asked, "Another issue is, should we let Susie and Raven look for the clue with us?"

"I don't think we should let girls in on our adventures," Purty said.

"That's why you don't have a girlfriend," I said.

"I do, too. Rhonda," Purty shot back. "Remember the kiss?" Purty added.

"Do you consider Bernice your girlfriend?" I asked Tucky.

"No," he answered.

"Just because you've kissed a girl doesn't mean she's your girlfriend," James Ernest added.

"Guys, we haven't answered the question." Randy tried to regain control over the meeting.

"Susie and Raven have been on this adventure since the beginning. It wouldn't be right to not let them continue now," James Ernest said.

"It should be Wolf Pack members only," Purty argued.

"Well, it's not going to be that way," I said back.

"I think we should vote on it," Purty said.

"You need a unanimous vote, and I'm voting against it. You can take all the votes you want," I said as I was getting upset.

"Why do we need a unanimous vote?" Tucky asked.

Randy explained to him our club rules and told him that we felt if someone is strongly opposed to something then we shouldn't do it.

"Okay," Tucky agreed.

"I think it's pretty lousy. We'll have to share our treasure with the girls," Purty stated.

"Is that all you're worried about? There is no treasure yet, and there may not ever be a treasure. You're acting just like the man who shot the two men in the cave," I said.

"Okay. Okay. I'm sorry. So, what now?" Purty repeated.

"I guess we go on with our plans tomorrow," Randy said.

Later, Mrs. Tuttle knocked on the door. When Randy opened the door she was standing there with a plate full of oatmeal cookies. Mrs. Tuttle looked around the room and said, "Thank you, boys, for cleaning up your room. It looks nice."

I would have been grounded for a week if my room ever looked like their room looked at that moment. I couldn't even imagine what it had looked like before they cleaned it.

After the oatmeal cookies had been passed around and Mrs. Tuttle had left the room, Randy said, "I like your haircut, Tucky."

"Yeah, me too. I'd like to get my hair cut like that," Purty jumped in.

At that point I was thinking how differently people look at things. I looked over at Tucky's head. The mohawk was standing one inch tall to the back of his head, and then hair began falling into a mullet that went down to his shoulders. It just wasn't right.

"I have an idea," Randy began.

I didn't like where it was going. I tried to eat a cookie. I would rather die than do what Randy was going to suggest.

"Why doesn't everyone in the club get a haircut like Tucky's?"

I knew it! I knew what Randy was going to say. Again, I was going to have to vote no against the club. Pretty soon I wouldn't be in the club. I wondered if the club could vote you out if you voted 'no' too many times. I wondered if I got to vote when they voted to throw me out of the club.

"It would be a way of welcoming him into the club," Randy continued.

What's wrong with a handshake, a pat on the back, or saying, "We welcome you to the club?"

James Ernest began to speak. I knew that James Ernest would be the voice of reason. He would tell them how silly and idiotic the idea was. But he would do it in a way that wouldn't hurt their feelings. He was good at that.

"I like the idea," James Ernest said.

What! Was I dreaming? This had to be one of my stupid dreams. My dumbest dream yet.

"But since we don't have hair long enough for the mullet, what if we all get a full mohawk? Tucky would have to cut his mullet off, and we would have our hair cut into a mohawk. That way we'd all look alike," James Ernest said.

I was right. James Ernest was the voice of reason. I actually liked the Mohawk and had always wanted to get one. But no way was I including a mullet in the back.

"I like the mullet," Purty argued.

"It's a good compromise," Randy agreed. "That way we all would have to cut some of our hair off."

We all looked at Tucky. He said, "I'm willing. When are we going to do this?"

"We can do it right now. We've got some electric clippers we can use," Randy offered.

"We need to take a vote," I said quickly.

"Okay. All in favor of everyone getting mohawks, raise your hand," Randy said.

Randy and Purty and Tucky's hands shot up into the air. I waited to see what James Ernest was going to do. I was trying to impose my will toward his hands so they would stay below his waist by staring at them. It did me no good. Slowly his hand began to rise, condemning me to a sentence of days of explaining and laughter, and a mom and girlfriend who both most probably wouldn't be too happy with me.

When his hand finally reached above his shoulder, all heads turned toward me. I shot my hand up into the air. There was no use prolonging the outcome that I knew I would succumb to. I might as well make it seem like I was all for it.

"I'll go get the clippers," Randy said excitedly. Purty followed him.

Now? We are going to do this now? We were going to get a mohawk in the middle of one the coldest winters in Kentucky's history? I'd be wearing a stocking hat all winter. Maybe I could leave it on all the time, and Mom wouldn't even notice the mohawk. Maybe I could borrow Purty's raccoon hat.

It wasn't but a minute before Randy was back with the clippers. Purty came back into the room with a towel for our shoulders, and a sheet to spread under us to catch the hair. I guess he didn't want to mess up his room. Sarcasm felt good at that point even if I kept it to myself. Randy pulled the desk chair over to the sheet and placed it in the middle.

"Who's first?" he asked. Purty leaped into the chair. It creaked.

"Can you cut hair?" I asked. I was thinking "Razor" McCall, the local barber, might do a better job.

"I cut all of my family's hair all the time. I enjoy it," he said. I never imagined Randy being a hairdresser.

Randy placed the towel on Purty's shoulders and then plugged in the hair clippers. He began by removing the hair around Purty's ears and the sides of his head. Purty looked like a monk with only the top of his head covered with hair. James Ernest, Tucky, and I were laughing so hard it hurt.

"Maybe this was a bad idea," James Ernest was finally able to say between his laughter. "I think I change my vote," he teased.

I definitely wanted to change my vote. I wasn't sure being in the Wolf Pack was worth the agony I was going to have to endure.

214

"His head looks like a weird acorn," I said.

"How wide do you want your Mohawk to be?" Randy asked Purty.

"The same as Kentucky's," Purty answered. I looked at Tucky's Mohawk. The Mohawk part was around two inches wide. Randy combed Purty's hair to the right.

"Okay," Randy said as he began to cut the left side of the Mohawk.

"Does it look straight?" Randy asked as he finished the first side. All four of us stood in front of Purty, eyeing the worst looking straight line I'd ever laid eyes on.

"Not very straight," James Ernest proclaimed.

"Hey, this is my head you're talking about," Purty complained.

"It's hard to cut a straight line on a curved head," Randy explained.

"I guess it would be," I said.

"I'll get better as we go," Randy said. "Oops."

"What do mean, oops?" Purty said.

"I can fix it," Randy assured him.

"I'll go last," I volunteered.

"Who's going to cut your mohawk?" Tucky asked Randy.

"Whoever thinks they can."

Randy tried to straighten the line and the 'oops' the best he could. Then he combed Purty's hair to the left and cut the other side. It was a bit better. He then cut the hair to the correct length using scissors. It looked okay for a first try, except it didn't look like it was centered on his head. Randy took the towel from his shoulder and shook the hair off. Purty went to the mirror over the dresser and looked at his Mohawk. He turned around with a big grin on his face. He must have been as blind as Uncle Morton. At least Uncle Morton wouldn't make fun of my haircut.

"I like it. You done good, Randy. How do you get your hair to stand up so straight?" Purty asked Tucky.

"I use hog lard," Tucky answered.

We all cracked up at the look on Purty's face.

"I think we have some Brylcreem we can use, Purty," Randy said.

"There's nothing wrong with hog lard. We use it for a lot of things," Tucky said.

James Ernest jumped into the chair next, and Randy did a better job on him. He decided to leave the top longer. He went for two inches. As Randy was cutting Tucky's mullet off and lengthening his Mohawk down the back of his head, James Ernest was putting Brylcreem into his hair and spiking his Mohawk to a point. I thought it was really cool looking.

I was hoping not to be grounded again for getting a mohawk without my Mom's permission. But I couldn't back out now. I took the chair and told Randy to make my Mohawk fourteen inches wide. I figured that might go from ear to ear. Randy paid no attention and began cutting my hair off. I finally settled on three inches wide and an inch high. I jumped out of the chair and went to the mirror when Randy told me he was done. I looked in the mirror and was actually very happy with the way it looked. I thought it was really neat looking.

The only club member left to do was Randy. Coty was going to be spared. Purty volunteered to do the cutting. James Ernest saved him by saying that he would also do it. Randy went with James Ernest. James Ernest went slow but did a very good job. Randy decided to go with the same cut that James Ernest got.

When Randy's Mohawk was done and he had put the Brylcreem in his hair, we all stood before the mirror and admired what we had done. We looked like a band of Indians ready to go on the warpath. All we needed was some war paint.

Purty went to the door and cracked it open and yelled out that we had something to show them. "Everyone needs to come to the living room and close your eyes and then let us know when you're ready."

"What is this all about?" Loraine said as she neared the room. Purty slammed the door shut. "Please, just do it."

"Okay. But you better not pull any pranks, and you had better have some clothes on—not like the other time you did this."

We all looked at Purty. He smiled.

"Okay. We all have our eyes closed and ready," Forest announced.

Purty opened the door, and we filed into the living room and stood in a straight line in front of the family. "On three, you can open your eyes. One, two, three!"

The family opened their eyes. The reactions that we saw were all over the place. Sadie began laughing. Francis looked surprised. Eight-year-old Billy yelled out that he wanted a Mohawk, too. Four-year-old Trudy laughed. Loraine looked like she might faint. It was the first time I had seen her speechless. Forest's look took on a tone of disappointment but not all that surprised.

"You look cuter," Sadie told Tucky. His face turned red.

"I want a mohawk like Randy and James Ernest have, Mom," Billy screamed out.

"We'll talk about it," was all Loraine could say.

We determined that we would meet the next day at two in the afternoon to climb down into the cave to look for the clue. Forest said he would like to drive us home, and he wanted all the boys to go along. He had Loraine call the store to tell my family to line up in the living room and wait.

When Forest pulled into the lot I saw that Clayton's pickup was there. I wondered what Susie would say about my mohawk. I wondered what my mom would say.

Forest walked through the door first and told everyone to close their eyes. We went in and stood before them. It felt like we were lining up for our execution. Before Forest told them they could look, Delma screamed out, "What a bunch of goofballs!"

Everyone then opened their eyes to see our new hairstyles. The expressions were from frowns to laughter. The twins were laughing and pointing at us. Papaw and Clayton were staring with open mouths. Mom looked like she was going into shock. Monie smiled and shook her head in what I thought what disbelief. I noticed that Susie and Brenda weren't there. I was somewhat glad.

"You boys somehow always surprise me," Clayton said.

"Apparently Kenny is now part of the Wolf Pack," Mom said. Kenny shook his head 'yes' and smiled. "I can't believe you boys did this."

Mamaw was the one who surprised me. She sat there with no real shocked look on her face or disbelief in her eyes. She finally said, "I like the haircuts. I don't see anything wrong with the Mohawks. You're all good boys."

We smiled big, wide smiles. That's why I loved Mamaw so much. She always thought I was a good boy. And I wanted to be because of that. I didn't want to let her down. I could always count on Mamaw to love me when others wanted to throw me into a hole and fill it up.

Papaw said, "Well, the good thing is that hair will always grow back. It's not like they have to wear their hair like that forever." I wasn't sure if that was an okay or a put-down.

Monie, Mom, and Mamaw got up and headed for the kitchen. I heard Monie say, "I'm glad I have all girls."

Delma cried out, "They do something that stupid, and that's all you adults are going to do about it!"

Thelma added, "They should be whipped, or grounded, or punished, or made to cut it all off…"

Monie then said, "Maybe I shouldn't have had kids at all, or at least stopped at two."

"That is so mean," Delma said.

Thelma was still rattling off what the adults should do to us.

Donna (Susie), Delma on Brenda's lap and Thelma, 1957

21 THE MAP

Papaw & Mamaw (Martin & Cora Collins) inside store

SATURDAY, FEBRUARY 3

Papaw was at the store early Saturday morning. It was snowing again. Papaw said it was the worst winter for snow that he could remember. Snow was piled up everywhere.

Mud and Louis had some success ice fishing the day before. They said they had fun and caught four catfish and a few bluegills.

I woke up that morning with a cold head. James Ernest said he didn't feel good and slipped into my bed to get more

221

sleep. I slipped a stocking hat over my mohawk haircut and went into the store to help Papaw.

"I always wanted a mohawk when I was a kid," Papaw said.

"Really?"

"Yep. Never did it, though. I envy you guys," Papaw said.

"Why?"

"You're making the most out of your youth. You're not wasting it. You're having the time of your life. You'll grow old and remember these years for the rest of your life. You'll have tales to tell your children and grandchildren. You guys certainly aren't boring," Papaw said.

"No. I guess we're not," I said. I had never really thought about what Papaw told me. I felt pride that Papaw envied me. It was strange—because I envied him. I loved everything about my Mamaw and Papaw. They loved me. They were kind to me. They cared about me. They liked spending time with me. They weren't afraid to discipline me. They made me want to be good. I wanted to earn their approval. What more could you ask from a person?

"So you aren't mad about me getting the mohawk?" I asked.

"Heaven's no. I don't think anyone is mad," Papaw said.

"You don't think Mom is mad at me?" I asked.

"No. I don't think so. She may be a little disappointed that you didn't ask first," Papaw said.

"Do you think she would have said I could get a mohawk if I had asked?"

"Probably not. But let me tell you a secret." Papaw walked over next to me and whispered, "Adults don't always do the right thing. Sometimes we say 'no' too fast. We should let kids make mistakes, make decisions. It's a way to let them grow and also to give them confidence and let them know that their thoughts are important. I see a lot of parents automatically say 'no' to children when they didn't even take time to consider the question. There's nothing wrong with you having a mohawk. But most parents would have quickly said 'no'. I guess it's somehow stuck in them."

That was one of the reasons why I loved Papaw. How many other men would tell a kid that adults didn't always know what was best, or that they were sometimes wrong?

"Thanks Papaw," I said. "Oh, by the way, you should probably stock up on some Brylcreem."

Papaw laughed as I walked away toward the kitchen.

Mom was frying eggs and bacon when I walked into the kitchen. "Why do you have on that hat?" Mom asked.

"My head is cold," I answered.

"You look better with the hat on," Mom said.

"That wasn't very nice," I told her.

Mom laughed and said, "I was just kidding. It was such a shock last night to see all five of you with mohawks. Kenny looked a lot better, getting rid of all that hair that hung down in the back."

"Probably," I said.

"There's no 'probably' about it," Mom said.

I began telling Mom about all of Kenny's brothers and sisters and their names. Papaw came into the kitchen when he heard us laughing. We told him about the names.

"Her name is Sugar Cook Key? I don't believe you," Papaw said.

"I promise. That's her real name," I said. "I would rather have that name than Monk Key."

"One of them is named Monkey?" Papaw said.

"The oldest son," I confirmed.

"And I gave that family credit at the store," Mom said as she shook her head.

James Ernest finally rolled out of bed around noon, saying he felt a little better. Mom thought maybe he was coming down with the flu or a cold. She told him he should stay in bed and rest.

"I can't. We have a Wolf Pack adventure this afternoon. I'll be fine," James Ernest told Mom.

Clayton drove up with Susie and Raven around one-thirty.

James Ernest and I were standing in the store when they walked in. I had taken my hat off once I had warmed up. The girls stopped and smiled at us. I was anxious to hear what Susie would say about the mohawks.

"I like it," she said. "It's pretty cool."

"I do, too," Raven said as she walked over to James Ernest to get a better look at his taller mohawk. "I should get one," she added.

"Why don't we all get one?" Clayton said as Mom entered the store while wiping her hands on her apron.

"That's a good idea. We could change the name of the county from Morgan to Mohawk County," Mom laughed.

Randy, Purty, and Kenny walked into the store followed by Forest and Loraine. Loraine began, "I ain't ever seen anything like these boys. All five of them getting mohawk haircuts. What will they do next?" Of course she wasn't really wanting an answer because she never took a breath before she continued. "Betty, what do you think of it? Have you ever seen such a thing? They look just like a band of Indians. It's a good thing we're living in this century. They went and did this without us knowing it. I hope you don't blame us because it happened at our house. Forest and I had no idea what they were up to. I am so sorry. Martin, have you ever?"

Mom grabbed Loraine's arm and led her into the kitchen, and I heard her say, "We don't blame you and Forest. We're okay with the mohawks. They look like a nice band of Indians."

We all burst into laughter.

"What are you Indians up to today?" Papaw asked.

"We're doing some exploring," Randy answered.

"Which way are you going? In case we need to send out a search party," Clayton asked.

"We're going to be up around the swimming hole," James Ernest answered.

"You don't plan on going swimming, do you?" Forest laughed.

"No swimming," Susie said.

Papaw then looked at Tucky and said, "Tell me what your brothers' and sisters' names are, Kenny."

Kenny smiled.

"Papaw doesn't believe me," I said.

"My brothers are Chuck Key, Luck Key, and Monk Key," Kenny began. The men laughed and shook their heads side to side.

"My sisters are Chero Key, Rock Key, Adore Key, and Sugar Cook Key. Of course, my name is Ken Tuck Key," Tucky finished.

"I don't know if it's any stranger than Delma and Thelma," Clayton said.

"You better not let them hear you say that." Papaw laughed.

"And then we have our family with Coal and Raven," Raven said.

"This county is getting a little weirder all the time," Forest said.

We all agreed.

"We like it like that," James Ernest said. We all agreed again.

The seven of us headed toward the lake. James Ernest had found the rope ladder and placed it on the back porch. He and Randy carried it. I carried a long rope that James Ernest wanted to bring in case we needed it. I had my flashlight, and others had brought their own. Randy took a lantern.

We all were bundled up with winter coats and gloves and hats. I had on my high-top hiking boots. Kenny had on the least—a fairly light jacket, no hat or gloves, and he wore old tennis shoes in the deep snow. Mom tried to get him to put on one of my spare hats and a pair of gloves. But he told her he was fine. James Ernest told me he was feeling better after sleeping the whole morning.

The trail around the lake was covered with deep snow and we had to be careful about not slipping down the banks onto the ice-covered lake. I mentioned to everyone that we should have walked across the lake. They agreed. I saw the spot where Mud and Louis had fished the day before. The hole had refrozen and was being covered by the falling snow. The lake was beautiful with the heavy snow-covered limbs sagging toward the frozen lake. The green pines contrasted against the pure white snow.

I saw two cardinals flying from tree to tree. The bright red showed up against the winter scenes. I knew that a prettier picture had never been taken. The slanted rock was nowhere to be seen. It was covered with two feet of snow. We began the walk along the stream to the swimming hole.

When we arrived at the hill that we would have to climb to get to the cave entrance, we realized that climbing it might be tough with all the snow covering it. James Ernest said that was why we brought the rope. He had me climb the hill and tie the rope to a tree so that everyone else could use it to help them climb up the hill. I made it up the hill within a couple of minutes and tied the rope to a cottonwood tree.

Raven came up next by using the rope to help her. Purty said he didn't need the rope. After struggling to get half-way up, he slipped and slid all the way back down. Susie came up the rope next. Purty began his second attempt up the hill. Susie, Raven, and I watched him slide down head first that time. Kenny scampered up the hill, using the rope in no time flat. Randy came next as Purty was making his third try. James Ernest followed Randy and we all yelled at Purty to grab the rope. He rolled down the hill on that attempt.

He grabbed the rope, and we had to pretty much pull him up the hill because he said he was tired from all the work he had done.

We walked over to the three boulders that stood guarding the cave entrance. I went over to the hole and cleared the fallen limbs and leaves and snow from the entrance to show everyone where the entrance was. Tucky had never seen it before. Raven also said she had never seen it. We tied the rope ladder off to the same tree that I had tied my rope off to the first day I went into the hole.

"Who wants to go down first?" I asked.

"Why don't you go down first? You have the most experience at climbing it without anyone holding the bottom," James Ernest said.

He was right. It seemed like I always went first and always had the hardest time climbing down. They said it was because I was the lightest and would have less trouble, but I thought they were using me as their guinea pig. I didn't really mind. Each member of the Wolf Pack needed to feel needed. This was why they needed me.

"I'll go ahead and light the lantern, and we can lower it to you," Randy said.

Tucky said, "I'll go get the rope." He turned and ran excitedly.

I took off my bulky winter coat. I had on a Reds sweatshirt under it, which I thought would be all I'd need in the cave. I crawled backward to the hole and slowly placed my legs over the rim of the hole until I could place my feet onto the rungs of the ladder. I made it down the ladder within a couple of minutes, and Randy lowered the lantern with the rope Tucky had gone back to get. I removed the snow and limbs from the floor of the cave below the opening. Susie said she would go down next. I held the ladder tight so it wouldn't swing as she climbed down.

When she placed her feet on the stone floor she turned and gave me a big hug and then kissed me on the lips. "This is so exciting," she said. I was suddenly excited, myself.

Tucky came down the rope ladder next. He seemed just as excited when he reached the bottom, except he didn't kiss anyone. Raven had no problem climbing down next. It was Purty's turn, and of course he bumbled and fumbled his way down the ladder. He complained that we weren't holding the ladder tight enough. His excess weight made it harder to hold it still.

James Ernest and Randy had no trouble making it to the bottom of the cave. Purty, James Ernest, and I had been in the cave in the fall of 1960. Randy had quit the Wolf Pack at that time over racism, so he had never been inside the cave.

After everyone had climbed down the ladder I said, "I don't think we'll find anything in here."

"How come?" Raven asked.

"I've searched this cave twice. Purty, James Ernest, and I searched it a little over a year ago." No one asked where Randy was.

"Yeah, but we weren't looking for a specific clue. We need to reach into all the crevices and crawl into all the little tunnels," Purty told everyone. "It has to be here. It has to be."

"Everyone split up and begin searching every square inch," Randy directed.

Susie and I went to the west side of the cave. It was the section that I hadn't searched before I had escaped from the cave. Randy search by himself, and Raven went with James. Tucky and Purty began searching under rocks and the crevices of the floor.

Susie and I found a small opening that headed back into the wall. We shined the flashlight into the hole but didn't see anything. The opening turned to the left. "I'll climb in and see where it goes," Susie said.

"You sure you don't want me to do it?" I asked.

"No, I want to do it. This is exciting," Susie said.

She put her hands and head into the opening and began crawling in. She had the flashlight in her right hand. I pushed on her feet to help her slide in. Her entire body was in the hole when she said that the hole stopped after it turned to the left. There were no clues or anything else in the hole. She had me pull on her feet to help her get out.

James Ernest had found the same tunnels that I had found before when I was trapped in the cave. He asked Kenny to crawl in to see if he could find anything. Tucky was as skinny as I was. He was a couple of inches taller than me, though.

As Tucky was getting ready to climb into the tunnel Raven asked him, "What did your parents say about your haircut?"

"They didn't even notice," he said. Maybe with eight kids it's harder to notice things or they figured it didn't really matter. If education didn't matter to them, I didn't figure their haircuts would matter much at all. Tucky didn't find anything in the two tunnels. We were shining the flashlights in every crevice we could find hoping the person had stuck it somewhere for safe-keeping.

We all ended up sitting on the large rock that I had rested on when I prayed. I told everyone that I searched the area where the Indian cave opening was. I didn't want them finding it and asking questions again. I had shown it to Susie. She couldn't believe I had fit my body inside it.

"I guess it's not here," Randy said dejectedly. "Either it never was here, somebody already found it, or we're overlooking it."

"I can't believe it," Purty complained. "So close to being rich."

"We never were close to being rich," Susie said.

"In my world I was," Purty said.

"In your world you're smart and good looking, also. And those aren't true, either," I said.

We laughed.

"You guys want to see something neat?" I said.

"Sure," Tucky said.

"Purty don't you dare scream," I said before shining my light on the ceiling, lighting up the bats that clung there. It looked like there were even more bats on the ceiling than the last time I had been in the cave. The room grew silent except for Purty's heavy breathing. I knew he might start screaming soon, so I dropped my light from the bats and onto the wall just below the bats. My mouth almost hit the floor.

"Guys, look at that," I whispered as if not wanting someone else to hear.

Six feet below the ceiling was a small hole. Two carved wooden sticks stuck out from the hole. I could see something light colored inside the hole.

"That's it!" Purty said in a muffled scream. "That has to be the clue."

The hole was approximately eleven feet above the stone floor. The next thing was figuring out how we could get up to it.

"If I stood on someone's shoulders I think I could reach it," Raven said. Raven was fairly tall, around five feet and seven inches, and she had long arms.

"Randy and I could get on our knees side by side, and you could put a foot on each of our shoulders. With two of us there would be less chance of you falling. We're about the same height. Then we could stand up and you're right, you should be able to reach it," James Ernest reasoned.

"Let's do it," Raven said. I felt the excitement return in the cave. Everyone had the feeling that this thing we could barely see was what we had come looking for.

Randy and James Ernest got down on their knees facing the wall right under the opening we were looking at. Raven started to climb onto their shoulders when I suggested, "You may want to take off your shoes."

She took them off. "You guys stand right behind us in case she falls off backward, okay?" James Ernest said. I knew that James Ernest really cared a lot for Raven and didn't want to see her get hurt.

We helped Raven as she stepped up onto their shoulders. She was able to balance herself by leaning forward and placing her hands against the wall. The two guys then slowly began to stand. They tried to rise at the same speed by looking at each other sideways. Raven was thin and, therefore, not that heavy. Susie took the flashlight from me and shined it up to the hole so Raven could see it. She was able to snatch the contents out with her fingertips.

"I got it. Go back down slowly," she directed.

"Throw it down to me," Purty said.

"Would you just wait, Purty?" Randy scolded his brother.

We helped Raven from their shoulders once the guys were back down on their knees. It had gone exactly as planned.

We went back to the large rock where we had been sitting before. Randy held the lantern up to give us the most light. We all were antsy with anticipation to see what the scroll would say. The scroll was rolled up tightly and tied together with a piece of string. Raven carefully untied the string.

"Who's going to read it?" Raven asked.

"I will," Purty cried out.

"Let Timmy read it. He found it," Randy said.

"Oh, man," Purty cried again.

Raven handed me the scroll. My hands shook as I reached for it. It felt strange in my hands—like I was holding something old, something sacred, something that held so much great importance to all of us. I slowly unrolled it, making sure not to rip it. The paper was connected to wooden spools at the top and bottom. I held it open in my hands.

There was nothing to read. Opening it up revealed a hand-drawn map. I spread it down on the top of my legs so everyone could take a look at it. I knew exactly where the map would lead us if we followed it. It was like looking at an old friend, something I'd never forget. The map would lead us to the old cabin where the Tattoo Man had hidden out, the cabin with the rag bed, the cabin where I knew I would die if I had been caught in it. I didn't say a thing as the others tried to figure out where the map led. My mind was back in that same cave again with the Tattoo Man reaching for my head and my arm going up and slamming my knife down into the Tattoo Man's foot. I handed the map to James Ernest.

I quickly got up and went over to a cave wall and threw up. Everything was flashing through my mind—the gun, the smells, the threats, the cabin, the cave, "Duck Tim," the escapes, the worrying, the bats, the Tattoo Man screaming for help as he lay at the bottom of the cave, dying not more than ten feet from where we sat. I had to get out of the cave—right then! I ran to the ladder and began climbing as fast as I could. I couldn't hear my friends' questions as they were trying to figure out what was wrong.

The rope ladder was swinging all over the place as I climbed. Suddenly it tightened. I looked down to see James Ernest and Randy holding it taut. I made it to the top and climbed out of the cave and flopped onto the deep snow on my back. Snow fell on my face as I lay there. It felt good. I was hot and sweating. I was sure I knew what had happened; I knew why the Tattoo Man had come to Morgan County. I knew!

A few minutes later Susie's head popped out of the opening, and she asked, "Are you okay, Timmy?"

"Yeah, I had to get out of there. I think a lot of bad memories overtook me."

"I had no idea you were still affected by what had happened," Susie said.

"I didn't, either. But I almost died in that cave, and the Tattoo Man did instead of me."

"Wow, I never thought of it like that." Susie laid down by my side in the snow, and we looked up into the falling snow.

"Did you guys figure out where the map leads?"

"I didn't," Susie said.

"It leads back to the old cabin. The treasure is buried inside the cabin," I told her.

22 BOBSLEDDING

On the way back to the store we decided to walk across the frozen lake. I wished there wasn't a foot-and-a-half of snow covering it. We could have gone ice skating—if any of us knew how or had ice skates. I saw Mud and Louis's tent on the lake again. We sneaked up to it. I could hear music coming from inside. They were listening to country music on a transistor radio. We all began screaming at the same time, scaring the two fishermen out of their wits.

Mud came scrambling out of the tent to see who was bothering their afternoon.

"Louis almost broke his pole in half jerking it up against the top of the tent! You guys have probably scared every fish in the lake. Wait till I tell your Papaw," he threatened.

"I'm going to beat him to it. Besides, the fish probably needed to be woken up," I said.

Mud scratched his head as Louis poked his head out of the tent.

"How many fish have you guys caught?" James Ernest asked.

"So far?" He began counting on his fingers and then said, "None. But I was getting a nibble before you guys scared it away," Louis said.

Susie looked at them and said, "His Papaw sells fish sticks in the store if you end up needing some."

We all cracked up, laughing. Even Louis and Mud starting grinning.

"You're such a cute, little thing to be so mean," Mud said as we walked away.

Papaw was in the store sitting and talking with Robert and Homer around the pot-bellied stove when we walked in.

As we walked through the store, Purty told Papaw, "Louis and Mud will be down in a while to buy some fish sticks."

I heard Homer say, "That boy is a strange one," as I left the room. The three men laughed. Mom and Mamaw were quilting in the living room—a good day for it. We went straight to the kitchen table and spread the map out on the table. We had decided not to talk about the map until we were back at the house.

Randy began, "I think the treasure is somewhere on the other side of Licking Creek."

"Timmy knows where it is," Susie blurted out.

Everyone looked at me. "It's inside the old cabin where the Tattoo Man stayed," I told them.

They each looked back down at the map. I pointed and explained, "This is Licking Creek. This line is the old logging road. This line here is the creek that runs from Blaze. These squiggly lines represent the waterfall that we saw on our hike. The X marks the spot where the cabin sits. The treasure that the slave lady buried is inside the old cabin."

"How did you figure all of that out so quickly?" Raven asked.

"It's all been in my head for over two years. It's almost all I think about. I'm also sure the reason the Tattoo Man came here in the first place was to find his Dad's body and search for the clue himself. That was why he roamed the woods all the time," I explained.

"He was so close to it and didn't even know it," Tucky said.

"Let's go get some shovels and go to the cabin," Purty said.

"It's going to be dark within an hour. Maybe we could do it tomorrow afternoon," Randy said.

"Oh, man," Purty said. "Where is all our adventure and risk-taking?"

"If it's there, it will still be there tomorrow," James Ernest said.

"Someone could have already found it," Susie said.

"Don't say that. That's why we don't let girls in the Wolf Pack. Too much negative thinking," Purty told Susie.

"It would be more like you guys don't want anyone smarter than you moronic idiots." Susie reddened. I quickly decided to stay out of it.

"Why don't you let girls in?" Raven asked, folding her arms across her chest.

"We decided we would let them in the club if we could find girls who would parade in front of us naked," Purty said just as Mom walked into the kitchen. I sank as deep as I could into my chair.

Mom stopped mid-step and turned toward the table and said, "What did you say, Todd?"

"I said…"

"Don't you dare say another word. If I ever hear you say anything like that again I'll break up the Wolf Pack. I'll go straight to your mom and dad, and I'll find the biggest switch I can find from the apple tree and whip your butt myself.

When you're in my house you will respect girls and women. Do you understand?'

"Yes, I und—"

"Didn't I tell you not to say anything? Do you have something wrong with you? I think it's time for you to go home. Go call your dad. Now!" Mom yelled. Mamaw had come into the room to see what all the yelling was about. I had never seen Mom so mad at anyone else other than me and Dad.

Purty jumped up from the table and scurried like a scared mouse to the phone inside the store. I almost felt sorry for him. After making the phone call, he went out to the front porch by himself to wait for his dad.

"Now, who else was part of this scheme to see naked girls?" Mom asked. Mamaw's eyes nearly popped out of her head.

The three of us were smart enough to let Purty hang out there on the falling edge alone. He was the one with the big mouth, and it was time for him to learn a lesson. We all shook our heads like we knew nothing at all about what he was talking about. We had jokingly talked about naked girls being allowed in the club when we first started the club. But it was all a big joke. Apparently Purty thought we were serious. He always took nakedness seriously.

It wasn't long before Forest was in front of the store to pick them up. Snow was falling like crazy. Clayton and Monie were walking into the store soon after Forest left with the three boys.

"It's a good thing I've got chains on the truck. I don't think a person is getting up the hill without chains tonight," Clayton said. Papaw said he had chains on his truck.

Clayton and Monie decided to visit for a while, so we got out a deck of cards and began playing Five Hundred Rummy. Susie and I were on the same team against James Ernest and Raven.

The adults were inside the store, talking, and Janie was watching television.

"I've never seen your mom so mad," Susie finally said.

"Not since Dad died and she moved back to Kentucky," I said.

"I think Purty almost wet his pants he was so scared," James Ernest said.

"I almost felt sorry for him," Raven said.

"Me too," I agreed.

"Did you guys really say that?" Susie asked.

"What?" I asked, knowing full well what she was talking about.

"That you would let a girl in if she would parade in front of you naked," Susie whispered.

I dropped my head to look at the cards I held in my hands. Susie looked from me to James Ernest.

He answered, "When we were making the rules for the club we voted for the club to be boys only. Someone joked that we would change the rule if we could find a girl that would—you know what."

"We all laughed about it, and that was it. We didn't actually mean it," I added.

"Who came up with the idea?" Raven asked.

James Ernest and I looked at each other. We both knew that James Ernest was the first one to bring it up and that I had continued it at that first Wolf Pack meeting.

"Can't remember. We were just joking because Purty wanted to make our club initiation that we all had to run around the lake naked on a Saturday," James Ernest explained.

"Then someone suggested that if we were involving nudity, it should be a girl," I continued.

"But why won't you let girls in the club?" Susie asked. "I think the club would be fun."

I had learned over my past twelve years that those types of questions were almost impossible to answer without someone getting mad. And usually it was someone getting mad at me. I tried my very best not to say anything. Susie stared at me, waiting for an answer. Raven stared at James Ernest.

"We never said that girls couldn't be a part of the Wolf Pack. They just can't be a member," James Ernest said, saving me from having to say anything, I wrongly thought.

"But why can't we be a member if we can be a part of the Wolf Pack, Timmy?" Susie asked me face to face.

"I think because girls wouldn't want to do the things we do. Girls may not be able to go on overnight hikes with four guys. Would Clayton and Monie let you go on an overnight hiking trip in the mountains with us?" I tried to throw the answer back into Susie's court.

"I guess you're right," she finally said after thinking about it.

"That's why we still wanted to be able to invite girls to do some things with us like finding the treasure chest and searching for the buried money. We're not against girls. Some things are awkward if you have boys and girls. It would be the same if you had a girls club. You guys would want to do things that you couldn't have boys," James Ernest continued.

"Like what?" Raven asked.

"Like getting together and talking about your boyfriends," I said.

"Who said we had boyfriends?" Raven said.

James Ernest and Raven ended up beating us at the card game, and we went out to the front porch to watch the snow falling so hard that it looked like we were getting two or three inches an hour. Mom came to the door and told us to gather some snow and they would make snow cream.

We had a great evening eating snow cream, throwing snowballs and rolling down the hill from the dam into the back yard.

Later that evening we got a call telling us that the church service for the next morning had been cancelled due to the heavy snow fall. It snowed all night. I had never seen so much snow in my life.

Sunday, February 4

The next morning outside my window looked like a winter wonderland. It looked like pictures I'd seen in magazines of the Colorado ski resorts. I had no idea if we were going to try and walk to the cabin to find the buried treasure. I knew it would be hard to get there through all the snow. Papaw said that there was close to two feet of snow on the ground with all the old and new snow combined. We were pretty much snowed in.

Papaw didn't think he would be able to get to the store until the roads were either plowed or melted, and the gravel roads were almost never plowed. I didn't think it would be right to go to the cabin in search of the treasure without Susie and Raven.

Sheriff Cane called Mom to check on her. He said that traffic was almost non-existent in town or on the county roads. We didn't figure to get any customers at the store. James Ernest and I tried to call Randy and Todd, but their phone was out of service. We figured their phone line may have been knocked down by the snow.

"You think we need to walk to their house?" I asked James Ernest.

I flopped onto my bed, and James Ernest followed me, and we lay there talking.

"I don't know. You know Purty will be champing at the bit to go. He wanted to go yesterday," James Ernest said. "It might be fun to go for a hike in the snow."

"I think it sounds like hard work," I said. "That snow is deep."

"Well, we need to do something. I can't stand to be stranded in the house for very long," James Ernest said.

"I have an idea, but I'm not sure how we could do it."

"What idea?" he asked.

"I was watching Wide World of Sports, and they had on bobsledding. We have enough snow to build our own bobsledding track," I suggested.

"I've always wanted to try that," James Ernest said excitedly.

"But how would we do it?"

"We need a hillside with a gradual slope that we could use to shape the tunnel," James Ernest said.

"We have a million of those in the county. We can use one of the valleys on Papaw's farm. We could use that first one on the right at the top of the hill."

There was a V-shaped hollow that had been cleared to become a crop field. It started at the point where the lane met SR 711. The old mailbox stood there. It gradually sloped and dropped probably sixty to eighty feet until you came to the bottom. It would be perfect for what we needed. But I had no idea how to build such a thing.

"Maybe you should call Martin and tell him what we want to do. He may have an idea," James Ernest said.

I ran to the phone and dialed Papaw's number. He answered the phone, and I told him what we wanted to build. We talked for a while, then I hung up.

"Papaw is going to bring the tractor down to pick us up. He said he would come up with some ideas. He thought it was possible," I explained to James Ernest.

"I guess he's bored being stuck in the house," James Ernest said.

"Probably, just like we are."

I went to find Mom to tell her what we were going to do. I explained to her what we wanted to do and that Papaw was on his way to pick us up.

"I was hoping you would watch the store this afternoon," Mom said.

"But Mom, we're not going to have any customers today."

"Okay. Be careful and dress warmly," she said.

James Ernest suggested that we take some cardboard boxes with us to use as bobsleds. We found some large boxes on the back porch and took them out front. We tried to call the Tuttle's house again. But their phone still wasn't ringing. I called Susie and told her what we were going to do. She said she would try to come and help.

Although there was two feet of snow on the ground, the temperature was fairly mild. It was in the upper twenties and didn't feel as cold as it looked. Papaw took longer than I expected. We finally heard him coming down the road in his green John Deere tractor. He parked it and came into the store to warm up. Mom and Janie came into the store to see him.

"Did you come up with any ideas?" I asked.

"I didn't. But I went to see the smartest man I know, Mr. Ulysses Perry. I told him what you guys wanted to do, and he said he might be able to help. He's going to meet us up there. I'm sure he'll come up with something," Papaw said.

James Ernest and I couldn't have been more excited. Papaw said he had warmed up and asked us if we were ready to go. He didn't have to ask. He could see how antsy we were to go. We jumped onto the tractor and hung on. It was hard to believe that we were in Morgan County, Kentucky. I had never seen snow as deep as it was. I expected to see elk and moose along the road.

We got to Papaw's lane just as Ulysses Perry arrived, also. He was driving a tractor with a wagon attached. Inside the wagon were two fifty-five-gallon drums. I wasn't sure what was going on.

"Hello, Mr. Perry," I shouted when he was close enough. He waved.

When he had come to a stop and stepped off the tractor he said, "This is the best I could come up with at the spur of the moment. You might be able to roll these drums down the valley, forming a half tunnel for your sleds. I filled the drums halfway with water. They're heavy, but you need something to compact the snow to be able to slide on it."

"What do we do, just let the barrels roll down the hill?" I asked.

"No. You want to form turns and curves in your track. You'll need to stand in front of the drums and turn them as they roll down the hill. You should be able to handle them," he explained. "It will probably take both of you to handle one."

"Why are there two barrels?" I asked.

"The first one is to form the track, and the next one is to pack it down harder," Ulysses told us. You can push the drums to the side and leave them down there. I'll come get them once the snow has melted.

Susie, Raven, Samantha, her sister, and Henry Junior, her brother, arrived as we were unloading the drums from the wagon.

"It's not going to be easy," Mr. Ulysses Perry told us.

Papaw tried to explain to Susie and Raven what we were going to try to do. We maneuvered the drum near the oak tree that stood next to the lane. We began rolling it toward the V-shaped beginning of the valley. We quickly switched to the other side of the drum to make sure it didn't take off down the hillside. Henry Junior asked if he could help us.

"Sure you can," James Ernest said. He ran over and got in the middle between us. We began walking backward down the hill. We tried to stay in the bottom of the V. James Ernest reasoned that this would enable us to pick up some speed at the start. We slowly backed down the slope of the hill. We then decided to turn it to the left a little and form a small curve. The weight of the water-filled drum was smashing the snow down really well, forming a hard bottom.

I was getting more excited with each step. We heard another tractor coming up the road from the store and saw Purty waving as they went by. Randy was driving. We turned the barrel to the right and created a small turn, and we turned it so it would roll over to the other side of the hill. We formed a large turn this time and then let it straighten out into a long stretch of tunnel where we figured we would be at top speed. We decided to roll the barrel to the bottom of the valley, and that would complete our first bobsled track.

We looked up to see that Randy and Purty were following our path and rolling the other barrel down the hill. I heard Randy yelling at Purty. It figured. We stood at the bottom of the hillside and looked up at the path we had made for our bobsledding track. I knew we didn't have real bobsleds, but the cardboard boxes would be just as much fun. The biggest problem was we had to climb back up to the top.

We waited for Randy and Purty to make it down to the bottom where we were. It didn't take them nearly as long as it had taken us to make the original track.

We rolled the drum out of the way and began our climb to the top. It was really hard in the deep snow.

"So how did you two know where we were?" I asked.

"We came to the store, and your mom told us what you guys were doing. Purty insisted on getting everyone and going to the cabin," Randy explained.

"Not today," James Ernest said.

"What? Why?" Purty cried out.

"We can't go without everyone. It's too difficult with all the snow and the ground inside the cabin would be frozen like a rock. We couldn't dig for a buried treasure if we wanted to," James Ernest said.

I hadn't even thought about the ground being frozen. James Ernest was right. We would have to wait until the ground thawed out.

"So instead we decided to build a bobsledding track," I said.

"And you didn't invite us," Purty said.

"Your phone line was dead. We tried calling," I said. "We're glad you're here."

"This looks like it's going to be fun," Randy said.

We were finally at the top when I looked at Ulysses and said, "The drums were a good idea. You don't have any bobsleds, do you?"

"I don't have any today. I could build one, but it would take a few days," he answered.

"Who's going to try it out first?" Papaw asked.

"Papaw, why don't you go down first?" I said.

"I'm not going to be your test dummy. I'm smarter than that. You need someone a lot dumber than me," he said just before Purty walked up and said, "I want to go first."

"There you go," Papaw said and winked.

"Be our guest," I said and handed him one of the cardboard boxes.

The boxes had been taken apart where you could sit on it and hold the front up off the ground. Purty took his makeshift sled and laid it on the track near the oak tree.

"How about a push?" he asked.

James Ernest and Randy placed their hands on his back and began pushing him down the track. They stopped just as he reached the top of the hill. We all ran to where we could get a good look. Purty began screaming as he picked up speed in the straight-away. The screams only ended when he came to the first curve and he went straight up and over the turn and went head first into the pile of snow. I was sure he was screaming, but if he was we couldn't hear him. All we could see was his legs dangling and kicking above the snow.

"Maybe we should have banked that first curve a little more," James Ernest said and laughed.

"I think it was perfect," I said.

"Do you think he needs help?" Raven asked.

"Nope, he'll dig himself out. If not, I'll help him on my way back up the hill," Randy told us.

"You can go next then," James Ernest said.

Randy got on his cardboard sled and took it to the top of the hill and took off slower by not having anyone push him. He wasn't going nearly as fast when he got to the first curve, and he was able to go through the turns with no problem at all. He then made it to the last straight-away and reached full speed. When he reached the bottom his sled came to an abrupt stop and Randy tumbled off the sled. Purty's legs were still kicking in the air. I figured that was a good sign; it meant he was still breathing.

Junior was next to jump on the track. He also made it to the bottom without falling off. Raven went next. She flew off her sled when she lost grip of the cardboard in the curves. She rolled across the field. We all laughed at her. Samantha went down the hill next with no trouble.

James Ernest also lost control of his sled and ended up off the track. He and Randy began pulling Purty out of the snow.

Susie went next. I was so proud of the perfect trip she made down the track. I was the last to go down. Papaw and Ulysses gave me a small push, and I guided my cardboard sled all the way to the bottom without falling off. Susie and I walked back up the hill with Henry Junior and Samantha. We all stopped at the first curve and tried to build the curve up higher with more snow. We could see that the track was getting icier and harder as each sled went down. It was as much fun as I had ever had.

Ulysses decided he had to make a run down the track. We all laughed as he went down the icy runway. He was screaming like Purty and placing his hands on the ground, trying to slow down. Papaw said, "If he can do it, I can do it." Papaw made it to the bottom but crashed and flew into the snow face first. When he had made it back to the top of the hill I noticed that his glasses were missing.

"Where are your glasses?" I asked.

"They got smashed a little," he said. He pulled his glasses from his pocket and held them up. They were mangled and twisted.

"But it was tremendous fun," Papaw said. "I think I'm heading for the house now."

"Thanks, Papaw," I said as he climbed up onto his tractor.

Ulysses said he'd had all the fun he could stand, and he left also. The rest of us spent the entire afternoon playing in the snow and sledding down the track. We had to stop when most of our sleds had ripped and torn apart. Randy took Susie and the Washington kids home and then came back to get Purty, James Ernest, and me. We hung onto the tractor all the way to the store.

It was nearing dark by the time we got back to the store. Randy and Purty took off for home.

An Eye for a Coin

Saturday, March 3

A month had gone by since we built the bobsledding track. We slid on it for the next two weeks. We improved it; we built up the walls when they fell down. Almost every kid within ten miles had come to slide on it. Some of the kids brought fancy sleds, some brought burlap sacks, and some went down the course on their butts. The track became faster as it got icier. All eight of the Key kids even came one day to slide down it. There were pictures of the course in the "Licking Valley Courier," our weekly county newspaper, and an article telling about it. Mom cut out the article and added it to our family scrapbook. I didn't even know we had one. I figured it had to be getting pretty thick.

The entire month of February had been bitterly cold with snow every week. The snow began to melt by March, and the temperatures were even in the mid-forties on Thursday. We decided it was time to go to the cabin and dig for treasure.

We were supposed to meet at the Tuttle farm at noon. Clayton was driving us up to their house. Kentucky was going to meet us there. James Ernest and I each carried a shovel. Raven carried one of Papaw's picks. Susie brought a couple of small flower-hand shovels.

When Clayton dropped us off I walked past his window. He rolled it down and asked me, "What are you kids up to this afternoon? Planting a garden?"

I looked at him and grinned and said, "We're looking for buried treasure."

"Good luck with that. Remember your girlfriend's pa if you find it," he said and laughed.

Tucky was sitting on the porch when we walked up the steps. Todd and Randy came through the front door, and we headed off the porch and around the house toward the path. Loraine came out of the back door and began telling us something about how glad she was to see us. We all waved and kept walking. We knew there wasn't enough daylight to stop and listen to her; we only had seven hours.

We were walking across the field when I heard a familiar caw. Within seconds Bo had landed on my left shoulder. He had been around more in the last week, perhaps because the weather was breaking. We ended up having enough shovels and picks for everyone to dig at the same time. We knew we might have to dig up the entire dirt floor inside the cabin.

Purty was bouncing all around the path and talking almost as much as his mom. He couldn't shut up about how much money we would find. It was driving me crazy. I was so glad that this would be the last day we'd have to listen to him go on and on about the treasure. It would be over one way or the other, and we could go on with our lives.

I asked him, "Purty, what are you going to do with all this money?"

"I'm going to put it in the bank until I'm out of high school. I may take some of it out to buy a car when I'm sixteen. Then

I'm going to open up an office, and I'm going to be a private eye in Lexington or Frankfort—some big city somewhere."

"How did you choose that?" Susie asked.

"As you know, I'm really good at finding clues and figuring things out. It's only natural for me to become a private eye," he explained. "Plus, I'm really good at sneaking around without being seen."

I always knew Sadie was delusional, but I never knew Purty was the same. It was strange how he stole all the traits that others in our group possessed and applied them to himself. I looked at him and decided not to say anything. Susie looked at me like she couldn't figure him out, either. The trail was still covered with some snow, but it was melting and leaving puddles.

A hundred yards ahead of us stood the cabin. Our treasure awaited us. Bo clung to my shoulder as I entered the old cabin.

"Where do we start digging?" Raven asked.

"It doesn't matter. Just dig!" Purty said as he tried sticking his shovel into the dirt floor.

"We ought to think, Where would we hide money so we could remember where it was?" Randy said.

"It had to be someplace easy so she could dig it up every time she needed to add to it," James Ernest added.

"She wouldn't want the guy to see it," Susie said.

"Maybe under her bed," Tucky suggested.

"Probably, but we don't know where her bed was," Raven said.

"Probably in a corner of the room," I said. "It would be easy to remember."

"Let's try that," Randy said.

Purty was still digging in the middle of the room.

"I don't think it would be very deep. Probably not more than 6 inches deep," James Ernest reasoned.

Susie and I went to one corner away from the fireplace. Randy went to another corner. James Ernest went to another with Raven, and Tucky took the other. Purty kept digging in the middle of the room.

Susie and I were digging in the corner where the rag bed was when I was trapped under the rags hiding from the Tattoo Man. I felt as though I could smell the same foul stink and feel the bug that crawled up my leg. I reached down and swiped at my leg. Susie looked at me. Bo had flown from my shoulder and perched on the mantle over the fireplace, cawing every once in a while. He finally flew to the floor and began scratching as though he was helping in the search.

Susie and I had dug out a section that was probably three feet by three feet in the corner and about eight inches deep. We had found nothing. I looked at Purty. I had never seen him work so hard at something. He was standing knee deep in a hole and digging deeper.

"Purty, I don't think she would have dug that deep every time she added to her money," I said.

"Has anyone else found it?" he asked me.

"No."

"Then leave me alone. My way is just as good," Purty said almost as if he was going out of his mind. He actually scared me a little. I decided to leave him alone and let him dig to China if that was what he wanted to do. I looked around the room. I had an idea. I took out my flashlight. There wasn't much light around the edges of the room. I began shining the light around the bottom of the building, searching for a clue.

There it was. Around half way between where we had dug and the corner that Randy was digging I found a notch that had been carved into the wood at the very bottom. I thought maybe it was placed there to remind the girl where she had hidden the money. I showed it to Susie by pointing to it. We grabbed our shovels and went to the spot and began digging. No more than four inches down I hit what I thought was a rock. I ran over to the small hand shovels and grabbed one and came back and got down on my knees and began scraping the dirt out. I soon discovered that it wasn't a rock. It was a small, metal box.

Bo hopped over to the hole I was digging and looked inside.

"Move Bo," I commanded. Bo wasn't happy with me as I shoved him away from the hole.

"Caw, caw, caw!" he yelled.

Everyone stopped digging to see what Bo was screaming about. They saw me on my hands and knees, and they laid their shovels down and came over to watch me dig.

"What did you find?" Purty almost yelled.

"I think I may have found it. It looks like a metal box," I answered.

Everyone had their heads hovering over me as I dug out from around the box. I finally uncovered the top. It was probably six inches long and three inches wide.

"That ain't it," Purty yelled out. "It's not big enough to be a buried treasure!"

I figured everyone's expectations were different. I knew that Purty expected great riches, but I thought there couldn't be much money. How would a slave girl come up with a lot of money? I figured that anyone who lived in this one room cabin wouldn't have much money to begin with. So how could she steal very much? I wasn't sure what the others expected. I was hoping that maybe the coins and money would be worth a lot because they were old.

I could sense the excitement and anticipation as Susie and I uncovered the small box. We lifted the tin box from the dirt once we had dug around it. The blackened tin box had a lid with hinges on the back side. I hesitated opening it. I wasn't sure if I should open it or let someone else.

"This is so exciting," Purty said as he rocked back and forth.

"Who should open it?" I asked.

"I will," Purty announced.

"Let Timmy open it. He found it," Randy said.

"Well, hurry up. What are you waiting for?" Purty begged.

I was sitting in the dirt with the box in my lap. I looked at Susie, and she raised her eyebrows as if to tell me to go ahead and open the box. I started to open it, but the hinges were rusty, and the top didn't open easily. I had to force the top to open to where we could see inside. Inside the box we could see silver coins—very few silver coins. It looked as though they were mostly silver dollars.

I emptied the coins onto the dirt beside me so everyone could see the treasure. Bo quickly swooped off the mantle and gathered one of the coins in his beak and flew out of the cabin. Purty screamed at Bo as he flew away with the coin. Purty fell to his knees and began counting the coins. He counted twelve silver dollars and a few smaller coins. In total there were fourteen dollars and sixty-two cents. Purty deflated and said nothing.

James Ernest said the coins were dated from 1829 to 1870.

"Some of the coins may be worth more than their spending value. People collect these. Some of these may be rare." James Ernest tried giving Purty some hope.

"We could take them to the bank and have Mr. Harney tell us what they are worth," Susie suggested.

Purty slowly got up from where he had deflated and said, "There could be more boxes. Maybe she buried them all over the room. That's it." He grabbed one of the long shovels and began digging again. "C'mon, guys, keep digging."

We knew the box was the only box. The only one who didn't believe it was Purty. He randomly dug holes in the cabin. Randy said that James Ernest should place the coins into his pocket to carry them home. We quickly filled up the holes we had dug and decided it was time to head back home. I picked up the tin box.

"Let's go, Purty," Randy said as Purty continued to dig.

"You guys stink. We need to keep digging!" Purty shouted.

"You can stay if you want to. We're leaving," Randy said.

Purty took the shovel with both hands and threw it as hard as he could against the inside wall of the cabin. The shovel ricocheted back toward Purty, and the shovel blade hit Purty in the face. Instantly there was blood flowing down his face. He was standing in the back doorway, and the daylight lit him up, and we could see the blood dripping from his hands that he held over his face.

Randy and James Ernest ran over to him. The rest of us were frozen in fear. James Ernest quickly took off his coat and shirt and gave his shirt to Randy who applied it to Purty's face, trying to slow the bleeding. Susie and Raven began crying while Tucky and I stood there staring at the scene, not knowing what to do.

"I'll run and get the tractor if you guys can get him down to the logging road. I'll meet you there," Randy said.

"We'll get him there," James Ernest assured him.

Randy took off running. I knew it wouldn't be an easy run through the snow and puddles. I slowly made my way over to where Purty was sitting on the floor. I was going to help James Ernest get Purty to the logging road.

"Purty, we need to get you to your feet so we can get you to your house and to the doctor," James Ernest told him. Purty took the shirt from his face so he could try to stand up. I saw that the shovel had hit Purty in his left eye and across his nose. A big gash went across the bridge of his nose, and blood was also pouring from his eye. I felt sick to my stomach. I looked away.

As soon as we got Purty to his feet, he passed out.

Raven ran out of the cabin and came back with snow in her hands. She applied the snow to Purty's forehead and to the cut.

"How are we going to get him to the road if he can't walk?" I asked.

James Ernest looked worried. "Help me get him up. I'll carry him."

"You can't carry him," Raven said.

"I have to," he said as he tied the shirt around Purty's head to slow the bleeding.

Tucky and I helped lift Purty to his feet, and James Ernest placed his arms behind Purty's knees and his armpits and picked him up in his arms. I tried to carry some of the weight by lifting Purty's legs.

We had talked about what a person could do when their adrenaline kicked in. Well, on that day I saw it firsthand. It was the greatest feat of will power I ever saw in my life. Purty outweighed James Ernest by thirty pounds or more, but James Ernest carried his friend all the way to the logging road without ever having to put him down. I was so in awe of what James Ernest was doing that I almost forgot that Purty was possibly bleeding to death.

By the time we made it to the road we could hear the tractor coming up the lane. Soon we saw Randy and Mr. Tuttle on the tractor pulling a wagon. They placed Purty inside the wagon and took off toward the house with him. Mr. Tuttle drove the tractor while Randy held his brother's head in his lap as they went. We were left standing there and listening to Bo call from the tree above us, "Caw!"

We walked back toward the house slowly. I don't think any of us wanted to hear Loraine wail and scream. When we finally got to the Tuttle yard, we could tell that no one was home. We had heard the sirens of the ambulance as we walked toward the house. We figured all of them had piled into the car and followed the ambulance to the hospital in Morehead.

I thought about taking the trail through the woods and across the swinging bridge, but decided it might be too slippery with the snow. Besides, it wouldn't be right not to walk with Tucky as far as we could, so we headed down the Tuttle lane.

"Why was Todd so angry?" Raven suddenly asked.

KenTucky Snow & the Crow

"He thought we were going to find some great treasure that would make him rich. He doesn't take disappointment very well," James Ernest said.

"He's been counting the money in his head since we found the chest in the cave. I don't know why he does that," I added.

"Did any of you guys really think we would ever find a lot of money?" Susie asked and added, "I didn't."

"Maybe when we opened the treasure chest, I did. I didn't think we'd find much in the cabin," I answered.

"I never thought we'd find any money at all," Tucky said. "I don't know what I'd do with money, anyway. You can't buy happiness with it, can you? Purty did not have any cause to do that, no how."

Tucky was right. I had everything I had always wanted. I was living in Morgan County with the people I loved. I had the most wonderful girlfriend in the world. I was as happy as I could possibly be.

"The best things in life are free," James Ernest added to our celebration of being poor.

"I hope Purty will be okay," Susie said.

"His eye didn't look very good," I said.

When we got to the bottom of the hill where the lane meets SR 711, Tucky said his good-byes and headed right toward his house. We told him we would let him know something when we heard from Purty's family.

As he started to walk away I asked him, "You want to go to church with us in the morning? We can pick you up."

"I don't go to church. Snakes scare me," Tucky answered.

"What do snakes have to do with church?" Susie asked him.

"I went once about a year ago, and the preacher had folks come up and handle snakes. They had rattlers and copperheads and cottonmouths in this big glass box. They told me that I had to hold the snakes to demonstrate my faith in God. I told them I didn't have that much faith. I ran out of the building and told them I'd never come back," Tucky told us.

We all stood there in disbelief. I had never heard of such a thing.

"I've heard of snake-handling churches. Dad said there was a colored church that did it for a while before most of them were bitten," Raven said.

"Our church doesn't do snakes in church. We don't even like spiders," I said.

"I always thought all churches had snakes. But that was the only church I've ever been to," Kentucky said. "Nearly scared me to death."

"No snakes," I promised.

"Okay, then. I'll try it once more."

"We'll pick you up around a quarter 'til ten," I told him.

"See you tomorrow," I said as he turned and walked away.

As we walked toward the store I looked at James Ernest and said, "We ought to go catch a small snake and take it to church tomorrow."

"That would be so mean," Susie said.

"It was just a joke," I said. I really did think it, though.

When we walked into the store we saw Susie's parents, my mom, Mamaw, and Papaw standing inside. "How is Todd?" Mom asked.

I could tell by the expressions on everyone's faces that they weren't happy. Loraine must have called someone before the ambulance arrived.

I didn't know what to say. James Ernest answered Mom, "He's cut across the bridge of his nose, and his left eye is pretty bad."

"What happened?" Papaw asked.

"He was mad, and he threw a shovel against the wall, and it bounced back and hit him in the face," James Ernest explained.

"What was he mad about?" Clayton asked.

"We were in the cabin digging for money that we had been told was buried there. We found it, and it wasn't very much. Purty thought there should have been more, and he got mad when we told him we were leaving. He wanted to keep digging," Susie chimed in.

"So you really were digging for a buried treasure?" Clayton said, looking at me.

"Yes, sir," I said, remembering the conversation we had when he dropped us off.

"Purty thought there would be some great treasure," Raven said.

"So, how much money did you find?" Mom asked.

"Fourteen dollars and sixty-two cents," James Ernest said as he pulled the money from his pocket and laid it on the counter. "But all the coins are around a hundred years old. They could be worth more."

Papaw and Clayton walked over to look at the coins.

"We were going to have Mr. Harney look at the coins to see what they're worth," I said.

"I know someone better to look at them," Papaw said.

"Who?" I asked.

"Fred Wilson?" Clayton asked.

Papaw said, "Yep, he collects coins. He's very knowledgeable when it comes to what they're worth."

24 Church without Snakes

I woke up with howling and cawing going on outside my window. I looked out to see Bo trying to land on Coty's back. Coty was jumping into the air, trying to catch Bo with his mouth. I was pretty sure Coty still didn't care much for Bo.

Mr. Tuttle had called late the evening before to let us know that Purty had to get seventeen stitches in his face and that they still weren't sure about his eye. They had to wait for the swelling to go down before they could test it at all. Purty was going to be in the hospital for at least a couple of days.

I felt bad for Purty, but he had done it to himself. I knew that his greed and desire to be rich had caused his accident. I wasn't sure why Purty was acting that way. Generally he was happy, but I also knew he was strung a little tight. Of course, Papaw always said that Purty was a weird kid.

I sure hoped he was going to be okay. Purty brought a lot of laughter into my life. I walked into the living room and noticed that James Ernest was not there. I wasn't sure where he was. Mom was already up and getting ready for church. She had placed cereal boxes on the table. I knew that was a hint. I had told her the night before that Kenny Key was going to church with us and that we needed to pick him up.

I sat at the table after getting the milk out and poured myself a bowl of Cheerios. I put four large scoops of sugar over the Cheerios and poured a little milk on them. I never liked milk. I never drank milk unless it was chocolate. But for some reason I could eat cereal with milk. But I left the milk in the bowl.

Janie soon walked into the kitchen, and I fixed her a bowl of Sugar Pops.

"I heard Coty and Bo outside our window," Janie told me.

"Me, too. They woke me up. Bo was trying to ride on Coty's back, and Coty wasn't very happy about it," I said, and Janie laughed.

"I think Bo has been stealing stuff," Janie said.

"Why do you think that?" I asked.

"He flew down and took my baby doll's silver shoe," Janie said.

"Did you see him do it?"

"Yep, he almost took it out of my hand. Then he flew away with it in his mouth," Janie said.

I thought about how he had swooped down and taken the silver coin in the cabin. I wondered what Bo was doing with the things he took. Mom had mentioned that she had lost some silverware. I wondered if Bo was the culprit.

"I'll try to find it," I told Janie as I got up to get dressed for church.

I had gotten to where I really liked my mohawk. The first time the Wolf Pack walked into church we got a lot of comments and stares. But people were used to it now. We all still had the haircuts and had even trimmed them up in the past month. Mrs. Holbrook huffed the first time we walked into the classroom with them. But then she said she had seen worse, probably Kenny's mohawk and mullet. Other younger boys in the one-room school had talked their parents into letting them get mohawks. Henry Jr. and Mark Daniel both got mohawks.

I thought theirs looked the best with the kinky black hair. The mohawks stood up perfectly on their heads. They were so proud of their haircuts. We had started a fad. Daniel "Sugarspoon" Sugarman wanted to get one, but his mother told him that he was not going to look as silly as we did. She said to him, "Would you jump off a cliff if they did?" But then she remembered that he had, and that he had shattered his arm doing it. She really didn't want him doing anything that we did.

Mom was finally ready to leave for church. Papaw came down to watch the store. Mom and Janie got in the front seat, and I rode in the back.

"Don't forget to go pick up Kenny," I said as Mom put the car into reverse.

"I did forget. We're running late. Why didn't you remind me?" Mom asked.

I didn't answer. It wouldn't have made any difference, but I wasn't going to tell Mom that. I had learned a couple of things in the past two years.

Mom pulled into the Key driveway within a couple of minutes. Kenny and his twin sister, Rock, came out of the door and headed toward the car door. They both jumped into the back seat with me. Kenny was barefooted.

"Hi," I said.

Mom said hello, and I quickly made introductions as Mom was backing out of the driveway.

"That's an unusual name," Mom said to Rock.

"Yep, everyone says that," she answered.

"I'm glad you decided to come with Kenny," I said to Rock.

"I'm not afraid of snakes. So Kenny wanted me to come along just in case," Rock explained.

"Wh…what are you talking about?" Mom said as Janie turned around in her seat to look at the twins in the back seat.

"Are there going to be snakes at church?" Janie asked.

"No. No. There're not going to be any snakes at church," Mom promised everyone.

I couldn't promise for sure. I never thought there would be an invasion of snakes in Mamaw's living room, either. I thought it would be interesting if a large family of snakes crawled up the center aisle between the pews. There would be as many arms going up as the day I said the memory verses. I could imagine folks dancing on the pews. I began laughing.

Rock Key had on a flowered dress, and it looked like she had washed her hair. She was even prettier than I thought she was when I had first seen her. We pulled into the parking lot just as we saw the last person enter the church. We hurried into the church. All eyes were on us as we walked up the aisle. I looked ahead to see if Susie had saved us seats. She was waving us forward. We had to squeeze into the seats, but we were able to do it. I introduced Susie and Raven to Rock. Susie told Rock that she liked her long hair. We then rose to sing the first song. James Ernest was there standing next to Raven.

"I like your dress, also," Susie said to Rock. Rock smiled back.

After the song and a prayer Pastor White had those who had brought visitors to introduce them. Of course, I was the only one who had brought visitors, so I stood and had them stand, also. I said, "These are my friends Tucky—I mean Kenny Key—and his twin sister, Rock Key." A murmur went through the church. "They live close to me near the tunnels."

I quickly sat back down. I noticed Kenny looking toward the pulpit as he was being introduced. I knew he was scanning the place, looking for the box of snakes. It would have been a good time to have a collection plate that had a snake that sprung out. I would suggest that to Pastor White. After the collection plate was passed around, the preacher got up to sing and invited James Ernest to come up and sing with him. Another murmur spread through the church because the congregation loved hearing the two of them sing together.

Pastor White asked the church to pray for Todd Tuttle because he was hurt in an accident, and I couldn't believe it, but Pastor White then preached on Eden and how the serpent lied and tempted Eve in the garden. Kenny sat there with his eyes popping out of his head. I knew he was expecting Pastor White to reach under the pulpit and lift a serpent into the air.

When the service was over, Kenny had the biggest grin on his face. No snakes. Kenny and Rock shook the Pastor's hand. He thanked them for coming and told them he hoped they would come back.

"Do you ever have snakes in the church?" Kenny asked Pastor White.

"I've never seen one in here," Pastor White answered. I noticed the pastor glancing quickly at Tucky's bare feet.

Kenny nodded his head in approval and smiled and walked down the steps. Pastor White stared at Tucky and Rock as they walked away.

We waved good-bye to everyone and got into Mom's car. Mamaw had ridden to church with Homer and Ruby, but Mamaw asked if Mom would take her to the store where Papaw was.

Mamaw sat in the front seat with Janie on her lap. I introduced Mamaw to Rock. On the way home Mom asked, "So how did you two enjoy our church?"

"I really liked it. The singing was just 'bout the best I ever heard," Rock politely answered.

"The pastor and James Ernest have great voices. It's always a treat to hear them sing together," Mom agreed. Then she asked, "How about you, Kenny?"

"I didn't like him talking about a snake, but I was glad there weren't none there," Kenny told her.

"We had snakes in Mamaw's house one night," I said.

"You didn't need to bring that up," Mom told me. "It was absolutely the worst night of my life. I didn't sleep a wink that whole night," Mamaw added.

Tucky began squirming in his seat.

I explained, "It was raining cats and dogs that evening, and Papaw said they came in through a crack under the door to get out of the rain. It was just a garden snake and her babies."

"Maybe instead of cats and dogs, it was raining snakes," Janie said and laughed.

"Kenny would die if it rained snakes," Rock said.

"I'm gonna die if y'all keep talkin' 'bout them," Tucky said.

I think he was serious. I had never seen someone more scared of snakes than he was, especially for being such a country boy. I knew Purty was really scared of them also, but I thought Kenny hated them more.

MARCH 10

Papaw had called Fred Wilson and told him about the silver dollars and other coins. He had come by the store and looked at them on Tuesday. He said he would be back on Saturday to let us know how much they were worth. I had looked forward to his return the rest of the week. I knew it wouldn't amount to great riches like Purty had hoped for, but I figured it would put some spending money in my pocket.

Fred walked into the store at eight thirty that morning. James Ernest and I were in the store, straightening up the shelves, when he walked in.

"Good morning, boys," Fred greeted us.

"Morning, Mr. Wilson," I said. James Ernest nodded toward him.

"I've got good news for you, I think." Fred went right to business. He pulled a folded piece of paper from the front pocket of his bibbed overalls. He carefully unfolded it and said, "The silver dollars are each worth between fifty dollars and one hundred dollars. For all twelve silver dollars you can get around eight hundred and twenty-five dollars."

James Ernest and I high fived each other, and I said, "That's great!"

"That's not all. The smaller coins are also worth something. In fact, one of the coins is worth over two hundred dollars. All the coins together are worth one thousand two hundred and fifty dollars."

"That is fantastic," James Ernest told Fred.

"Thank you so much. How do we sell them?" I asked him.

"I already found a buyer. All you have to do is give me the coins, and I'll bring you the money next week."

"Are you going to wet a line today?" I asked.

The weather was fairly nice. It was supposed to be close to seventy. Fishermen were already up at the lake.

"I thought I might give it a try this morning," he said.

"It's on the house today. Thanks for your help with the coins," I told him.

"We'll call the guys while you're fishing and give them the news and have the coins ready when you're done," James Ernest told him.

I ran to the back porch and got Fred a dozen nightcrawlers, and he headed for the lake. I headed for the phone and dialed Purty's number.

Purty had to wear a patch over his eye to protect it until they determined if he was going to regain the sight in his eye. The doctors weren't sure if his eyesight would return or not. They told him he was lucky the shovel didn't cut his eyeball completely out of his head. Purty liked strutting around like he was a pirate. He thought the patch was cool, especially with the mohawk haircut.

Sadie answered the phone, of course. I asked if I could speak to Randy. She dropped the phone and left me hanging there. I had no idea if she was getting him or not.

After a couple of minutes Randy came to the phone. I told him what Fred had said, and he agreed that we should go ahead and sell the coins. We decided Tucky and the girls would be okay with it. James Ernest had figured that each of us would get $178.60. I was rich.

We gave Fred the coins that afternoon as he was leaving.

A week later we had our money.

April 15

Kenny had begun coming to school almost every day since he became a member of the Wolf Pack. He even brought Rock, Adore, and Chero with him at times. Kenny finally admitted to Mrs. Holbrook that he couldn't read very well. She already knew it, and Mrs. Holbrook started working extra with him and his sisters.

Susie and James Ernest had offered to help them after school, as Susie had done with Raven. Within only a couple of weeks they had improved a lot.

The redbuds around the county were in full bloom. The valleys and woods were beautiful. Trees were turning green. Spring was in the air, and warmth had returned. The snow and our bobsled track were distant memories now. The worst winter in anyone's memory was now something of the past that we could tell kids and grandkids about one day. Men could sit on the front porch of the store and talk about enduring the winter and snows of 1962.

Daffodils and tulips had sprung up along the roads and in flower gardens around the homes in the community. Women were happy to be out of the house and tending to their gardens and flowers. Fields and hillsides were being plowed and readied for planting. Fishermen were catching catfish again at the lake.

I was so looking forward to the end of school and summertime. The Wolf Pack had lots of plans for the summer. Adventures awaited us and our tree house still had to be built. There was swimming and hiking and picnics and fishing. I couldn't wait!

25 COYOTE

Saturday morning arrived with lots of commotion and excitement. The morning light was shining through my bedroom window. I heard Papaw in the store already waiting on fishermen. Mom was yelling through the bedroom door for me to get up and help. I looked at my clock, and it was a quarter 'til seven. I heard James Ernest as he went to the back porch for bait. James Ernest had been helping more in the store, trying to earn his keep, which was fine with me. I had fewer chores to do with James Ernest volunteering to do some of them. He made a lot of trips to the spring for water, and even cleaned up around the lake at times.

But this also meant that we both had more time to work for different farmers in the community, planting the spring crops and putting out gardens. It seemed like every weekend was filled with farm work, and then school the rest of the week. There had to be a law against this.

But Mom had told me that I could take this Saturday off from work. Susie and I had been planning a hike to the big waterfalls up toward Blaze, the same waterfall that the Wolf Pack had found after leaving the butterfly field. Susie was also excited about seeing the butterfly field again, especially in the springtime.

272

Raven and James Ernest had thought about going with us until it was decided they had too much to do. Raven needed to help her mom and dad on their farm, and James Ernest was going to help at the store and then help Homer on his farm. I had a day for fun. I felt a little guilty, but not much.

I walked into the store, and there stood Fred Wilson, Mud McCobb, and Louis Lewis.

"A lazier kid I've never laid eyes on. It's almost seven o'clock, and you're still in bed," Mud started in on me.

"He should be ashamed of himself. James Ernest is working his fingers to the bone doing his job. His grandfather is up before dawn waiting on customers that he should be helping with," Louis said as he lowered his head and shook it side to side.

"Are you two jerks ice fishing today? I sure hope so. Maybe you'll drown," I said.

Fred and Papaw laughed.

"And now you're insulting the customers. What has become of the nice Timmy we used to know?" Mud asked.

"They woke him up to wait on bait wasters," I answered.

Everyone laughed as I turned toward the kitchen.

I ate a bowl of corn flakes and drank a glass of orange juice. Mom walked into the room and asked, "When are you leaving for your hike?"

"Susie is supposed to be here around nine," I told Mom.

"And where are you going again?"

"We're going to hike to the butterfly field and then on to the waterfalls. We'll be gone almost the entire day," I said.

"You'll have to tell Hagar how to get to the butterfly field. Maybe he would walk me there one day. I'd like to see it."

"I will."

"It is supposed to be a beautiful day. It's a good day for a hike. I wish someone else was going with you two," Mom said.

"We'll be okay. Nothing to worry about," I assured Mom.

"I've heard that before," Mom said and walked out of the room.

I loved May in Kentucky. The weather was great. The summer heat was on its way but was not there yet. Flowers were blooming everywhere. I looked, and new life was being born on the farms and in the woods. Susie's goats had multiplied to where they now had ten. Three new baby goats were born the month before. When you drove out the ridge and looked into the pastures you would see calves and foals and fawns running and playing. I felt like one of them on this day. I wanted to play in the sunshine, and play and explore, and enjoy the day.

I packed my backpack with a couple of sandwiches and snacks and filled two canteens with fresh water. I had my walking stick and was waiting on the front porch, waiting for Susie to arrive. James Ernest loaned me his walking stick and canteen for Susie to use. Coty was in the yard, chewing on an old stick. He sensed something was up, and he seemed anxious to go.

Clayton's pickup finally pulled into the gravel lot at one minute past nine. I jumped off the porch and ran to the truck. We traded hellos, and then I asked if Clayton would drive us up Morgan Road to where the trail started. He said he would. I ran back to the porch for our things and yelled for Coty. I hollered good-bye through the screen door and then hopped into the back of Clayton's truck with Coty.

Mom and Papaw came out onto the porch and greeted Clayton and then waved as we pulled away from the store. Five minutes later Susie, Coty, and I were walking on the stones crossing Licking Creek to the logging road that led to the cabin. Susie was so pretty. She had on jean cut-offs and a blue-and-white-checkered, sleeveless blouse. Her strawberry-blonde hair hung down between her shoulder blades in a ponytail. She had bangs hanging almost to her eyes. Her face had light freckles that would darken during the summer months. I figured I had the prettiest and sweetest girlfriend in the world.

We climbed the opposite bank of the creek and stood on the small trail that would lead to the logging road.

"I've been looking forward to this since the day we planned it," Susie said.

"Me, too."

"I'm kind of glad it's just me and you and Coty," Susie said as she blushed.

"I was hoping Purty could come with us," I teased.

Susie stared at me, and then I laughed and said I was joking. "I'm glad it's just us, also."

It wasn't long before we were walking on the familiar logging road heading toward the cabin.

"Are you looking forward to school being out and summer getting here?" I asked.

"Not really. I like spring. It's not so hot."

"I do, too. But I like being out of school. And I'll be turning thirteen this summer, a teenager."

"I don't think I want to become a teenager."

"Why?" I asked Susie.

"I don't know. I don't want to get too old too fast. I like being young. It's hard to explain. I like being a kid and not having worries that adults have. I know how hard Mom and Dad work to have a great home for me and my sisters. I know how much they worry about stuff. It seems harder when you're older."

I hadn't really thought about it before, but I knew Susie was right. I knew someday I would be worrying if the rain didn't fall for weeks at a time. I would worry if the money was short and my kids needed clothes or food. What if the tractor or truck stopped running? But I also knew that it was a part of living, a part of growing up, a part of being an adult and taking on responsibilities. I knew that life wasn't a bowl of cherries— or cherry dumplings—as much as I would like for it to be.

We had only been hiking twenty minutes, and my mind was already wandering to other thoughts besides how wonderful it was to be hiking with Susie in the wilderness. I changed the subject.

"Any new rumors or juicy gossip at school?" I asked.

"I think Tucky likes Bernice the skunk," Susie said.

"Really!" I said, wanting to tell Susie about Kenny kissing Bernice in the outhouse. But I knew I couldn't. It was a secret of the Wolf Pack. "I thought Sadie had a thing for Tucky also."

"She does, but Kenny is a little scared of Sadie."

"Of course," I agreed with Tucky.

"I think it's causing trouble between Bernice and Sadie. I saw them arguing at recess one day," Susie said.

"They have to remain friends or neither one of them will have a friend to their name," I said.

"Bernice said something mean to Delma and Thelma Friday, and Delma told her, 'You're nothing but a dumb, ol' pole cat!'" Susie told me. We laughed.

"Called her a pole cat? That is so funny. What did Bernice do?" I asked.

"She started to run after them, but you know how clumsy she is, she fell on the gravel and skinned her knees and hands."

"I remember seeing that," I said.

"She was pulling small pebbles from her knees during class," Susie said.

"So what does Tucky say about Bernice?" I asked.

"He said she was a better girlfriend than no one."

"I don't think that's true. I'd rather be the loneliest guy in the world than have Bernice as a girlfriend."

We had come to the turn that led down the path to the cabin. We could see it up ahead. We hadn't been back to the cabin since we dug up the buried tin box. Coty was running ahead of us, smelling the spring scents. The forest floor was covered with ferns and mayapples and various flowers. I saw a Jack-in-the-pulpit and showed it to Susie. We opened the flap to see Jack inside. The walk was absolutely wonderful. But it was twice as good because I was with Susie.

We got to the cabin. Coty walked through the door and we followed him. We stopped in mid-step. The entire dirt floor of the cabin had been dug up. Holes were everywhere. I looked at Susie and at the same time we both said, "Purty."

Coty was carefully walking around the holes and sniffing at each one. I wanted to ask him if he smelled Purty, but I knew he did. Apparently Purty still believed there were more boxes buried in the cabin, and he had been sneaking back to dig when he could. He was determined, I gave him that. I kind of felt sorry for Purty for wanting to find more money so badly.

Purty had worn the patch for a month while his eye healed. The doctors said he had recovered most of his sight and that he was very lucky. They said he probably should have lost all of his vision. To me, his eye still looked a little strange. It wasn't normal. But then, neither was he.

We left the cabin and continued toward the butterfly field. It wasn't long before we came to the field. It was breathtaking. The field was covered with so many different flowers and colors. Susie's smile stretched across the field. She began naming the ones she knew.

"This is Indian Pink. This one is Baneberry. Here is Lily of the Valley. Look at the beautiful Blue Flax. This is Yellow Coreopsis, Purple Thistle. Look at the orange Poppy and the Buttercup. They are all so beautiful. There's Spiderwort and Shooting Stars. This one is called a Cat's Paw. This is Yellow Cornflower, and this one is Crimson Clover." Susie went on and on. I was laughing with joy as I saw how happy she was dancing around in the flowers. She was smelling them and touching them. I couldn't imagine anyone any happier than she was.

Butterflies and dragonflies and damselflies were scurrying across the top of the field. It was a multitude of life and color rolled into one big, happy moment. There were no deer in the field that morning. But it didn't dampen the thrill of the visit.

"This is so wonderful and beautiful!" she yelled out at the top of her lungs.

Bluebirds and finches and chickadees flew all around the field, singing along with Susie.

We spent close to a half hour in the field before I suggested that we needed to go on if we wanted to see the waterfall. Susie reluctantly agreed, and we headed on up the trail toward the small mountain stream.

Susie talked non-stop until we made it to the stream. She talked about the flowers, the birds, the butterflies, and the dragonflies. I loved hearing Susie go on and on about the field.

We turned left and began the climb up the slope toward the falls. This would be the roughest part of our hike. I figured it would take us another two hours to make it to our destination.

"This brook is really pretty," Susie told me.

"Not very far from here is where we saw the bear and cubs," I said.

"Timmy."

"Yeah?"

"Thank you for bringing me on this hike. I love doing this with you." Susie reached for my hand, and we walked on.

I would do anything to be with Susie. I knew we were still young, but I knew I would be lost without Susie as my girlfriend or without her in my life. No matter how bad a day I was having, if I thought of her it brought a smile to my face.

I had shivers and goosebumps running up my arms as we walked up the path while holding hands. Coty ran over to the stream and got a drink of water. Susie pointed out the blue-eyed grass and purple columbine that grew near the path.

"Imagine what heaven will look like if Morgan County looks like this," Susie said.

"Maybe heaven will look just like this. Maybe God put Morgan County on earth to give us a taste of heaven. I hope so, because I love it here," I told Susie.

"I do, too. But I think heaven will be even better."

As we came to the crest of a hill I heard Coty bark ahead of us. We hurried the few feet to the top and saw a coyote standing in the middle of the path sixty feet away. Coty was standing around twenty feet in front of the coyote, and they stared at each other. The coyote looked from Coty to us and then back to Coty. I wasn't sure as to what I should do. I didn't want to put Susie in harm's way. If she wasn't there I would possibly run toward the coyote or throw rocks at him to scare him away. We remained silent as we stood as still as possible.

The coyote growled at Coty. Coty took a step backward. Coty then dropped to the ground in submission. It was really strange to see Coty do that. He hadn't even backed down from the roaring bear. The coyote took a few careful steps toward Coty. Coty whimpered. I was terrified at what the coyote would do to Coty if they fought. I didn't believe Coty would be a match for a wild coyote.

Susie's hand gripped tight between my fingers. The coyote continued sauntering toward Coty while keeping an eye on us. Coty rolled over on his back as if he wanted to play. The coyote continued until they were face-to-face. Coty whimpered again, reminding me of the whimpers I heard the day I found Coty in the den.

The coyote whimpered back and then licked Coty's face. Was I really seeing what I was seeing? Susie's fingers relaxed their grip and I heard her say, "Awww."

The coyote then raised her head and looked at us and then turned and walked into the woods. Coty stood and looked back at us and then whipped his head around and watched the coyote vanish into the trees. Coty trotted toward the spot where the coyote disappeared, following her scent. He smelled the ground and barked, and then he raised his head to the sky and howled. Not his usual howl. But a different mournful howl. It was almost painful to hear.

Coty then slowly turned and slowly came back to where we still stood. I bent down to rub his head and let him give me a kiss. He licked my face as Susie dropped to the ground to pet him.

We walked on, and Coty stayed by my side for the next half hour. Susie and I walked in silence as we thought about the scene that had taken place, and took in the beauty of the stream to our right. Coty finally left my side to lead the way as he usually did.

"Do you think that could have been Coty's mother?" I said. I had noticed when the coyote walked away that it was a female.

"I was wondering the same thing. I didn't expect that to happen," Susie said.

I didn't think we would ever know for sure. She could have been Coty's mother. Coty could have come across the coyote at some time before when he explored the woods without me. Perhaps James Ernest had introduced them to each other. I lived in a strange, wonderful place. I was glad they were friendly and that a fight hadn't broken out.

We had passed the spot where we had seen the bear, and then we stopped when we came to the Big Butt rock. Susie began laughing when I pointed to the rock, "There's the Big Butt rock that Purty kissed."

"What is wrong with him?"

"No one knows," I said and laughed.

Susie just shook her head.

WATCH OUT

Susie and I left the Big Butt rock behind and continued up the slope. We had to be careful due to the rocks and roots that were on the path. The morning was gone and the afternoon had arrived. The temperature was in the seventies. It was nice, but still warm when hiking while carrying a backpack. We decided to take a break and eat lunch. We made our way to the stream and found a rock that we could both sit on to eat.

Mom had made sandwiches for us and I ate mine as if I hadn't eaten in a week. Susie politely ate hers and then we got out two banana flip cakes to eat. We shared them with Coty. Mom had sliced a few slices of boloney for Coty, which he gobbled down. I figured Coty knew the coyote wouldn't have given him boloney if he had followed her.

We watched the minnows swim in the brook as we ate. We saw Jesus bugs skating across the water and dragonflies fly from rock to rock, their wings sparkling with blue and green. The water slid over the moss-covered rocks, causing bubbles to rise to the surface. The scene was perfect, especially with the beauty that sat beside me. I was a lucky guy.

"I guess we had better be going," I finally said. I could have stayed there all day.

We continued the climb up the slight incline. It was getting close to one in the afternoon. I knew even if we didn't stay very long at the waterfall, it would be near dark before we returned home.

"How is it going with Kenny, Rock, Adore and Chero? Are they learning to read?" I asked as we walked.

"They're doing great. All of them are smart. They just never had anyone try to teach them before. They even seem to be enjoying it. James Ernest is really helping Kenny. He wasn't real thrilled with a girl trying to teach him anything."

"I can tell by some of his comments."

"Oh, I found out something. Oh, my gosh. I meant to tell you. You won't believe this."

"What?" I asked.

"You know how we were talking about Kenny liking Bernice?"

"Yeah."

"I heard that Bernice and Kenny were kissing inside the outhouse at school. How gross is that?" Susie said while making a gross face.

"No way! In the outhouse?" I said, faking surprise.

"I heard it from Rhonda who overheard Bernice telling Sadie about it. I was so grossed out."

I kept the Wolf Pack promise and didn't say anything about knowing about the kiss already. I heard a caw and looked up to see Bo circling above us. He made one flap of his wings and then glided down and onto my shoulder. I was glad to see him.

"Where have you been, Bo? I've been missing you." I reached up to rub his chest. He seemed to like it when I rubbed his chest.

Susie stepped in front of me and said, "Hi, Bo."

Bo bobbed his head and said, "Caw."

We continued our walk up the trail toward the falls. When Coty returned from the woods, he didn't notice Bo until Bo yelled out at him. Coty looked up, cocked his head sideways, and took off for the woods again with Bo right behind. Susie and I laughed at the two of them. I wondered if they would ever get along.

Later we could hear the muffled faraway sound of the waterfall. Bo had returned to my shoulder. We knew we were close. Susie's tiredness was replaced by excitement as the sound became louder.

"Do we have time to swim for a while?" Susie asked.

"Yeah, maybe a half hour or so. We can get cooled off, anyway," I answered. Susie had worn her swimming suit under her clothing.

The trail finally came upon the overlook high above the stream and the waterfall. My excitement was suddenly replaced by fear when I looked toward the waterfall and saw six guys in the pool of water.

"Get down," I whispered. I quickly fell to the ground and pulled Susie's arm with me, leading her down with me. Bo flew up into the air, startled by my sudden movement. He landed in the top of a small dead tree that stood next to us.

We peeked over the edge of the overlook and down toward the boys in the pool.

"Who are they?" Susie whispered to me.

"They're the boys from Blaze, the boys who attacked us on top of the cliff, the same ones who cut our rope ladder and left us for dead in the cave. See the one on the left next to the rock?"

"Yes."

"That's Hiram. He's like the leader of them. He started the fight."

"He's the boy who attacked Purty at church," Susie remembered.

We watched them for a couple of minutes. I saw that most of them were skinny-dipping. Susie hid her eyes in the green moss when one of them would get out of the pool in full glory.

Finally I said, "We can't let them see us. No telling what they would do." I hesitated and then said, "Neither one of us would be safe."

Susie looked at me with alarm on her face, knowing what I meant.

We started to scoot backward when Bo flapped his wings and swooped down the cliff toward the boys from Blaze.

"Caw, caw," he called out as he glided toward the rock where the boys had undressed. We could see Bo grab something from the rock with his feet and start to fly off. I heard Hiram yell at Bo and then saw him reach up onto the rock he was standing next to. He strained his body until he reached something, and he held it at the sky, and a shot went off. Hiram was firing a gun at Bo.

Susie yelled out, "No!"

I pulled Susie back down into the moss. She realized what she had done and she stopped screaming. The bullet missed Bo, and Bo flew right over our heads. I could see a watch clutched between his toes as he flew overhead and upward into the sky. Another shot rang out, and a bullet hit a branch of the tree that Bo had just flown over not more than ten feet from us. We kept our heads down. Chances were that they hadn't heard Susie's scream with the sound of the waterfall around them. The roar of the falls was loud.

Suddenly Coty appeared by my side. I reached up and pulled him down to me, hoping the gang hadn't seen him. I could hear the boys yelling at one another. It seemed like one of them was mad over losing his watch, and was blaming Hiram for the loss. Then Hiram turned toward the boy who was yelling at him and pointed the gun toward him. The boy ducked under the water as a shot rang out, and it looked like Hiram had fired over the kid's head as a warning shot.

This had turned serious. These boys were liable to do anything. This wasn't just a fistfight between two groups of boys. They had guns, and I knew they would use them. Susie and I and Coty crawled backward as quickly as we could. We got up once we couldn't be seen, then ran back down the trail. We had to be careful due to the rocks and roots on the trail. Susie tripped once, and I was able to catch her arm, keeping her from falling. Coty began barking, but I was sure the gang couldn't have heard him.

We continued running until I thought we were safely away from the boys. We stopped and bent over trying to catch our breaths.

"I've never been that scared in my life," Susie said.

I knew what she meant. The sad thing was that I couldn't say the same thing. I had been that scared many times over the past three years.

We walked in quiet for the next few minutes as we calmed from the escape and the run. I looked around me and saw the beauty that was there. The mossy creek, the green pines and giant oaks, the deep blue sky above our heads, and the quaint trail that we were walking down. I reached for Susie's hand, and all was okay again.

"I'm sorry we didn't get to swim," I told Susie.

"The waterfall was beautiful. The view from the overlook was amazing."

"It's even more beautiful looking up at the overlook from the pool."

"I couldn't believe Bo stole the watch. I was so scared that he was going to get shot," Susie said.

"Bo stealing the watch didn't surprise me," I said.

"Why?"

"He's been taking stuff all winter and spring."

"Really?"

"I think he has a stash somewhere. Mom has had silverware come up missing. He stole a shoe from one of Janie's dolls one day as she was playing with it. Bo likes shiny things. He probably could see the face of the watch glistening in the sun from his perch in the tree," I explained.

"It was actually funny… if Hiram hadn't had a gun."

I agreed and laughed.

Coty stayed by my side as we walked down the trail. He was either tired of exploring or wanting to protect me from the danger behind us. I liked him being there. Coty was such a faithful, loyal dog. He meant so much to me.

"Maybe since we didn't get to swim we could spend some more time at the butterfly field," Susie suggested.

"Okay," I said.

Susie smiled. Her freckles sparkled in the sunshine.

Suddenly, I thought I heard voices behind us. I stopped and held onto Susie's hand tightly. Then we both heard the voices. The hairs on the back of my neck stood on end.

"Hurry, this way." I pulled Susie off the trail and toward the woods. "C'mon, Coty."

We hurried into the woods and hid behind a large oak tree. I picked Coty up and held my hand around his snout so he couldn't bark. Within a couple of minutes Hiram and two other boys stood on the trail across from us. Coty was trying his best to squirm out of my arms.

I recognized the other boys as Hiram's smaller brother and one of the other guys we fought with.

I could hear Hiram say, "I know I saw two heads up there. It was probably two members of that stupid Oak Hill gang. If we ever get our hands on them again, they will die. I'll shoot them myself."

I wanted to throw up. I stood there praying Coty wouldn't slip out of my arms. I looked toward Susie, and she had her face covered by her hands. I couldn't tell if she was crying or not. I wanted to step out from behind the tree and bravely take care of the three guys. But I wasn't that strong, or that brave. Hiram had the gun in his hand. I had a walking stick and a dog. I didn't know what they would do to Susie if they caught us. I didn't want to know.

"What are we going to do?" Hiram's brother asked him.

"I guess we'll head back. They probably ran all the way home like scared mice. We'll get them sooner or later. Maybe Billy Taulbee can help us."

They turned and headed back up the trail toward the waterfall.

27 WHAT WAS I THINKING?

We stayed behind the trees for the next ten minutes. We wanted to make sure they were completely gone and out of hearing distance. I didn't want Coty barking and bringing them back. I finally slipped down the tree to a sitting position. Susie did the same. It was as if our bodies had tightened into a ball with all the tension that ran through our veins. I knew Susie felt the same. I let go of Coty. He turned and began licking my face. He knew something was wrong.

I finally said, "I didn't know we were called the Oak Hill Gang."

"If I were you I'd be more worried about them wanting to kill you guys. And what was that about Billy Taulbee?"

"I don't know." My mind was racing. The thoughts were tangled in my brain. I couldn't think about anything because my mind wanted to think about everything at the same time. I was brain-tangled.

"You've got to tell Sheriff Cane."

I looked at Susie. What did she just say? I have to plant sugar cane. My brain was in a hissy-fit.

"I'll tell him then. I'm not going to worry about you getting killed because you won't tell the sheriff. I'm sure Sheriff Cane will want to know about Billy Taulbee still being around."

Susie just kept talking about stuff I couldn't make out. I needed time to think. I needed time to untangle the string of

Christmas lights in my head. That's what it felt like. I held my head with both of my hands until my head stopped swimming. I wasn't sure if Susie was still talking or not.

After twenty minutes or so my mind began to clear. I stood up and began walking out of the woods toward the trail. Susie and Coty followed me as we continued our hike home. I continued thinking about Billy Taulbee. It made sense that he took refuge in Blaze. The boys of Blaze probably knew him from their relationship with the moonshiners. He probably was hiding out in Blaze recovering from his injuries.

"I think I need to tell Sheriff Cane about the threats and about Billy Taulbee," I told Susie.

"Are you okay?" Susie asked as if she was concerned about me.

"Yep," I answered.

"I've been telling you that for the past half hour."

"I didn't hear you," was all I said.

When we got to the bottom of the mountain and we were about ready to make the turn right toward the butterfly field, I said, "I need some water."

We walked over to the stream, and I got down on my hands and knees and stuck my head under the water. The cool water felt good running over my head. I threw my head back, and the water sprayed onto Susie. Coty was drinking from the mountain brook. I took my canteen from my neck and filled it up.

"Do you need any water?" I asked, pointing to her canteen.

"No thanks. I'm fine."

I got up, and we began following the flat trail. We finally came to the butterfly field. When we got to it I saw deer at the edge of the woods in the same spot we usually saw them. We watched the fawns play and leap into the air as they chased each other. One of them seemed to be chasing a butterfly.

We stayed at the field for probably an hour. I needed it. I needed a rest. I needed for my mind to clear. I needed time to think about the fact that the boys of Blaze wanted us dead.

I needed time to watch Susie in the flowers. She was singing as she looked at each flower and played with the butterflies. She reminded me of a beautiful fairy in one of the fairy tales that Mom had read to me as a child. I played with a praying mantis that I found on one of the branches lying on the ground.

I knew that it was getting late. The sun was getting low in the western sky. It wouldn't be long before it dipped behind the mountain.

"We'd better be going," I said.

We walked hand in hand toward the cabin. When we got close to the cabin, Coty took off toward it. He began barking. We hid at the side of the cabin, unsure of what was inside. We couldn't be too careful. Then I heard a familiar voice say, "What are you doing here, Coty?"

It was Purty. We walked around the cabin and looked inside. Purty had a shovel and was digging.

"You're not giving up, I see," I said.

"What are you guys doing here?"

"We came to look for buried treasure," Susie said.

"I've dug up the entire floor. All I can do now is go deeper," Purty said.

"You're wasting your time," I said.

"You don't know for sure," Purty came back.

"You're right. But I think I'm sure." I knew there was no use in arguing with Purty. I knew there was no use in explaining sensibly to him. "I hope you find more," is all I said.

"Thanks," Purty said.

Before we left I said, "Be careful. I've heard that snakes like to burrow deep under the ground in old cabins." I turned to leave.

Susie and I hadn't walked fifty feet before Purty caught up with us. "It's almost supper time," he explained. When we got to the logging road we saw Bo flying above the road toward us. He circled us and landed on me again. He seemed to like my left shoulder. He always landed on the same one.

I decided not to say anything to Purty about our encounter with the boys of Blaze. I would tell the Wolf Pack all at once. We needed to have a meeting.

I began playing fetch with Coty. I had picked up a small stick on the road and threw it ahead so Coty could go after it. He would chase it down and then bring it back. The third time I threw it; Bo flew from my shoulder and beat Coty to the stick. He grabbed it and flew on ahead and dropped it. Coty chased after it. Bo flew back toward us and landed on the road. Coty started to bring it back to me, but Bo blocked his way and began cawing. Coty dropped the stick. Bo grabbed it and flew on down the road and dropped it. Coty ran to it and picked it up again. Bo intercepted the path to me again, and again Coty dropped the stick.

This went on until we came to the turnoff. We decided to go with Purty and take the path across the swinging bridge. Bo was actually playing fetch with Coty.

Bo then landed on Coty's back, and Coty let him stay there as we walked down the path toward the Tuttle house.

"Tell Randy he needs to call a meeting. I have something important to share," I told Purty as we turned toward the bridge. "Also, call my mom and tell her we're almost home. I know they are probably worrying about us."

"Okay," Purty said.

"I can't believe what we just saw," Susie said.

"I believe anything anymore."

It was almost dark by the time we crossed the bridge. But we were only fifteen minutes from the store. We hurried across the bridge and down the gravel road to the store. Before we got to the store Susie stopped me and said, "Thank you for taking me on an amazing hike. I'll never forget it." She wrapped her arms around me and gave me a big kiss on the lips. It made the day complete. We should have done that more on the hike. What was I thinking?

28 Telling Sheriff Cane

The red and green pickups were in the gravel lot along with Sheriff Cane's cruiser. Papaw, Clayton, and the sheriff were sitting on the porch.

Clayton spoke first, "It's about time you got my daughter home."

"Yes, sir," I said.

"Did you two have fun?" Sheriff Cane asked us.

I had a hard time answering that question. We did, but we didn't. "We need to talk to you guys." That was all I knew to say.

Susie said, "Yes, we do."

We opened the screen door and walked through. The women came from the kitchen to greet us. The phone rang. I answered it. It was Purty calling to tell Mom that we were on the way home. "Thanks a lot," I said and hung up.

Mom asked, "Who was that?"

"Purty. He was supposed to call you a half an hour ago to tell you where we were. He decided to eat supper first," I explained.

The men who had entered the store began laughing.

Papaw said, "Sounds just like that boy."

Delma and Thelma and Janie entered the room. Delma said, "We really didn't think we'd ever see you again, sis." She ran over to hug Susie. Thelma then did the same. Janie stood there not knowing what to do.

"We had a great time. Betty, the butterfly field was unbelievable. You have to get Sheriff Cane to take you there," Susie said.

We then told everyone that we needed to tell them about something. We had them tell the girls to go to the bedroom while we talked. Mom looked worried. We then proceeded to tell them what had happened at the waterfall and what we had heard as we hid behind the trees - about how Hiram was going to kill the Wolf Pack.

"He said he would kill you?" Sheriff Cane confirmed.

"His exact words were, 'If we ever get our hands on them again, they will die. I'll shoot them myself,'" Susie told the sheriff.

"They called us the Oak Hill Gang," I said.

"Oh yeah, that's not all," Susie said.

"Oh, no!" Mamaw moaned.

"They then said they could get Billy Taulbee to help them," I told him.

"Billy Taulbee?" Papaw exclaimed.

"That means that Billy took cover in Blaze. He has to still be there," the sheriff reasoned.

"That's what I think, also," I said.

"Something has to be done about these people," Mom cried out.

"I agree," Sheriff Cane said.

Susie and I grabbed drinks from the cooler. I took an RC Cola, and Susie took an Orange Crush. Mamaw made us sandwiches, and we went outside. I took Coty a couple of slices of boloney. He was lying on the front, curled up, and asleep. He woke long enough to eat the meat.

We walked up to the lake and sat on one of the benches. The half moon had risen, giving us some light. We could hear the bullfrogs croaking and the hoots of the owls from across the lake. This had been one of my favorite days of my life until we saw the boys of Blaze. It was still a great day. I wondered what the summer would bring. School would be out soon. I knew I wanted there to be many more days with Susie.

Walking back toward the store we looked over to see Bo perched on top of Coty's dog house. Coty barked a greeting and Bo cawed. They had finally become friends by playing a game. I figured it was a lot like humans.

That night I lay in bed and thought about the day I had. I wondered if Sheriff Cane would find Billy Taulbee somewhere in Blaze. I wondered if he could do anything about Hiram saying he would kill us. I wondered what adventures awaited me and the Wolf Pack during the coming summer. I knew they would be great and exciting, whatever they were. I soon fell into a deep sleep, hoping to wake up and let the next adventure begin.

THE END

Pictures

*Aunt Ruth, Aunt Ola & Great Aunt Mildred, Joe Jr.
(Ruth's son) on steps*

Clayton holding Thelma & Delma

Brenda with Delma, Donna (Susie) with Thelma

Mamaw with her father Robin Easterling at reunion

Papaw (Martin Collins) inside store

Dad holding Janie & Mom and me (Timmy)

Uncle Morton with Della Collins (Clayton's sister)

Brenda & Timmy & Donna (Susie),
Thelma & Delma, in front

The Perry Cemetery

Timmy with his catch for the day

Dear Readers,

Please visit my website: www.timcallahan.net for pictures and information.

You can e-mail me at: timcal21@yahoo.com with questions and comments.

I love hearing from readers.

Blessings and happy reading,
Tim Callahan